Our Final Winter

CHARLÈNE BOUTIN

Cover illustration by Sierra Ward
Cover design (font) by Rotoscope Design
Developmental Editing by Swati Hegde
Line Editing and Proofreading by LTT Editorial Services

E-BOOK ISBN 978-1-7382847-6-4
PAPERBACK ISBN 978-1-7382847-7-1

www.irisbookspublishing.com

To anyone grieving someone who is still alive…
You're stronger than you know.

Author's Note

This book takes place both in the Canadian provinces of Québec and Newfoundland. Because part of this story occurs in a Québecois college setting, I want to clarify a term you'll see often: CEGEP.

CEGEP is an acronym for Collège d'Enseignement Général et Professionnel, which is French for College of General and Professional Education. They are a type of public educational institution that is unique to the province of Québec in Canada.

In Québec, secondary schools end at the eleventh grade. Students who wish to attend university then have two choices: one, take a two-year degree at a CEGEP in order to then take a three-year university degree, or two, attend a single year in a CEGEP and attend a four-year university degree in another province.

CEGEPs also offer standalone three-year career degrees that don't require further education, like nursing, paramedic, police technology, biopharmaceutical production technology, and more.

Students who attend CEGEP straight out of high school will typically be 17, 18, and 19, depending on your birth month. I'd also like to note that the legal drinking age in Québec is 18. This should give you enough context to enjoy the story!

I also want to note that although I wrote this story with the ultimate goal of warming your heart, there are difficult topics that may be triggering for some readers. If you feel like the following themes may be triggering to you, perhaps it would be best for you to pick up this book another time:

- Explicit, on-page sexual content
- Abusive parents (both on and off page)
- Meltdowns and panic attacks
- Separation anxiety
- Depictions of undiagnosed post-partum depression
- Momentary suicidal ideation

Please take care of yourself first and foremost!

Chapter 1

I can hardly believe it, but for the first time in months, my husband is coming out with me.

My 'phone pings, distracting me from my search for the perfect earrings. Tania's name pops up in our group chat.

Tania

I seriously CANNOT wait, you guys better be ready

A hint of glee bubbles from my stomach. Oh, I am ready. I go back to rummaging for earrings in the jewelry box I keep on my wooden dresser and finally snag the simple emerald-studded ones I was looking for. Karan got me these for our thirteenth anniversary last year, saying he thought they'd bring out my eyes.

I adore the fact that we celebrate the anniversary of the day we first kissed and not the day we got married.

I hate that he forgot about it this year.

But tonight's different. He's making time for me. For us. As I put on the earrings, I'm so elated I could float away.

And yet, I'm still waiting for the other shoe to drop.

Now fully ready, I step out of our bedroom and stop short at the sight of Karan's broad back in the middle of the hallway. He's facing away from me, standing still, his head hunched over. It looks like he's checking his phone.

He's already got his deep navy winter jacket on, and no hat to cover the thick black hair he's pulled back into a bun. Raised in Abitibi, this stubborn man won't wear a hat unless we intend to spend some real time outside.

"Ready to go?" I ask, placing a hand on his shoulder and moving past him to grab my own coat.

But his locked jaw, guilty eyes, and lack of a response as he looks away from his phone turn my elation to ashes on my tongue.

"Rachel…"

He gazes back down at his phone and starts typing a quick response to whoever he's chatting with.

I can already guess who's name is on the screen.

"I'm sorry, but I'm going to have to bail."

I knew it.

I should never have gotten my hopes up.

"You're seriously not coming?"

My husband stares back at me with an apologetic look. He may take up nearly the entire entry hallway with his tall and broad shape, but at this moment, he's never looked smaller.

Karan knows what he's doing to me. And I know he hates it as much as I do.

So, why does he do it?

"Mom's internet is down again, and she tried fixing it, but she can't," he starts with a sigh. "If I don't go and help her now, they won't have internet for the whole evening. Worse, my dad might try to fix it himself and mess it up more. Mom won't have her TV, she'll get bored, and she'll blow up my phone anyway."

"Okay, but we have *plans*." I cross my arms, attempting to stand tall. "Tania and Nolan made the drive to make it, too. Don't you think it's rude to blow them off?"

Karan's jaw tightens, a muscle jumping beneath the skin. His fingers drum once against his thigh before curling into a fist. Those brown eyes dart away from mine, then back, then away again.

Our gazes lock. We share a strained look.

After seven years of marriage and twice that time together, we can read each other like a book.

Or, at least, we used to be able to.

Karan's gaze falls to the ground. "I can join you guys after." The deep timber of his voice is so low it's almost a whisper.

"Your parents can live one night without TV or the internet." Frustration balls itself up like a tight fist in my chest. "It's really not that serious."

I hold onto a lock of my long chestnut hair flowing over my shoulder and grip it tight, my knuckles turning white.

This man is literally going to make me pull my hair out.

Ever since Surinder and Martine moved to Montréal earlier this year, Karan has been like this; running right to his mommy whenever the tiniest thing is wrong. It doesn't matter if the twins have soccer practice, if he literally just walked in from doing overtime at work, or, like tonight, if we have plans with *other people*.

Most of the time, I let it go. Although the doctors have assured us that Martine is almost completely out of danger, she's still undergoing the final bouts of treatment for cervical cancer.

But this isn't about her cancer. I don't know what it's about, but the weight of it has been suffocating me.

Karan drags his hand down his thick beard. "It'll give me a chance to say hi to the boys. You're always saying I don't spend enough time with them."

I close my eyes and sigh. There's no use. His mind is made up. And frankly, I don't want to fight with my husband. I see him so little as it is. The last thing I want is to poison what little time we have together.

Or to hand that time over to his mom, but hey, beggars can't be choosers, apparently.

"The reason the boys are with your parents in the first place is because we were supposed to go out," I let out, teeth clenched. "But whatever. Fine."

"Rachel…" He grabs my arm before I can reach for the door handle.

Once upon a time, the sensation of his hand on my skin would light me up with stars. Make me forget everything else plaguing me.

Now it feels like nothing more than… just a hand.

I turn back to him. With more than a foot in height difference, I have to crane my neck up to meet his gaze.

"I said fine, Karan. Just go. I don't want to fight."

He lets my arm go.

I hurry out the door without another word, the cold December evening air hitting my face with a thermal shock.

Karan follows sheepishly behind me as I make my way down the winding staircase leading to the sidewalk. I turn left to head toward the metro station.

"I'll join you guys as soon as I'm done!" Karan calls out to me, waving with the car keys in hand.

He's taking the car to head to his parents' place, since the metro doesn't make it all the way to Pointe-aux-Trembles.

I muffle a quick sound of affirmation, but I don't look back.

I cross my arms to protect myself against the cold winds of the oncoming winter. Gritting my teeth, I try to get my mind on something else—anything else—besides my husband and his antics.

I never wanted to be *that* wife. The nagging wife. The wife who complains about her mother-in-law. A mother in law who has *cancer.*

When I stood on the altar and said "I do," I didn't only vow to love Karan in sickness and in health. I vowed to myself to stay true to who I was. I refused to let the difficulties of life slowly poison me and turn me into a frigid bitch.

I wouldn't say I'm at "frigid bitch" levels yet, but damn do I feel myself getting there sometimes.

I can't let myself get there. I'm not... I'm not them.

To get my mind off my argument with Karan and hopefully arrive at karaoke night in a better mood, I take out my phone and dial my sister Océane's number. She picks up almost immediately.

"Why are you calling, you weirdo?"

"Because I'm walking and don't want to have to type out a text?"

"You know what voice memos are, right?" She's being snarky, but I can hear the smile in her high-pitched voice.

"Yeah, yeah, I do." But I wanted a more immediate connection to her. Hearing her voice, knowing she's all right, will always soothe me.

"So… what's up?"

I stop at a red light and sigh. "Today's one of those days."

"Oh." I hear the rustle of movement on the line as Océane's breath hitches. "Do you want me to come see you?"

"I'm not home." The light turns green, and I start walking again. "Just wanted to commiserate with someone. Also, you don't always need to be the one coming to me."

I don't know why she insists. I don't think I've been to her place in over a year, even when her flare-ups would make it much easier for me to go see her there.

"I know, I know." She pauses. "Want to play 'Wish they were our parents'?"

I chuckle right as I push on the heavy doors of the metro station, my hair flying out from the gust of warm wind that escapes from below.

"Hmmm… so, Cayce and Corey's teacher this year is this lovely old lady nearing retirement. She's the sweetest, patient teacher I've ever met. She's especially patient with the boys' separation anxiety."

I pause when I reach the crowded escalators. To my despair, the metro is crowded tonight.

"I wish she were our mom," I mutter.

"There's this new guy at art therapy," Océane continues. "He can't stop talking while he paints. And he's weirdly obsessed with painting mangos for some reason?"

She sighs. I wait for her to say the line I know is coming. The line we've repeated countless times during these games.

"I wish he were our dad."

We keep going like this for a few more rounds as I wait for the metro. On days like today, being estranged from our parents feels so deathly lonely. Especially when I see how close Karan gets to be with Surinder and Martine.

But I never regretted my decision to get Océane out of that house. Not for one second.

The metro arrives, and I walk inside, using my free hand to grab onto the support pole. It's not extremely crowded tonight, but there are enough people that no free seats remain. From the corner of my eye, I spot an elderly woman sitting in one of the seats, a worn paperback in her hands.

I squint to make out the cover and have to stifle a pleased giggle when I notice the bulging pecs and biceps of the half-naked man on it.

"There's an old lady reading what seems to be a spicy billionaire romance sitting in the metro. I wish she was our mom."

"Oh my God. I love that for her," Océane laughs. "I wonder if she's reading a spicy scene right now."

"She's got a complete poker face. She could be reading anything."

I can only aspire to reach the level of bold confidence dripping from this sweet-looking old lady.

Soon, the friendly feminine voice of the metro calls out my station. I can finally get out of here.

"I'm almost there," I say as I make my way closer to the doors. "Talk soon, okay?"

"Okay." Is that disappointment I hear in her voice? "Love you, Rach."

"Love you, Ann."

Putting away my concern for now, I exit the metro station and walk to Crescent Street, which is already alive with foot traffic. By the time I walk into the karaoke bar, my mood is a bit better than it was when I left my condo.

"Bonjour hi!" A giant of a man greets me at the entrance, his cheery demeanor a stark contrast to his nearly scary appearance.

"We have a group reservation under Sophie Côté?"

"Ah, yes, they're already here."

I buy myself a beer before the man escorts me to our karaoke room. The booming bass of music erupts from the doors we pass down the hallway, until we stop in front of a door that is clearly ours. Our friend Avery's voice, belting an Adele song, echoes through it.

"Have a good evening!" the man chimes before leaving me to it.

I burst into the room in the middle of Avery's song; she doesn't stop singing but shoots me a big smile and doubles down in intensity while everyone else in the room whoops out to greet me.

Her smile turns to a knitted brow when she realizes I'm alone, but she doesn't stop her song.

Tania is sitting on Nolan's lap in one corner. Next to them, Logan marvels at his partner and the mother of his child's singing. Sophie and my brother, Will, are seated on the other side of the room, Sophie's ridiculously long legs propped up on Will's lap. Both their concerned gazes don't leave me as I sit next to Sophie and wait until Avery's song is done, slowly sipping on my beer.

When Avery huddles back down against Logan with a bashful grin, the questions begin.

"Where's Karan?"

"Is he running behind?"

"He didn't bail, did he?" My brother's question holds a tone of accusation.

Will stares at me, his eyes hard. He'll hate my answer.

"He did, in fact, bail."

My reply elicits a groan from pretty much everyone in the room.

What is it this time?" Tania asks. "Don't tell me his mommy called for help for something tech-related."

When all I give her is a deadpan stare, she shakes her head in exasperation.

"This man! Seriously, this man!"

"I mean, I can't be too angry," I say, although I don't know why I'm defending him. "She's still got a round of treatment to go, and—"

"She's basically out of the woods, though," Nolan interrupts. "I'd be upset if Tania bailed on me for such a cop-out reason."

"Yeah…" The room listens with rapt attention as I retell the evening's events.

"How long has it been like this?" Logan asks as he readjusts his glasses. "I remember last spring when we went to Tania's family's sugar shack, you guys had an argument then, too."

"That's when the in-laws moved to the city," Will adds, sharing a concerned look with me.

He loves his brother-in-law, but he's also privy to how much Karan's behaviour has been affecting me these past several months.

"Yeah," I confirm. "Karan's dad retired. And with the whole cancer thing, I think they just really wanted to be closer to their son."

"Does she still keep showing up unannounced or making plans with the twins without your approval?" Sophie asks.

"Yep." I pop the 'p' and take a sip of beer. "Seriously, I love this woman, but now that she doesn't live six hours away, I'm realizing how… intense she is with Karan."

With my estranged parents, Karan's family is more important to me than I ever expected for in-laws. Sophie and Avery constantly rave about the beautiful mother-daughter connection they have. Even when we were on speaking terms, my mother and I never had that.

Love, it seemed, was always conditional in our household.

"How intense?" Tania asks.

I sigh and lean forward in my seat. "Well. For one, it's not only with Karan. It's with the kids, too. It's hard to explain without seeing it. And ever since the job thing…"

"Oh, yeah, the job thing," Logan recalls.

Last spring, Karan and I had a huge fight about his new job while we were out at Tania's sugar shack.

Watching him come home from his job as a game developer every single day, a smile on his face and his spine held straight with pride… it was bliss.

But it wasn't *serious* enough for his mommy and daddy, so he transferred to a software startup instead. Now, those smiles are gone, replaced with bags under his eyes and a stooped figure.

I hate what it's doing to him.

"He's always tired," I continue, chewing my bottom lip. "He comes home late more often than not. When he's there, he's zoned out."

I sigh again, rubbing my hand against my mouth. "Guys, this fucking sucks."

"At least you're here," Nolan chimes in with a mischievous grin. "So let's get your mind off that bullshit. I've got a show for you ladies."

Tania arches an eyebrow, then yelps when Nolan pushes her off his lap and stands.

"I'll take that." He grabs the microphone from Avery, then removes his shirt in one graceful movement.

All four women, me included, whoop in encouragement at the sight of his broad, tattooed chest. He leans over the karaoke machine, types in his choice of song, and as soon as the beat comes on, he starts bouncing his shoulder provocatively.

I can't help the giggle that escapes my lips. Nolan starts singing the first lyrics of *I'm Too Sexy*, continuing his provocative moves as his gaze switches from person to person.

Nolan's strategy works; for a moment, my mind is taken off the shitshow I've left at home. There's only room for laughter with my friends. Then, it's suddenly my turn, and I lose myself to the music, fully leaning into my shitty performance that makes everyone laugh even more.

But as the evening wears on, and Karan fails to show up at all, the nagging thought creeps back into my head. It's a constant companion that won't leave me alone.

This relationship is dying.

Chapter 2

Karan

I wince at the sound of the cupboard door slamming shut. I don't move, putting all my attention on the sounds in the condo. Will this stir Rachel from her sleep?

A sigh of relief escapes me when I hear nothing.

I didn't intend to slam the cupboard door like that. But sometimes, I can't control my strength. The only time I feel gentle is when I'm with Rachel and the boys.

The last thing I want is to wake her. Or our sons. It's still pitch black outside, and even Cayce and Corey never get up at this hour. If Rachel were to wake up, it would only sour her mood even more.

I'm trying to make it up to her, not make things worse.

I fucked up last night.

Badly.

I now have all the items and ingredients I need on the counter to make *Aloo Paratha*, Rachel's favourite of all the breakfast recipes passed down from my Punjabi father. I've already boiled potatoes last night after coming back from my parents' place, which means I can now mash them with a fork and blend them with spices before preparing my *Paratha* dough to stuff everything inside.

Rachel seemed *pissed* last night. I'm not exactly sure why it affected her as much as it did. Our group of friends gets together relatively often. Sure, it's not every day that Tania and Nolan make the trip, but they only live an hour and a half away.

Still, I can own up to my mistakes. I *have* to, if I'm to remain the good husband I've always vowed to be.

My Rachel deserves better than what I've been giving her.

Weariness seeps into my bones as I knead the dough. With the prepping of the potatoes and getting up early this morning, I haven't slept nearly enough. Still, it's important for me to make it up to Rachel. It's not her fault if she doesn't understand the duty I have to my mother and father. Although my mother is Québécoise like her parents, we still grew up in very different households.

Dad's droning lectures—whether given in a calm demeanor or in frustrated screams—have etched his traditional values straight into my skull. He and his sister Anjali were the only ones from their family who immigrated to Canada for work, which means there's no one else to inherit our culture. The last thing he wants is for his values to die with him.

And if there's one thing he taught me above all else, it's to respect—no, honour—my mother. I owe her my life, and given her health over the last couple more years, there's no limit to what I should be doing to uphold my duty to her.

I spent so long living six hours away from my parents, and I still haven't grown accustomed to our new proximity. Of course it's natural for me to rush to their aid whenever something comes up. It was so much easier to give Rachel everything she deserves when my other responsibilities lay so far away.

But I can't let myself forget that Rachel won't understand. Not after what her parents did. My stomach still roils at the thought of how she was robbed of the solid parental presence that I've come to rely on.

And either way… I have a responsibility to care for my wife just as much as I have a responsibility to care for my parents.

A bead of sweat drips down my forehead as I finally finish prepping the *Aloo Paratha* for cooking. It's still pitch black when I look outside. I've got time.

I pan-fry the *paratha* one by one. The aroma of spices and bread fills the air, and I smile to myself, knowing that nobody can get up in a bad mood when it smells this good in your home. While one of the *paratha* cooks, I start a pot of coffee, adding to the scrumptious aroma in the kitchen.

I leave most of the *paratha* in the oven to keep them warm for me and the boys, then place two of them on a plate for Rachel. I pour her a cup of coffee in her favourite mug. I got this mug for her for our anniversary two years ago. It says:

I'm a

~~*Farmacist*~~

~~*Pharmasist*~~

~~*Pharmasyst*~~

I sell drugs

She adores it, even if Cayce and Corey can now read and have started to ask what it means.

Carefully, while being mindful of my typically clumsy demeanor, I carry the plate and the mug toward our bedroom.

I have to set the mug down on the hardwood floor to free my hand and open the door, and in doing so, I spill a few scalding drops on my hand and have to bite back a yelp.

When I finally manage to cross the door, both items in my hands, my gaze falls to my sleeping wife. She's sprawled across the bed with her arms above her head, her delicate chestnut hair fanned across her pillow.

A pang flares in my chest. She's even more beautiful than the first moment I laid eyes on her. And I love her so much that it hurts.

She's my angel.

Slowly, so as not to wake her yet, I deposit the plate and the mug on her nightstand, then walk around the bed to the left side—my side—and crawl into the blankets next to her. I wrap an arm around her chest and slide in close. Despite our size difference, her small warm body fits perfectly into mine, as it always has. I nuzzle into her neck and inhale her sweet strawberry scent.

I'm exactly where I should be.

The problem is, I haven't been here enough as of late.

God, I miss her.

Rachel stirs at the touch, emitting a soft whimper that sends a shock of arousal directly down my spine. I desperately wrestle against my inner urges to make this moment about more than simply being close to her. It takes everything in me to resist, especially when she slides in closer and wraps one leg over my hips.

She's warm, and soft, and I know all too well how good it feels to have my hands all over her, to be inside her, to watch her writhe and gasp above me.

Fourteen years haven't doused the fire of my desire for her.

It has only fanned its flames.

"Mmm?" she whispers, her eyes still closed as I wrap my arms around her back and revel in the sensation of her lips against my chest.

I kiss her forehead with a smile. "Good morning, love. I made you breakfast."

She leans her head back and sniffs. "I can smell it. Oh my God." She sighs and nuzzles her head against my chest.

"I'm really sorry about last night." I press my lips to her forehead again. "I know I haven't been spending a lot of time with you lately. And I know breakfast doesn't make up for it, but I hope you know that I'm trying."

Rachel stiffens in my arms.

Fuck.

I said something I shouldn't have.

"Did you have fun?" I ask, hoping she'll be excited to tell me all about the fun evening I missed.

Instead, she rolls away from me and sits up before rubbing her eyes. "I don't know. Did your mom get everything she needed?"

The pointed way in which she says 'mom' confirms what I thought.

She's still pissed.

I sit up and move to wrap my hands around her shoulders but stop short. I know Rachel is still as attracted to me as I am to her. Just feeling her response to my cuddle a moment earlier—before she fully woke up and remembered she's pissed at me—tells me everything I need to know.

But now's not the time to try to win her over with affection.

When she's upset, Rachel withdraws. Until this year, the root of her upset was almost always an external source. Nothing to do with me.

It happens on her mother's birthday. Or on days when the twins have overstimulated her. A plethora of things can hurt Rachel, and my role in these moments was always clear to me.

I support her. Protect her. Do everything in my power to make sure nothing can get to her when she's fighting against her demons.

But now that I'm the root of her upset, I have no fucking idea what to do. And it's been happening more and more.

"I'm really sorry," I repeat, already knowing that these are just words. "I promise I'll go next time, unless someone is actively dying."

A deep sigh moves through Rachel's body. Because her back is to me, I can't see her expression. I wish I were still in touch enough with her to be able to instinctively know what's on her mind, like I used to.

"Whatever. It's fine." She reaches for the plate on her nightstand and shimmies back against the headboard. "Thank you for breakfast, Karan."

A soft smile appears on her pillowy lips. My heart lifts at her expression but sinks right back into my stomach again when I lift my gaze to meet her green eyes.

She looks… tired.

Of course, she woke up seconds ago, but I detect another layer of weariness in those eyes that I love so much.

"Uh…" I place the blanket back over her legs before she deposits the plate of food on her lap. "It's a pleasure, love. There's more in the oven if you're still hungry."

"Okay. This is nice." She smiles again and takes a bite, her eyes closing as she savours the bite. "And really good."

The sound of a door opening, followed by quick footsteps, alerts us to the twins' presence.

"I'll get them ready this morning." I shuffle to my feet and shoot a final look at my wife. "You enjoy your breakfast."

"Okay. Thank you."

"I love you."

"... I love you, too."

I walk out of the bedroom to go greet my boys, unable to get that sinking feeling out of my chest that my efforts this morning will not be enough.

Chapter 3

Karan

As I watch my parents drive away from the John Abbott residence parking lot, a single thought makes its home in my mind:

For the first time in my life, I'm free.

Yes, my throat is knotted, and I had to hold back tears when my mother was bawling her eyes out in my arms. If it had been up to her and Dad, I would have stayed in Val-d'Or for my two years of CEGEP.

But despite the pain of missing them already, I can't help thinking it was about damn time.

The only way I managed to convince my parents to come to Montréal for CEGEP, instead of waiting until university to leave home, was the reminder that pursuing my studies in English would improve my chances of getting the job they'd always dreamed of for me—software engineer.

Is it true?

Absolutely not.

I'm here to become a video game developer.

I turn and head back inside the century-old red-bricked residence building, guilt gnawing through my insides. It's not that I don't want to serve my parents in the way Dad has taught me to do. Game development still pays well. They won't have to worry about a thing.

By the time Dad retires, I'll be a senior developer, and I'll make enough to support them.

Them, and the family I'll hopefully have by that time.

Instead of heading back to my room, which is on the second floor, I decide to walk around instead. The hallways are busy with other families helping their kids move in, and I have to watch my large, clumsy self so I don't bump into anyone.

I'm doing the right thing by being here.

Yup. I am.

The more I tell myself that, the more I'll believe it.

Sniffling sounds interrupt my thoughts, and I slow my pace before turning the corner of the hallway. The sight in front of me stops me short.

The tearful sounds are coming from a little girl with chestnut hair, probably around eight or nine years old. But that's not who took my breath away. The culprit is the stunning girl holding her against her chest.

Silky peach skin. A shiny cascade of chestnut hair. Bright green eyes framed by dark lashes. And pouty pink lips I can't stop looking at.

I'm far enough away that she hasn't seen me. And I don't want her to, either. From the looks of it, this is a heavy moment. The two adults, who must be her parents, have puffy eyes from crying, but seem to be impatiently waiting for the little girl to calm down. And this beautiful girl looks so brave, so caring, as she tries to soothe the child.

There's just something about this girl. Now isn't the time, but I know I have to see her again.

***

It takes four days before I see her again.

Well, not technically.

I do notice her sitting way at the back of my humanities class on Tuesday, but by the time I manage to wrangle myself out of the stupid desk-chair combo that definitely isn't designed for someone my size, she's already gone.

On Thursday night—or as the rez kids call it, *Jeudredi* (a French portmanteau of Thursday and Friday)—I attend my first party with my three roommates. The music is loud and the beer plentiful, purchased by those who have had the pleasure of turning eighteen already. It's the cheap kind, but I don't turn up my nose at the offer of free drinks by the hosts.

"Bro," my roommate Johann says with a bump on my shoulder, his German accent thick. "Now this is a party."

I wouldn't know. There isn't a universe in which my parents would have let me attend a party. In this universe, my sixteen-year-old roommate has seen more parties than me and can outdrink me by an entire six-pack, if not more.

To be honest, I'm not really paying attention to the vibes of this crowded party. Instead, I'm scanning the room for someone in particular. Someone that my thoughts have kept coming back to, over and over.

And there she is.

Leaning against the wall with a red solo cup in hand, she looks absolutely beautiful in the flowery summer dress that falls just above her knees, leaving her soft calves exposed. My mouth goes dry at the sight of her.

Yet, she seems so small. Not because she's particularly petite—she's about average height with a medium, lean build—but because of the way she's leaning into herself. Those chestnut locks of hair cover half her face, as if she's trying to hide herself away.

"I'll be right back," I tell my roommates before making a beeline for this girl.

I stop when I'm ten feet away. The last thing I want to do is come off as creepy or scary, so I lean up against the same wall as her and awkwardly slide along until I'm about three feet away.

She turns her head to me with a side glance, her pink lips pursed.

"Hey." I raise an eyebrow. "Do you come here often?"

Wow. Real smooth, Karan.

The girl looks around. "So, where's the wine?"

"Uh…" I look down at my red solo cup. "This is beer. I think that's all they have?"

She settles her bright green eyes on me. "Oh, that's too bad. I like some wine with my cheese."

It takes me a second to realize she just made a joke and for me to burst out into an awkward guffaw.

"Your joke was definitely better than mine," I tell her.

Being this close to her is messing with the chemistry of my brain.

"I'm sorry, this…" I gesture to the loud ambiance of teenage drunkards around us. "… is new for me. And I just saw you here, and I've seen you in my humanities class, and I just thought…"

My voice trails off when I realize I might come off as too stalkerish.

"I saw you, too." Her cheeks go red.

My heart skips a beat. "You did?"

"Yeah." She looks down at her glass. "This isn't really new for me, but I came with my roommates and they ditched me. I don't really like parties."

A surge of anger bubbles in my veins. We don't all get lucky with our roommates, and it looks like she definitely didn't.

Who would leave this angel alone?

"That's kind of fucked up." I slide an inch closer and smile. "Want to get out of here, then?"

My pulse speeds up at the audacity that just came out of my mouth.

She purses her lips again. "Presumptuous, sir."

Shit.

I slide a bit farther away, racking my brain for ways to make it seem like a joke. "Uh…"

The girl bursts into laughter, and it's one of the most beautiful sounds I've heard in my entire life.

"I'm just fucking with you, dude. Let's go." She starts to walk, but stops in her tracks. "Before I run away from a party with you, I should probably know your name."

My heart is in my throat when I speak. "I'm Karan."

The girl's face softens, and immediately, my insides turn to jelly.

"I'm Rachel."

Chapter 4

Rachel

"**R**achel?"

I look up from my prosciutto sandwich to find an alarmed Trey looking down at me from the door of the break room.

Whether it's at home or at work, I can't seem to catch a break.

"What's wrong?" I say, my mouth still full.

"Someone's on the phone for you."

Swallowing my bite in a hurry, I stand.

"Who is it?" I try to keep my voice calm, but an edge of panic still makes its way through.

A list of all the possible problems rushes through my mind all at once:

One of the boys got hurt at school.

Something's wrong with one of Sophie's kids.

Martine's cancer has stopped responding to treatments.

Trey steps aside to let me through the door as I waltz past him. "Your sister, I think?" he manages to say while I pass by him.

Océane.

I freeze.

What could be wrong with Océane?

Shit, shit, shit.

I rush to the pharmacist's counter, where the phone is on hold, and immediately grab it and press the button to push the call through.

"Océane? What's wrong?"

"Rachel!" My heart stops upon hearing the panicked tone of her voice. "I need help." She utters a small moan; she's in pain.

"Where are you? What happened?"

"I'm at home. I was trying to put stuff on a shelf…" She cries out. "Rachel, I'm stuck."

My blood goes cold. "Did it fall on you?"

"Yes. I can't move."

"I'm coming. Don't move."

I hang up the phone and see Sandrine, the other pharmacist on staff today, staring back at me with a worried look.

"I have to go," I tell her in a clipped tone.

"Everything okay?" she asks while I'm already scrambling to find my coat.

"No. My sister's hurt."

"Shouldn't she call an ambulance?"

I turn to Sandrine, who's getting on my already frayed nerves. I'm not going to waste precious time explaining why I'm not going to call an ambulance for my sister unless it's absolutely necessary.

Calm down, Rachel. You're not her. *You're not* them.

"Just hold down the fort while I'm gone, okay?" I manage to say, my tone still clipped.

"Uh, okay."

I wave a quick goodbye to Trey and the others before racing straight outside, ignoring the blast of icy air that stings the skin of my face. My mind scrambles to calculate the time it's going to take me to get to Océane's place.

I haven't been in a long while because she always insists on coming to my place instead. Finally, I manage to recall that it takes about thirty minutes by metro from downtown to reach her neighborhood.

That's thirty minutes too long.

My heart hammers against my chest in a frenzy while I sit idly on the metro, waiting to arrive at my destination.

Sandrine is right about the ambulance being the best choice in most cases. They'd certainly get to her faster.

But Océane is vulnerable.

My sister's fibromyalgia is the least of her worries. In the past, every time she was dragged to the hospital by force by paramedics, the panic and trauma set her back for *months*.

Thanks to the abuse from our parents, Océane's mental state is a fragile tapestry of PTSD, anxiety, depression, and dissociative amnesia held together with duct tape and a dream. And that's only what's officially on her list of diagnoses.

I can't count the number of times I've argued with a doctor who dismissed her symptoms, spent afternoons playing phone roulette to understand why her approval for disability was lagging behind, or screamed at her psychiatrist until tears ran down my face because he'd made rude remarks to her.

I know better than anyone what she's going through.

And it's none of my coworkers' business.

I shudder to even *think* of what would have happened to my sister if I didn't have the medical authority that comes with holding a doctorate of pharmacy. Being ten years my junior, she never gets taken seriously for her issues.

Except when I'm there.

The metro ride doesn't take that long, but to me, time crawls to a stop and chokes at me until I finally reach Crémazie Station and head back outside. Océane's apartment is a two-minute walk from the station. I arrive in under a minute.

My trembling fingers make it impossible to unlock the front door of the basement triplex with my set of keys, and I fumble the keys a few times, biting my lip to hold back the curses threatening to spill out. Gritting my teeth until my jaw aches, I force the door open and stumble in, immediately gagging as the foul stench hits me.

The apartment is *filthy*.

An oppressive heaviness hangs in the air, a mix of stale food and something else I can't quite place—something rotten, hidden beneath layers of neglect. My gaze sweeps across the single room, a chaotic blend of her life scattered haphazardly: dirty dishes piled high in the tiny sink, their contents congealed and unrecognizable, and dust motes dancing in the weak light filtering through grimy windows.

In the corner, the small couch sags under the weight of crumpled blankets and discarded clothes. I step further inside, and my foot crunches on the remnants of a broken picture frame, shards glinting like tiny, treacherous stars against the grimy wooden floor.

A double bed is pressed against the wall, unmade and tangled in a fortress of sheets. I can imagine her there, wrapped in that cocoon, battling demons that lurk beneath the surface of her consciousness. The tiny kitchen table holds a half-eaten takeout container and a scattering of old mail.

And then, my eyes land on the shelf. It lies sprawled across the floor, books and trinkets scattered like fallen leaves. Underneath the mess, I can only just make out her small body.

"Shit, Océane!" I rush to her aid, pushing past the mess of empty grocery bags and dirty clothes littering the floor as a pained groan sounds out from underneath the shelf.

Luckily, the shelf is not full size. I'm neither big nor tall, but I'm much stronger than Océane, and it takes me only a few seconds to push it back up against the wall. When I'm sure the shelf is secure and won't fall back on us, I kneel to the ground and start shoving the books and trinkets away from Océane.

Océane utters a sob of relief, then struggles to sit up. I help her by supporting her back, then grab her heart-shaped face in my hands. A small gash sits underneath her left eye where either the corner of the shelf or a book hit her, and I can tell from several red spots on her forehead and cheeks that she's going to have bruises.

I look into her green eyes, carefully stroking her cheek with my thumb. "Where does it hurt most? Did you break anything?"

"It hurts everywhere." She winces and lets out another sob. "My… my collarbone is really bad."

I carefully touch around her collarbone, feeling for a fracture, and let out a sigh of relief when I don't find anything.

"I'm gonna check out your ribs, too," I warn her before moving my hands lower.

She winces at the touch, but nothing is broken. If it were anyone else, I'd be concerned, but with her condition and what she's just been through, I unfortunately expected nothing less.

I shift my focus back to the gash on her face. "This is pretty deep…"

My heart sinks when I realize there's a good chance Océane will need to go to the hospital.

"I'm not sure if this will need stitches or not." I stand. "Stay here. Do you have any clean washcloths?"

"No."

Shit.

"Okay."

The most important thing is to clean this thing so it doesn't get infected. I look around, feeling despair claw at me from the state of this apartment. And from the messy state of Océane's hair, I can tell she hasn't showered in days. Her thick, waist-length chestnut locks are drawn back into a braid, but it looks like there's matting in the back of her head.

"I'm going to need to get you to your sink so I can clean this."

Océane attempts to stand but crumbles with a cry. I clench my jaw and consider my options. My sister is so small that helping her to the sink wouldn't be an issue for me, but I'm likely going to hurt her in the process.

And with that gash…

"I'm going to call an ambulance," I say, my tone firm, though I'm anything but certain.

There's no way I can bring her to the hospital via public transportation, and there's also no way I'm leaving her alone to go get my car at home.

Océane seems to be thinking the same thing as me, because she doesn't argue.

I make the call and grab her pillow and blankets from her bed to make her more comfortable while we wait. Like the rest of the apartment, the bed is filthy. I don't know when she cleaned her sheets last, but from the state of them, it must have been much too long ago.

I sit next to Océane and hug my knees to my chest. She looks at me with a frown, the pain still visible in her eyes.

"I know what you're going to say," she starts, tears welling in her eyes. "I'm really not in the mood for a lecture."

"A lecture?" I scoff, gesturing to the hovel of her living space. "Océane, we're way past a lecture here. I'm not mad about this. I'm worried. I'm really worried."

The part about not being mad is a lie. Truthfully, I am mad.

But not at my sister.

I'm pissed off at myself.

I should have realized something was going on with Océane. Ever since she's moved into this solo apartment to get away from her toxic roommate, she's always insisted on visiting me or Will, never the other way around.

And the way she hesitated before saying goodbye on the phone the other night…

How did none of that raise any alarm bells in my mind? She's got fibromyalgia, for crying out loud. It doesn't make sense that she'd never let us come to her, especially on bad flare up days.

Guilt gnaws at my insides. I've been way too focused on my issues at home. On my growing sense of disconnect from Karan. Meanwhile, my baby sister's been in crisis, and I didn't realize.

I can't blame Will, either. He only recently started to take a more active role in Océane's life; he doesn't know her like I do. For all intents and purposes, I'm more of a mother to her than our real mother ever was.

It's all on me.

Océane doesn't say anything. She's aware that telling me not to worry would be in vain. Instead, she pinches her small lips together and lets a tear fall.

"How long has it been like this?" I ask her as a dark thought begins to take shape in my mind.

"Um…" Océane looks around, her chin trembling. "The apartment thing… a while. I just… Living alone like this… I…"

"Hey, hey." I scoot closer to her and wrap an arm around her frail shoulders, careful not to hurt her. "You should have told me you were struggling."

"It's been getting worse," she continues. "Lately, I've just… I can't even get myself in the shower."

"Yeah, I can tell."

"I'm so sorry."

"No." I lean back so I can look her in the eye. "I'm the one who's sorry. I should have caught on."

"You're not a mind reader, Rachel. You have your own life to worry about."

"Well, you're a part of my life, too." I look around, then squeeze her closer. "You can't live like this anymore."

"I don't know what to do," she sobs. "I can't get a roommate. I'll only be a burden on them, and that's not a stranger's responsibility."

I open my mouth, but she interrupts me.

"I already looked into facilities for assisted living. There are some for younger people like me. There's one in Pierrefond, and another one in Petite Patrie." Her gaze falls to the ground. "But they have no room right now. The ones that do have room…"

A shudder passes through me at what she's implying. There's no way I'm letting Océane live in a place like that if it's anything less than wonderful. And some of these places are straight up awful.

The thought lurking in the back of my brain grows, until I have no choice but to face it.

"You're going to come live with us."

The words are out. I can't take them back now.

Océane blanches. "I can't do that."

"Yes, you can. I'm not leaving you here alone." I gesture around us again to make my point. "Clearly, this isn't working."

"Rachel, I'd love to live with you. But…" She shakes her head. "I'm not your responsibility. I can't impose like that."

"You're not imposing. I'm insisting. And you are my responsibility, whether you like it or not."

"I'm a grown adult."

"Who can't take care of herself!" My heart rate is getting faster. "Océane, this is dangerous. You could have gotten seriously injured, or… fuck, you could have broken your neck. And you're going to make yourself sick living in an apartment that you can't clean."

I'm the one who got her out of our parents' house. The one who's been making sure she's been surviving for the last several years. This responsibility is mine to bear, no one else's.

Especially not a stranger at some facility I know nothing about.

More tears escape Océane's eyes. "I can't do this to you guys. What about Karan?"

"What about him?" I pinch my lips. "You know how much he values family. He's not going to object to us helping out my sister."

At least, he better not.

Every time Martine comes by the house without warning, or plans an outing with the twins without telling me in advance, his response is the same.

She's my mom. I don't want to stir shit up and cause a fight in the family.

Or, the one I simply can't fault him for saying:

She's sick. I want her to spend as much time as she can with the boys.

If Karan keeps letting his mom do all this stuff without asking me… if he constantly cancels our plans because she needs him and she's family…

… then me bringing Océane home shouldn't be a big deal, right?

"Are you sure?" Océane asks, her eyes still watery.

"One hundred percent. We even have a room for you."

The guest room will be perfect for her. Right now, Cayce and Corey share a room, and with us still working through their separation anxiety, that arrangement isn't changing anytime soon. We hardly use the tiny guest room anymore, since Karan's parents now live nearby.

Before she can argue further, there's a knock at the door. The paramedics are here.

And our lives are about to change drastically.

Chapter 5

"**Y**ou look distracted, Beta."

I jump, ripped from my daze in a panic at the sound of my father's voice, but when I look up at him, he's simply staring back at me with a gentle smile.

I'm safe. I'm safe. I'm safe.

The decades-old chant soothes me back into my composed self.

As always, my father's salt and pepper hair is neatly combed to one side, not a single stray strand out of place. He gave me hell when I began growing my hair out and tying it back in a bun.

Years later, he's over it, but that tiny glint of judgment always hides in his hazel eyes.

"Uh…" I look around to center myself back in the moment.

It's just the two of us sitting on the couch in my parents' small living room. From my vantage point, I can see Rachel chatting with Mom in the kitchen.

So far, so good.

Rachel's smiling, a glass of beer in her hand as she sits at the kitchen table. I can't see Mom, but I hear her scurrying around at the kitchen counter. No matter how many times Rachel has offered to help Mom when she's making a meal, Mom always refuses.

But it's not about Rachel. Heck, I'm sitting here on my ass, not helping out, for a reason. Mom likes her space in the kitchen, and hell hath no fury for the poor mortal who gets in her way, cancer or no cancer.

"Yeah, I guess I am a little distracted." I rub the back of my neck with my hand as I crane it around. "Where are the boys?"

"I think they're downstairs." Dad squints. "What's on your mind, Beta?"

I inhale and lean back against the leather couch. The truth is, I can't really spew out everything that's on my mind. Not to Dad. That was never the type of relationship we had. My brain is still scarred from memories of his screams, the fear that would inhabit my bones, whenever I dared to step out of line or try to be someone he doesn't want me to be.

Even if I was open with him, I can't really share what occupies my mind right now. Not when it has to do with my mother.

I'm not blind about the fact that the amount of space Mom's been taking up ever since they moved to the city has been weighing on Rachel. Despite the long hours I work, it's still very clear to me. I lost a lot of points by choosing to help Mom the other night, and I was already in the negatives.

But I know what Dad would say. *A good son honours his mother.*

Ever since I was born, he has always drilled down this one value from his Indian heritage more than any other:

Love, respect, and serve your parents.

Mom may not be Indian, but she sure as hell wields that value, too. There's a good reason they fell in love and got married; they've got a lot in common.

But it's insanely frustrating not to be able to share what's on my mind. I can't share with Dad because he won't understand. Most of my friends from college slowly fell away when I had Cayce and Corey. The person I'm closest to apart from my wife is Will, but I can't be 100% honest with him, either.

I'm supposed to take care of his sister. I'm supposed to make her happy. And I'm too ashamed to let him know that I've been failing miserably.

The pressure of it all is debilitating.

So, instead, I force a smile and look Dad in the eyes. "Work is running me ragged. I'm just a bit tired, that's all."

Dad's smile gets bigger, wrinkling his eyes. "Good. You're working so hard. You should be proud of yourself."

"Hmm." I nod without too much conviction.

"It may be hard, but that's what the man of the family does," Dad continues. "They work real jobs that provide for their families."

"Ubisoft was a real job, Dad," I mutter under my breath.

Neither he nor Mom ever considered my work in the video game industry as a 'real job'.

Despite the healthy paychecks.

But software engineering pays more, and despite me doing almost the same thing, my work at True Keys is more legitimate in their eyes.

They're the ones who pushed me for the change. And Dad is right—the money I make at this startup is serious. We're already starting to consider finding a bigger home, and for the first time in years, I'm not constantly worrying about paving the way for our boys' futures.

Rachel provides just as much as I do. In fact, we're a pretty even split. My yearly bonus is what takes me over the top.

That bonus alone is what allows my father to see me as the true provider he has drilled me to be.

"Maybe your generation considers that a real job," Dad says with a roll of his eyes.

I freeze in horror. I didn't mean him to hear what I'd whispered under my breath.

"But it doesn't matter," he adds. "The job you have now is perfect."

Perfectly *suffocating*.

"Dinner's almost ready!" Mom calls out from the kitchen.

Dad's eyes light up and he stands before Mom's sentence is finished. While I stand, I spy Rachel heading towards the basement to find the boys.

Within a minute, the six of us are sitting at the dinner table with a steaming plate of Mom's signature *pâté chinois*. I turn my attention to Rachel. She's looking down at her plate with deep fondness in her eyes.

I know she misses her own mother's *pâté chinois*.

"Thank you, Mom, this is delicious," I say after swallowing my first juicy, beefy bite.

Mom smiles at me from across the table. She's wearing a long pink head scarf that drapes over her shoulder. Every time I get to see her like this is a blessing.

It wasn't that long ago that we were fearing for her life.

"Mom, I don't like the corn," Cayce frets, pushing at the creamed corn on his plate with his fork.

"I'll eat yours," Corey volunteers.

Before he has a chance to steal a bite from his twin brother, my mother grabs his wrist.

"Nuh-huh," she chides, patting Corey's head and mussing his straight black hair. "Cayce needs to eat his own corn. There's plenty leftover if you want more, honey."

"Cayce doesn't have to eat the corn if he doesn't want to." Though Rachel is sitting straight to my left, her voice sounds subdued.

Mom raises her eyebrows. "They're going to grow up picky if you keep catering to their whims."

"That's not how we handle food." This time, Rachel's voice is louder, more firm.

"Karan had to eat whatever was on his plate, or he didn't eat at all," Mom continues. "And now he eats basically anything."

The air is thickening with tension, and Rachel stiffens next to me.

"I'm basically a garbage truck!" I add, attempting to loosen the tension.

"Dad's a garbage truck!" Corey laughs. Cayce snickers too.

Dad shoots me a glance that makes my blood go cold. A memory of him screaming and sending me to my room for daring to talk with my mouth full rears its way to the front of my mind.

"Let's not bring talks of garbage to the dinner table, please," he says in a stern tone.

I lower my chin and keep eating in silence.

"Anyway, I wanted to talk about the Christmas plans." Mom takes a bite before she continues.

I give Rachel a sideways glance. She seems okay. At least, for the time being.

"I finalized the details with Jocelyne. We'll arrive at her cottage on December 23rd, and we can stay as long as we want up til January 3rd because she's headed to Mexico then. Anjali and Suresh will be joining us with their kids as well."

A bubble of excitement bursts in my chest. Jocelyne is Mom's sister, and Anjali is Dad's sister. It's not the first time Jocelyne has invited Dad's side of the family over to her cottage. One of my favourite years, Rachel and I were a brand new couple, and I was madly in love.

Still am.

I've been looking forward to Christmas this year more than usual, specifically for this. I have such sweet memories of Rachel and me in that log wood home, huddled near the fireplace with hot cocoa. Or that moment in the shower while no one else was home...

I can't let my mind go there. Not at the dinner table.

I peer at Rachel, eager to share my excitement with her. But my heart sinks a little when I notice her fidgeting hands and the way her gaze flickers away.

She's not as excited about this as I am.

"Are we gonna take the ferry?" Cayce asks, his eyes lighting up.

His grandmother smiles down at him. "Of course we're going to take the ferry, honey!"

The mental calculations start bouncing around in my head. Taking the ferry to Newfoundland is only going to make this trip longer—and more expensive—than it needs to be. Instead of taking flights directly from Montréal to Gander, we'll have to fly down to Sydney in Nova Scotia, then take the ferry, then drive up to my aunt's cottage housed on a small peninsula near Gander.

From Rachel's tense disposition next to me, I can tell she's running the same calculation in her mind.

"We… hadn't decided about the ferry yet, Mom," I stammer.

But it's too late. Both Cayce and Corey are nearly jumping up and down in excitement.

"I wanna go on the ferry!" Cayce whines.

"Me too!" Corey echoes.

Rachel shoots me a glance, and if looks could kill…

"It will be fun!" Mom adds, her eyes going dreamy. "Just think of the memories this experience will create for the boys. Spending the night on a ferry!"

"It's not like we can't afford it," I say, sighing and rubbing Rachel's shoulder in an attempt to convince myself as much as her that this is a good idea. "And we'll be asleep in the cabin most of that time."

"Will the boys even want to sleep?" Rachel retorts.

She's got a point. Keeping them under control will be a challenge for sure.

"We'll be four adults against two kids," Mom adds. "Plus, we'll avoid the layover."

"Yeah," Rachel sighs, defeated. "A single two-hour flight is definitely better than a four-hour layover…"

My chest swells with relief. Seems like she's coming around to the idea.

All I want is for her to be happy.

"Well, that's settled, then," Mom says with a happy smile.

Next to her, Dad has nearly cleaned out his entire plate already, having said hardly anything.

"Oh, Karan, I almost forgot to tell you!" Mom bites her fork, swallows, and points her utensil to the twins. "I'm taking the boys to the movie theater next Sunday."

"Uh, no," Rachel immediately pipes up, her tone stiffer than how she usually speaks to my parents. "We've got plans that day. We're visiting a friend in Estrie."

She turns to look at me, looking for support.

Oh, yeah, I'd almost forgotten we're going to visit Tania and Nolan in Roxton Falls that day.

"Yeah, sorry, Mom."

Mom chuckles without humour. "Well, then, why don't you go visit them on Saturday instead? I haven't taken them to the movies in ages."

"We can't Saturday," Rachel replies.

A hint of confusion blooms. What's happening on Saturday?

"Actually, if you took the kids on Saturday, it would work out great, so I've got no problem on that day," Rachel adds.

"Ugh… I guess I'm going to have to move stuff around on my schedule… but maybe I can make it work. You guys are always so busy!"

My brows furrow as I turn to Rachel. I'm almost scared to ask. Rachel already thinks I'm not present enough. If I start forgetting important events on top of it, I'm in trouble. "Sorry, what are we doing Saturday again?"

Rachel's sheepish look is not what I expected. "I was about to tell you later tonight…"

So I didn't forget anything.

Relief washes over me.

"Well, you can tell me now." I smile encouragingly.

Rachel's gaze darts around the room with a nervous energy before returning to me. "We're moving my sister in the guest room."

My eyes widen and my mouth goes dry, the shock hitting me like a bolt of lightning. The table goes quiet. Even the boys settle down at the bomb Rachel just dropped.

"Wait… what?"

I can't help the shocked tone of my voice. Maybe I'm misunderstanding, or I heard wrong. Maybe Océane is only coming over to spend the weekend. Or Rachel said something else entirely, and my overloaded brain fed me back mush.

Rachel's eyes go soft as she gives me an apologetic look. "Like I said, I was going to talk to you about this later… but something happened today."

"What happened to the poor dear?" Mom pipes up with a hand on her chest.

Mom has only met Océane a couple of times, and helped us out when Rachel got her out of their childhood home, but that didn't stop her from developing a sweet spot for her.

Rachel looks down. "She got hurt. She's struggling to care for herself. I… She can't be left on her own anymore."

"Oh, that poor child…" Mom covers her mouth.

Meanwhile, I can't utter a single word. A tight knot forms in my stomach, my pulse quickening.

I can't believe Rachel would invite someone into our home without talking to me about it first.

Actually, that's not it.

I can't believe she wouldn't trust me to say yes.

Does she not think I would be okay with this?

I love Océane like the sister I never had. The amount of pain this girl has had to endure is simply unfair.

Bringing someone new into our home is a big deal. A *huge* deal. It's a decision that should have been made by the two of us. Together. But we don't leave family behind. If this were my sister, I couldn't fathom leaving her in need, especially knowing that I could have helped.

The fact that Rachel didn't trust me with this decision… it triggers alarm bells deep into the recesses of my mind.

Something is deeply wrong between us.

For the first time, a doubt creeps into me about whether my wife still sees me as the man she loves and trusts with her whole heart.

I focus on that when I force a smile and grab Rachel's hand. "Family comes first, always," I affirm to her, my thumb tenderly stroking her palm.

She smiles at me in relief while I try my best to pretend I'm not panicking inside.

Chapter 6

Rachel

August 2011

The weekend couldn't come fast enough.

It's hot and sunny out, so I quickly put on a pink summer dress that I match with strappy sandals and make my way outside before any of my roommates wake up. I'm not really interested in making small talk with them. Luckily for me, it looks like they're sleeping in late.

Nothing like a nice walk out in beautiful St-Anne de Bellevue to clear my head of its trash.

I make my way past the rolling green hills of our campus, walking a bit faster than I intend to. The truth is, I need to burn some frustration.

A large part of me misses my baby sister like crazy. Every night, I fall asleep with an ache in my chest. I took care of her for the first seven years of her life, soothed her fears like she was my daughter. I intend to visit as often as I can, but I can't afford a bus ticket there and back every weekend.

But another part of my brain keeps circling back to that tall boy and our evening together two nights ago. Mostly, I'm obsessed with one vital question:

Why didn't he ask me for my number?

We had a perfectly pleasant evening playing hooky from that stupid party, wandering around campus in the dark and just… talking. By all accounts, it should have been boring, but there isn't a single thing Karan can say that bores me.

At least, not so far.

I don't even know why. But there's something about his aura, the deep, baritone sound of his voice… He may be a stranger, but the other night, he made me feel at ease.

At home.

Oh, and he made me laugh. Gotta give him points for that, too.

So, when it was past midnight and we both headed back towards the residence building, only parting ways to head to our respective rooms, I felt like something more should have happened. But it didn't.

I should have given him my number myself, or asked him for his, but I didn't dare. I was too swept up in the moment, basking in the exhilaration of walking next to him.

Maybe he felt the same way.

Or maybe he's decided he doesn't like me.

Above me, tall trees loom over, letting the sun filter through their bright green leaves. To my left is the glittering lake, and off in the distance, I think I see a sailboat passing by.

I focus on the calming beauty around me to settle down.

Within five minutes, I make it to the boardwalk bordering the St-Lawrence River—home of St-Anne's central commercial area, where old, quaint buildings decorate the edge of the water. It's too early for the boardwalk to be busy. Instead, I'm gifted with the vision of a sunrise across the water.

I lean against the railings on the boardwalk and take a

deep breath. My attention is so far away from my own body that I don't hear anyone approaching until his voice booms from behind me:

"Looks like you could use a break."

I jump and scream, then turn with a hand on my chest, my heart beating a mile a minute. Karan, looking sheepish, is nonetheless a pleasant sight against the backdrop of the restaurants and boutiques in my vision.

He wears the hell out of his crisp buttoned-up shirt decorated with dozens of tiny cacti, and his shorts let his long legs breathe. Instead of having his hair pulled up like the last two times I saw him, his wavy locks tumble free an inch past his wide shoulders.

"Shit, didn't mean to scare you," he says as he takes a step back.

I grip the railing and take a breath to stabilize myself. "You're a ninja, or what?"

"Absolutely not. I'm surprised you didn't hear me coming a kilometer away."

I chuckle nervously. "I was zoned out."

"Yeah, I should have thought of that and been more mindful of my approach." With that, Karan takes a step forward. "Are you okay?"

My toes tingle at the thought of him getting closer.

I'm okay now, I want to say, but the last thing I want to do is be too forward.

He's cute, and there's definitely something about him that makes me want to get closer, but there's a good chance he doesn't feel the same way.

"I just…"

How do I explain everything that's on my mind? The way I not only miss my sister, but feel this constant gnawing anxiety that she's not safe without me?

I don't have any proof. My parents are okay, I guess. They're not the warmest people, and they've been pushing me and my brother Will hard, but it's for our own good. There's just something about the way they are with little Océane, though…

I can't put my finger on it.

I decide to keep it simple. "I miss my family."

"Hmm." Karan walks up to the railing and leans against it, mirroring my previous pose. "I never thought I'd say this, but so do I."

I arch an eyebrow. "Never thought you'd say this? Why?"

Karan laughs, and the deep roar of it makes my heart soar. "They're kind of… overbearing. But they mean well."

"Ah." I turn and lean back against the railing, our forearms separated by a single inch of space. "Yeah, I get that. Mine said they'd help me through college only if I stayed on the honour roll for all five years of high school."

"And did you?" His warm brown eyes transfix me.

"Yes."

"Same. Even got the governor's medal."

"Oh, shit."

"But I'm from Val-d'Or. And I went to an English school."

My brow furrows. I know nothing about Val-d'Or, or any town in the Abitibi region, for that matter.

Karan smiles. "Nine of us graduated. Not much competition, you know."

"Oh."

"So…" Karan shifts his arm a tad, enough for the fine hairs on my forearm to feel his. I hold back a shiver. "I was right about how you could use a break."

"This is a break." I gesture around us, keeping my left arm in place so I don't break our closeness.

Karan smirks. "Want some company?"

"You're offering?"

"No, I'll call my roommate so he can hang out with you." Karan rolls his eyes. "Of course I'm offering, Rachel."

"Just making sure." I slip a loose strand of hair behind my ear. "There are probably a million better things you could be doing on a nice Saturday morning instead of hanging out with someone like me."

"Someone like you?" Karan looks at me, puzzled. "And what would that be?"

When he moves his arm away to cross them in front of his broad chest, I stifle back a soft whine.

"I dunno." I look down at the mirror-like surface of the water, thinking back to everything I've been called throughout high school. "Quiet. Nerdy. Boring. Goody-two-shoe."

"Hmm." Karan relaxes his stance. "So, in other words… Introspective. Smart. Grounded. Honorable. Yeah, no, I can't think of a better way to spend my Saturday morning."

A warm flutter spreads through my stomach. Maybe there is something there after all.

***

By the time we make it back to the residences, I'm exhausted and sunburnt. The whole day has passed us by, and it's almost midnight.

I can't stop giggling. And it seems like Karan feels the same, because his shoulders won't stop shaking.

I'm not sure why. Neither of us has said anything particularly funny in quite a while. But maybe, after a full day of walking along the canal, eating ice cream, checking out the cute shops, enjoying local foods, talking about everything and nothing, and laughing so hard Karan snorted his slushie up his nose, we're both a little giddy.

Or delirious from the sun.

We walk up the stone steps of the residence building, our pace slowing as we near the door. Once inside, we pause in the hallway.

I don't want this day to end, but we both have homework and studying on our to-do lists tomorrow morning.

I hate the idea of parting ways with Karan.

He just… gets me. He sees me, unlike anyone else ever has. Even the asshole I dated in high school, who ended up cheating on me anyway, never made me feel the way I feel now.

I turn to him and shyly twirl a strand of hair. "Thank you for distracting me today."

He turns, and we're so close our chests almost touch. I can detect the warmth emanating from him. He smells good, despite all the time we spent out in the sun. And the way he's looking down at me…

"Anytime," he says.

Neither of us move. The air is so thick you could cut it with a knife. An urge to rise on my toes and close the distance between our lips weaves it way through my skeleton.

But I could never. What if I'm reading this all wrong?

No. I need to let him make the move.

"So…" Karan backs away, and I try not to let my disappointment show as he fishes something out of his pocket—his phone—and hands it to me. "You should put in your number. So we can do this again."

"Oh. Yeah." My neck and cheeks warm up as I fumble with his phone and input my contact details, handing it back with an awkward shove. "There you go. Just… text me, and I'll have your number, too."

"Yeah."

We both stand awkwardly in silence, the moment stretching until I can no longer stand it.

"Okay, well, I gotta get to it." I pinch my lips and wave. "See you around, then?"

"Yeah," he repeats with a smile. "See you around, Rachel."

I swallow back the lump in the throat as I make my way back to my room. This time, I thought for sure we had a moment. It couldn't have been only me. I'm not that socially impaired, am I?

Or maybe we did have a moment, but he doesn't want to kiss me. Guys like him might prefer taller girls with fuller curves.

I reach my apartment and quietly make my way to my room before I change into my pajamas and crash on my bed. My roommate is asleep, and our two other roommates are likely sleeping as well in the second bedroom. I don't have anyone I can talk to about this.

My phone vibrates in my pocket. Puzzled, I take it out, only for my heart to skip a beat at the sight of the unknown number's message:

Unknown number
Rachel, it's Karan. Just realized I forgot to give you something. Can you meet me in the Western stairwell?

I quickly fumble on the tiny keyboard to type out my response:

Yeah omw

Karan
Cool

I look down at my pajamas—pink plaid shorts and a soft pink tee—wondering if I should change. I'm not even wearing a bra. Is it too early for him to see me like this? What if it makes him uncomfortable?

But I'm too wired and impatient to change, and so I rush out of my room just as I am, bare feet and all.

I don't know what he wants to give me. All I know is that I'll take any extra moment I can get with this boy.

I arrive at the stairwell first, but within seconds, the sound of the heavy metal door echoes from above. My heart thunders against my ribs, my hands trembling from anticipation. I do my best to remain motionless next to the wall, even when I catch a glimpse of Karan rushing down the stairs, red-faced and nearly out of breath.

"You're here," he breathes out in relief.

"I am."

He stops in front of me, hesitation painting his soft features. Only a second passes before he speaks, but it extends into infinity as I wait.

I don't dare touch him.

"I, uh…" Karan looks away, then back to me, a newfound confidence glinting in his eyes. "I forgot to give you this."

With one step, he closes the distance between us, pressing me up against the wall; his hand lifts my chin just as he leans forward to bring his lips to mine.

The tightrope wound up in my spine finally snaps at the relief of his body against mine, of our lips pressed together; my hands weave through his hair, his pulse quickening against my collarbone. His free hand tightens around my hip, and I'm drowned in the sensations of him, his clean taste, the roughness of his short beard against my face, the heaviness and warmth of his body contrasted to the cold of the wall at my back.

I'm floating, both ultra-aware of my body and so airy I could fly away.

This feels *so right.*

It's all over too fast when he lifts his head up, his hand still cradling my cheek. The warm brown irises of his eyes are nearly taken over by his blown-out pupils.

"I've been wanting to do that all day. I couldn't let you fall asleep without…"

"Hey!" a shrill voice calls out from above.

Karan jumps back. I look up to see a short and stout girl looking down at us from the railing. My stomach sinks when I recognize her as one of the RAs—residence assistants.

"No loitering around here after curfew! Go back to your rooms!"

I don't want this moment to end. Karan grabs my hand and squeezes.

"Now," the RA repeats.

I look into Karan's eyes, and we both giggle at each other, our gazes communicating everything our lips don't have time to say before we part ways.

Chapter 7

Rachel

By the time I finally allow myself to crash against Sophie's sectional couch with a cup of hot tea in my hand, I'm exhausted.

And it's only Saturday morning.

Sophie saddles up next to me, bringing her knees to her chest with one arm and holding her mug of tea in the other. All five of our kids are playing on the floor next to us while Will and Karan are changing the sink in Sophie's bathroom.

Playdates like this are common for us, but for the last couple of weeks, we've been so busy that we haven't been able to catch up. Between moving Océane into our guest room a few weeks ago and taking the kids to a bunch of Christmas activities, I haven't had much time to catch up with Sophie.

Right away, she detects something's wrong.

"Girl, talk to me." She scrunches her nose and frowns. "The guys are gone, and the kids are distracted, so tell me what's up."

I let out a deep sigh and straighten my back just enough so I can deposit my mug on Sophie's coffee table. Although Sophie has been in our lives for only just over a year, I trust this woman with my life. Already, she's like a sister to me. It helps that Will gushed about her for ten whole years before they finally got together, so it's like I got to know her before I even met her.

Still, bringing what I have on my mind out into the world feels like a betrayal of my vows. Right now, the man I love is somewhere in this house, performing manual labour despite his exhaustion from work.

Tendrils of shame creep up around my spine at the thought of giving an ounce of attention to these seedlings of ideas trying to implant themselves into my brain.

My eyes start to burn. I swallow the lump in my throat and look down at my hands, trying to focus on the sounds of my boys laughing in the background.

But Sophie is too perceptive. "Rachel? Oh, honey…"

She places her own mug down and scoots closer to me, her long arms enveloping my shoulders.

It would be easy to let the tears fall. Sophie is safe. But I don't want to alert the kids.

So I swallow again and take a deep breath, nestling my head against Sophie's shoulder.

"Things are fucked."

"Okay." Sophie pulls away from me to hand me my mug. "Drink. Then tell me."

I close my eyes, letting the warmth of the mug seep through my fingers. The aroma of chocolate mint tea wafts through my nose. It's a small comfort for the current turmoil fighting its way through me. I take a sip and let the hot liquid coat my tongue, then swallow to let it warm me from the inside.

"I brought Océane to live home with us without asking Karan first."

As soon as the words are out of my mouth, I shut my eyes in shame.

"Wait, what?" I open my eyes again, terrified of Sophie's reaction, but the look in those blue eyes of hers just seems… confused. "Like, permanently?"

"Yeah."

I proceed to tell her about the day I had to bring her to the hospital, and about the state of her apartment. With every moment, Sophie looks more and more horrified.

"Why doesn't Will know about this?" she breathes out. "He's trying to be more active in her life."

"Yeah, I know. That's why I haven't told him yet."

The last thing I want is to overwhelm Will with a sense of duty. He's already riddled with enough guilt for nearly avoiding Océane for years on end while he was struggling to come to terms with his own demons.

"And you didn't tell Karan?"

"I know." I cringe. "Well, I told him after I'd already invited Océane. But I didn't really give him a choice."

"Why?"

Once again, I detect no judgement in Sophie's tone. She's simply trying to understand.

I take another sip of tea to stabilize myself. It's a constant effort to keep the tears at bay.

"Well, part of it is that I couldn't live with myself if Karan said no. I can't leave Océane out to fend for herself. But…"

Julian toddles over to the couch, most likely bored with whatever the older kids are doing. He stretches his chubby arms out toward Sophie, who immediately picks him up.

"Hey, baby." She turns her attention to me while she places Julian on her lap. "But what?"

"But I guess…" That's the part I've been struggling to reconcile with. I tighten my grip on the mug. "I'm just so sick of Karan letting Martine push him around, but the worst part is how Martine keeps overstepping her boundaries with the boys, and Karan doesn't seem to mind. So I think I didn't tell him just to be petty. Which I hate."

I grit my teeth and take a steadying breath again.

"Okay. Yeah, there's a lot to unpack here."

Julian grabs a strand of Sophie's golden hair and puts it in his mouth.

"Yuck, Julian!" She pulls the strand back out and laughs, then wags a finger at him. "Mommy's hair isn't for eating."

Julian gives his mother a mischievous smile.

He's absolutely adorable, but I definitely don't miss those days. Especially with twins.

I look out at my boys on the living room floor, my heart tugging in my chest. They are their own people by now, and I love who they're becoming. I can't help seeing their father every time I look at them. He's in the light golden brown of their skin, the shiny gleam of their black hair, their large almond eyes framed by thick black lashes.

When I think of Karan, I think of home. I think of a sturdy boat keeping me safe in turbulent waters. I can hardly tell where I end and where he begins, our souls so deeply entwined that they might as well be one and the same.

The moment he came into my life, everything clicked

into place. It was never difficult. We naturally drifted to each other, and loving him became second nature.

What happens if that changes?

"You know we could take her, right?" Sophie says, her voice soft as she strokes Julian's hair. "I'm sure Will would agree."

"No." The word is immediate, reflexively bypassing my brain altogether. "She's my responsibility. I've always been the one to care for her. I'm not going to let her down."

"Okay, so what did Karan say? What does he think?"

"Does it matter?" The tears threaten to surface again when I look Sophie in the eye. "It's not like he asks me my opinion on much anymore. He just does whatever he wants… or rather, what his mommy wants."

Sophie cringes. "That attitude is *not* a good sign."

"I know."

"Just last year, it was like the two of you couldn't get enough of each other."

"I know."

"And now you're not even on the same team."

I nod slowly as I stare out into space. "I know."

And that's the problem. I know it all too well. That knowledge is an ugly thing, a weight settling deep into my bones, festering with dread as I keep wondering:

Am I the only one between the two of us who knows?

Am I the only one who cares?

Chapter 8

Karan

The old sink groans as Will and I wrestle it free from its mounting. My shoulders burn from the awkward angle, but we manage to lift it clear without anything catastrophic happening.

"Not bad for two guys who spend their days in front of a computer screen," Will chuckles, wiping sweat from his forehead with the back of his hand.

I can't help but laugh. "Yeah, who knew all those hours spent writing code would translate to actual manual labor? To be fair though, you do way more than stare at a computer screen all day."

On top of his work at a business consulting firm for small businesses, Will helps Sophie run her party planning business.

"Same shit, though. None of this." His eyes gesture to the sink as we both grab hold of it.

We set the old sink carefully against the wall, and I take a moment to stretch my back. The bathroom is small, and it makes every movement feel confined, especially at my size.

Kind of like my life lately.

Will's already examining the new fixture, but I can tell by the way he keeps glancing at me that he has something on his mind. That's the thing about Will. He's been my brother in law for so long that he's gotten terrible at hiding his thoughts from me. Rachel's the same way.

Rachel.

My chest tightens at the thought of my wife. Last weekend, we moved her sister into our guest bedroom. The move went fine, and if I'm being honest, it's sweet to see how happy the boys are to have their aunt with us.

The issue isn't Océane, though. It's the way Rachel seems to be icing me out.

"Hey, Will?" The words tumble out before I can stop them. "How do you and Sophie make it work? With the crazy schedules and everything?"

I don't mention the three kids. They may not be Will's children, but they might as well be, with the way he's been stepping up.

"It just seems like your life has been chaos for the past year," I add.

Yet, despite the chaos, he and Sophie are still going strong. After more than a year, they still look at each other like they did in those first weeks.

Will straightens up, his expression turning serious. "We make time. Even if it's just fifteen minutes of actual conversation while brushing our teeth."

Make time.

That simple statement hits me like a truck.

I grab a wrench for the sole purpose of having something to do with my hands.

He pauses, studying me. "Everything okay with you and Rachel?"

"I don't know, man. Something's off."

Will frowns. "Off how?"

"I don't know, but it's like… she doesn't talk to me like she used to."

I think back to the last conversation we had that lasted more than five minutes that wasn't about the kids or the minutia of running the house.

The answer has my heart sinking to my feet.

The fight we had at karaoke night nearly two weeks ago. That was the last time.

"Well, do you try to talk to her?" Will asks.

"I do, but it's hard." I deposit the wrench on the brand new sink, instead focusing on scratching my cuticles. "My job's been running me ragged. By the time I'm home, I'm exhausted, and Rachel is already done with dinner with the kids. I haven't touched my game project in, like, over a year."

"That's a damn shame."

Will enjoys playtesting the small game concept I've been developing on my own time.

When I had my own time.

"There's that, and then there's dealing with family stu—" I stop myself, but it's too late.

Will's eyes narrow slightly. "Family stuff. You mean your mom?"

I focus intently on the cuticle of my thumb. I don't know what Rachel has told Will, but my immediate urge is to come to Mom's defense.

"She means well."

"Yeah?" Will's voice is carefully neutral, but an edge hides underneath. "Does she mean well when she undermines Rachel's parenting decisions? Or when she shows up unannounced and expects everyone to drop everything for her? Or when she asks you to cancel your plans with us?"

"It's not that simple." I pull on a stray piece of cuticle and draw blood. "She's family, and—"

"I'm going to stop you right there, because I need you to understand something." Will sets down the pipe he's holding and turns to face me fully. "You need to remember where Rachel's coming from, man. And you know exactly what Rachel and I did when our parents became toxic. We went no contact. Cold turkey. It was the hardest thing we've ever done, but we did it because we had to protect Océane. And ourselves."

His eyes are hard. I let out a small grunt.

"So," he continues, "you can imagine that the type of blind devotion you have towards your parents is a bit hard for us to understand."

My large hand bangs against the counter as I set it down too hard. "That's different. Your parents we—"

"Abusive? Yeah. But toxicity comes in many forms, man." Will's voice softens. "Look, I'm not saying your mom is anything like our parents. That'd be completely ridiculous. And I know she's been dealing with a lot, with the cancer and all. But to me and Rachel, blood is *not* thicker than water. She might not understand why someone would let their family walk all over them."

"Yeah, but I wasn't raised that way," I say, my voice barely above a whisper. "Family is everything. You don't turn your back on family. No matter what."

I can't imagine being in the same scenario as Will, Rachel, and Océane, and having to choose to go no contact with their parents. My parents put a lot of pressure on me, but they've been my rock throughout my life.

Will picks up the pipe again, but his eyes stay locked on mine. "You married Rachel. She's your family too."

The words hit me as hard as if Will had struck me across the face with the pipe.

Of course, Rachel is my family. She's the mother of my children, the love of my life, my partner in everything. Or at least, she used to be.

When did I stop treating her that way?

Chapter 9

Karan

August 2011

I never would have predicted how much joy it brings me to see the two most important women in my life doing each other's nails, their smiles splitting their faces, both of them nearly out of breath from how much they keep talking to each other.

But it's one of the most beautiful things I've ever seen.

Aunt Jocelyne sits next to Mom and Rachel at her worn kitchen table, watching Mom's handiwork like a hawk. On the other side of the open-concept room of Jocelyne's cabin, Dad adds more wood to the fire stove while I'm refilling the plate of Christmas snacks and desserts at the kitchen counter. Jocelyne has put on some Québécois folk tunes from La Bottine Souriante, music she only plays during this time of the year.

"I have no idea how you keep such a steady hand," Rachel tells my mother. "You know, with you being ancient and all."

Mom guffaws. "Careful what you say, or I'll laugh too hard and ruin these candy canes."

"If she's ancient, what am I?" Jocelyne responds, pretending to clutch her non-existing pearls.

"Decrepit?" Mom volunteers.

All three women burst into laughter, and I can't help but chuckle to myself as I finish up the plate.

I bring it over to them with an infectious smile on my face.

"Here you go, ladies."

"Are you trying to give me diabetes?" Rachel exclaims, her eyes going wide at the sight of the plate filled to the brim with nanaimos bars, macaroons, fudge squares, marshmallow rolls, and sugar cookies.

"We only make these once a year!" Jocelyne reassures her. "They haven't killed you yet."

"Yeah. Yet." Rachel looks up at me with wide, innocent eyes, her hands still under Mom's care. "Love, would you mind feeding me a nanaimo?"

I oblige, feeding her a bite of the layered treat. As she closes her eyes to savour it, I take a moment of my own to close my eyes and bask in the moment.

When things between Rachel and me got serious, I was definitely nervous about her meeting my parents. They can be a lot for some people, and not everyone is comfortable with how intensely my mother can love.

But I had nothing to worry about.

Not only did Mom and Rachel get along great at first, but their bond has only gotten stronger over the years.

Yes, Rachel got a bit annoyed when my parents helped us move into our first apartment downtown together once we graduated from CEGEP and got ready for university. Mom got it in her head to be helpful and unpack all of our kitchen stuff, only, the way she placed things wasn't how Rachel would have done it.

But she knew Mom meant well, and she waited until my parents were gone to reshuffle everything back to how she wanted it.

Rachel isn't just the love of my life. She's everything to me. Having her in my life, from the very beginning, has felt as natural as breathing.

In the moments when all the doubt and guilt threaten to bring me under, she's there to remind me that I'm on the right path. She's even kept my involvement in the Ubisoft competition secret from my parents, at my demand.

I graduate at the end of the school year, and soon enough, I'll have to let my parents know what I truly intend for my career path. I'm not ready yet—I don't think I ever will be, even when it's time—but knowing I'll have Rachel to lean on soothes the terror that's been haunting my nights.

Speaking of the Ubisoft project, I should check up on our group chat.

I feed Rachel the last bite of her nanaimo bar, holding on to the sound of her laugh, before excusing myself to the guest room area upstairs. I left my phone in our room, at my father's insistence, but I've been itching to check in with the guys and make sure nothing's come up.

We're only supposed to reconvene on January 7th, at the start of our final semester, but not working on this project has been leaving me filled with nervous energy.

Once I find my phone lying on my bedside table, I turn it on, and my heart sinks all the way to my feet at the number of missed notifications.

Blood pumping, I read through them all. Every new

message sends another pinprick of adrenaline down my spine.

Fuck, fuck, fuck.

They want to reconvene before the new year. Derek has just gotten a surgery scheduled in February, which means we need to finish our next prototype earlier than expected.

What am I going to tell Rachel?

What am I going to tell my *parents?*

I don't realize I've been sitting on the bed, in the dark, nearly hyperventilating, before Rachel slowly walks through the door and gasps. She rushes to my side.

"Karan! What's going on?" Her soft hand slips under the fabric of my shirt to stroke my back in a calming motion.

In a monotone voice, I catch her up on the situation.

"Okay. Okay…" Rachel nods a few times. Then moves her hand up to my shoulder and squeezes. "What do you want to do?"

"I… I mean, we… have to go. I'm sorry, Rachel."

"Don't worry about it. I'm fine, so long as I'm with you, okay?" She leans her forehead against mine. "We'll go. We'll change our flights."

"I can't lie to my parents."

"Okay."

"But I can't tell them the truth."

Rachel hums. "Karan. I'm here. I'm always here. And I'm on your side, always. Okay?"

"Okay."

I allow myself to take in more of Rachel's touch, more of her presence, before I dare to stand and make my way downstairs with her. Even as we descend the stairs, I don't let go of her hand.

Mom, Dad, and Jocelyne are all seated at the table by down, drinking tea and chatting. Good. I won't have to try to capture their attention. I silently sit at the end of the table; Rachel sits next to me, not letting me go.

Mom is the first to notice my somber expression. "Honey, is everything all right?"

Dad and Jocelyne quiet down and turn their gazes to me. A familiar terror sinks its claws into my back.

That scrutiny is the heaviest of burdens when all I want is to simply be myself.

I'm safe. I'm safe. I'm safe.

"Something came up, and we have to leave tomorrow," I start.

"Wait, what?" Mom exclaims.

"Leave?" Dad adds.

"Oh, no, is everything okay?" Jocelyne asks.

"Everything's fine." I take a final look at Rachel, and the comforting warmth in her eyes will have to be enough. "Earlier this year, I joined a competition with three of my friends from McGill."

The four of us are hungry for much more than the $8,000 prize for best game prototype or $2,000 prizes for some of the other titles achieved at Ubisoft's annual Game Lab competition. Every team gets access to a mentor, but, perhaps best of all, creating something great can get the right people from Montréal's video game industry to notice you.

Last year, over a dozen internships and jobs were handed out, some of them by Ubisoft themselves, so we've got our hopes up.

But I can't tell them any of that.

"A competition?" Dad asks when I've been quiet for a moment too long. "That's my son. You're planning on winning, I hope?"

"That's the idea." I squeeze Rachel's hand. "But something came up, and we need to get back to Montréal earlier than planned to finish up our… stuff."

"What are you making? What kind of competition?" Jocelyne asks, stars in her eyes.

She's not the one I'm terrified of disappointing.

"It's the Ubisoft competition," I say, shifting my gaze downward.

"Ubisoft? Who's that? An important company?" Mom asks.

"Wait a minute…" Dad crosses his arms as he begins to figure it out. "Isn't Ubisoft that video game company?"

"Yes."

There's no point in lying. He'd see right through me. He always has. And I learned from experience that lying only made it worse.

"Oh," Mom says. "So, wait, it's a video game contest? You play games and stuff?"

"No, no, we make them."

That should make it slightly better.

"So let me get this straight." Dad stands, his voice climbing in volume. "We're helping you pay your rent, your groceries, all so you can afford tuition at McGill, and you do what with your time? Make stupid games?"

The guilt and shame fully takes hold now. I want to shrink away from Dad's booming voice. I sink so deep into myself that I barely realize it's Rachel's voice I hear next.

"I've been keeping him focused," she explains. "It's not that big a project. And every night, I make sure he's done his other homework and studying before I let him focus on the competition stuff."

That's partly true, but it's a bit more complicated than that. Rachel and I have always helped each other stay focused on our studies. But she's also fully supportive of this project. She knows that I'm holding out for an internship or a job at the end of this.

"Still. Video games?" Dad huffs, but his volume has gone down.

"Won't that distract you from what you really want to do?" Mom asks before turning her attention to Rachel. "And honey, you have to be careful with yourself. You've got your own plate full with your applications to graduate school. I don't want you to do too much."

"It's really no trouble," Rachel reassures her as she leans against me with a smile. "There's nothing I wouldn't do for your son. I've got my eye on him, I promise."

"Good," Dad says. "Because I wouldn't want all of our hard work, all I've sacrificed, to go to waste."

"It won't," Rachel adds.

The taste of shame is still persistent on my tongue. The only reason I can still live with it is the assurance that at the very least, Rachel has my back.

Chapter 10

Rachel

"**S**hit, shit, shit." Karan breezes past me to pour himself some coffee, knocking against my elbow in the process.

"Watch it," I spit out as I grab my own freshly poured mug and head to the table.

Océane, who's flipping pancakes in front of the stove, peers over at Karan with a worried expression. Her long hair is pulled back into a huge bun, but it looks like it's been brushed.

She's having a good day today. No—a great one. She had so much energy this morning that she simply insisted she had to make us breakfast to thank us for our hospitality.

"Are you okay?" Océane asks Karan.

"Yeah, I'm fine, but I'm going to be late." Karan sets his mug on the table, then walks over to Cayce and Corey's seats, ruffling their hair. "I think I might switch to a travel mug and go now."

"Why?" I look at the clock hanging over the stove. "You're right on time. What's the rush?"

I can't help the accusatory tone that slips between my teeth.

"You need to eat!" Océane says as she slides a stack of pancakes on a plate, walks over to the table, and places them at Karan's spot. "Here, you can have the first ones."

Karan looks at the pancakes, then at me, and back at the pancakes before taking a seat. "Yeah, these look too good."

"Can I be next?" Cayce calls out to his aunt.

"No, me!" his brother argues.

"You'll get yours at the same time," I firmly tell my boys before turning my attention back to Karan. "You didn't answer my question."

Karan is about to take a bite, but stops short of the forkful of pancakes entering his mouth. "Boss wants me in early to fix a bug."

My shoulders tense. "They keep making you stay late, and now they're going to make you come in early, too? Seriously, where does this end?"

"You know what'll make this better?" Océane chirps out with a big smile. "Orange juice!"

She pours a glass from the carafe of juice on the counter, then saunters over to Karan. It's been such a long time since I've since her walk with such a pep in her step. Inviting her over was the best thing I've done since…

Océane's face suddenly twists in pain, and she stumbles. I watch nearly in slow motion as the glass of orange juice slips from her fingers, falling onto Karan's lap and soaking his suit. Océane catches herself before she falls to the ground, her face still twisted in pain. But her look of pain turns into horror when she notices the mess.

"Oh, no, no, no," she whimpers. "I'm so sorry, Karan!"

Karan doesn't say anything at first. He's stuck in place, his face frozen in shock. Even the boys are quiet.

I'm the first to make a move.

"Let me find some towels."

Then, I head towards the bathroom.

"It's fine," Karan calls out. "I'm going to need to change anyway."

When I'm back, Océane is kneeling on the floor, her face still warped in pain.

"Boys, pancakes are canceled," I say.

They start whining, but I interrupt.

"Grab yourselves cereal instead, then go get dressed. No whining."

I place my hand on Océane's shoulder as I lean down. "Let me."

"No." Tears glimmer in the corner of her eyes as she keeps wiping the floor with paper towels. "This is my fault."

I kneel next to her and start mopping up the mess with the towel. "Océane, you're in pain. Just… go rest."

"I'm always in pain." She stops wiping; a tear drops onto the floor below her. "I just wanted to help, for once."

"Hey." I let go of the towel and cradle both her shoulders. "I appreciate the effort. I really do. Thank you for what you tried to do, but you're here so that I can take care of you. Not the other way around."

Our bedroom door slams shut. Karan, now changed into fresh clothes, rushes past the kitchen towards the front door.

"I gotta go, see you guys tonight!" he calls out right before leaving.

Just like that.

I reign in all the thoughts I have about his stupid job and his stupid boss. Right now, I need to focus on Océane.

"He's going to be pissed, isn't he?" Océane asks as more tears fall.

"Karan? I don't think so. Seriously, Océane, don't worry about it." I grab my towel again and finish wiping what's left of the juice on the floor. "Don't try to work through pain. Please."

She blinks away her tears and sits up. "I don't want to be a burden to you guys."

"You're not a burden. I promise." I kiss the top of her forehead and hope with all of my heart that she believes me.

***

I'm in the middle of filling a prescription when Trey walks up to me, his eyes wide.

Oh, God, what is it now?

"Hey, I think it's the school on the phone for you," Trey says with a shaky voice. "You can't catch a break, can you?"

An inkling of dread grabs hold of me. I look down at the prescriptions I'm working on, then gaze out to the waiting area, where Mr. Therrien is patiently waiting for his heart medication.

As much as I want to drop everything and run to the phone, I need to stay focused on finishing this task first.

A stray thought goes to my boys. So many things could be wrong. Maybe it's something minor. Or not so minor.

The anticipation is killing me.

I steady myself. "Tell them I'm going to call them back in five minutes, okay?"

Trey frowns. "It seemed urgent."

Fuck.

Don't you think I know that? I want to scream at the young tech.

But there's no use. He doesn't have kids of his own, and is likely years away from thinking about such things.

So, I breathe in through my nose to calm myself instead. "Okay. I need to finish this prescription first. They're aware of what my job entails."

That's why the school has been instructed to call Karan first whenever something urgent happens. They must have tried that.

And failed.

Trey nods nervously and heads back out to the phone.

I finish what I have to do, careful to move quickly without rushing anything or losing focus. Once I've spoken to Mr. Therrien and kindly sent him on his way, I rush to the phone. My fingers dial the number faster than my brain can recall it, the act having become almost muscle memory by now.

Once the secretary picks up, I can hardly contain my voice. "It's Rachel Béchard. You called about Cayce and Corey Bhatia?"

"Yes, Miss Béchard. I think it would be best if you came and collected the boys."

The dread strangles my heart. "What happened?"

"There's been an incident with a substitute."

The secretary refuses to go into more detail, telling me it's best for me to come down and discuss it in person. So I bottle up the anxiety and the fear and make my way to the school, leaving my work yet again.

Once I finally arrive, a wave of relief floods through me at the sight of Cayce and Corey sitting in the office, side by side on the uncomfortable couch, their little faces tearstained by otherwise looking okay. I rush to them and scoop them up into my arms.

They cling to me for dear life, apparently still shaken from whatever happened to bring me here. I stroke their hair and murmur calming words into their ears, our moment of unity broken only by the throat-clearing of a woman behind me.

I turn, lifting both boys on my lap, and only now notice the two other adults in the room. Principal Zaidi is sitting calmly at his desk, while a woman I don't know, a young, pale, nervous-looking girl, stands with her hands wringing together.

"Thank you for coming in, Miss Béchard," Principal Zaidi says, speaking in his usual calming tone.

"What exactly happened?" I ask, keeping a hand on each son for their comfort.

"I'm so sorry!" the young woman bursts out, wringing her hands more violently than before, her gaze flitting to us and then away frantically. "I didn't know… If I'd been told, I would have done things differently, I wouldn't hav—"

"Léa," Principal Zaidi interrupts, placing a hand on forearm. "Take a breath, okay?"

Léa's panic sure as hell isn't making me feel at ease, but I reel back the urge to go full mom-zilla and instead turn my attention to the principal.

"Léa's new, and she was replacing Miss Thérèse, who's out sick for the day." An idea of what happened starts forming in my head, and now I'm the one who starts to feel sick. "I take full responsibility for not briefing Léa appropriately before she took over the classroom this morning."

"She separated them." The words that come out of my mouth are a statement, not a question.

Léa stifles a sob. "I wanted to help the kids practice doing activities with a wider variety of people. I swear, I didn't know it would… they would…"

I take a deep breath and let out a sigh, slowly. I'm so tired. On my lap, Cayce and Corey are still slightly trembling.

I go on autopilot for the rest of the meeting, accepting the young substitute teacher's apologies without complaint. The truth is, these types of mistakes can happen. No matter how much I try to do to protect my boys, the world is bound to throw something at them to hurt them.

The best I can do is be there for them in the fallout, and make sure to bring them to every therapy appointment.

I only wish I didn't have to do it all alone.

The drive home is uneventful, the boys' usual energetic chatter tempered to a heavy quiet. To get their mind off the whole thing, I encourage them to 'help' me make dinner once we arrive home, tasking them with stirring the pot of pasta while I focus on a simple white wine sauce.

Océane joins us for dinner, then insists on heading to the living room to play with them. I make the most of the opportunity to catch up on some reading I've meant to do.

It's only hours later, at 8 PM, that the front door slams shut, louder than I'm accustomed to.

Karan's heavy footsteps echo through the condo, followed by the thud of his laptop bag hitting the ground. I peek my head out of our bedroom and into the hallway to find him running his hands through his dark hair. A few strands loosen from his usually neat bun.

"Hey," I call out softly, despite not feeling soft at all.

He got called in early this morning, and now he's back late.

As always.

"Dinner's ready. I kept it warm for you."

His only response is a grunt as he begins untying his shoes. Everything about his posture screams that today was rough—from the way his broad shoulders hunch forward to how his fingers fumble with his laces.

I return to the kitchen and pull his plate from the oven where I've been keeping it warm. The boys finished eating over two hours ago, and Océane is still in the living room with them. I try to focus on their laughter to keep myself from exploding.

Karan sits at the table and begins eating the pasta mechanically. It looks like he's performing a task rather than enjoying the meal me and the boys poured love and attention into. I busy myself wiping down the counter, stealing glances at him between swipes. Dark circles ring his soft brown eyes. His shoulders remain tense as he eats.

When he's done, he brings his plate to the sink. I follow with the dish soap, and to my surprise, he falls into line to help—me washing, him drying—a treat I rarely get nowadays.

But the tension in the air makes my skin prickle.

I hand him a plate, studying his face. His jaw is clenched tight, and a hardness lingers in his eyes.

A dark thought passes through me. I hope his foul mood isn't about what I think it's about.

"Are you mad about this morning?" I ask, careful to keep my voice low so the kids—and Océane—won't overhear.

"What? No." He practically snatches the next plate from my hands. "Of course I'm not mad."

"Really? Because you look mad."

The plate clinks against the counter as he sets it down with more force than necessary.

"Okay, fine. Yes, I'm mad. But not at Océane." His voice comes out in a harsh whisper. "My boss spent twenty minutes yelling at me for being late, then made me stay to fix someone else's mistake. So that's why I'm not feeling at the top of my game right now."

I turn off the water and face him fully. "Then quit."

Our life was perfect when he worked at Ubisoft. Well, okay, not perfect. Nothing ever is. But we had it *good*.

Yes, having twins threw a wrench in our plans, but we adapted and thrived because we were a team. Because we were living our truths.

I desperately want everything to go back to how it was before. And only one thing stands in the way.

This godawful job.

"What?" Karan gasps.

"Quit that stupid job that's slowly killing you." Keeping my voice low enough so that the kids and Océane don't overhear this fight is a challenge, but I do my best. "You hate it there. You're always exhausted or zoned out. When was the last time you actually played with the boys instead of just existing in the same room as them?"

"This job pays more than the last one," he snaps back, hunching his shoulder and shooting a panicked look towards the living room as he realizes how loud he spoke. "Or did you forget about that new house we've been looking at?"

His tone is quieter this time.

"I don't care about a bigger house!" I grab the dish towel from his hands. "I care about having my husband back. The one who used to light up when he talked about his work. The one who would spend hours building pillow forts with the twins instead of passing out on the couch every night."

"So I'm not allowed to be tired? To have bad days?"

"That's not what I'm saying and you know it."

I fold my arms across my chest, trying to contain the frustration—the rage— building inside me.

Is he purposefully not hearing me?

Even if that's the case…

I've got to contain the pressure, the heat, the ugliness stirring below the surface. Especially with the kids in the house.

I'm not like her.

"Every day is a bad day now. You're like a ghost floating through our lives. You're barely here even when you're home, Karan."

What happened to the man who would sweep me into his arms just because he felt like it? The one who couldn't wait to tell me about his day, who would spend hours debugging his code out loud to me even though I understood maybe every fifth word?

I used to anticipate every thought that popped into his head. Now, I look at him and only see a stranger wearing my husband's face.

"I'm doing this for us," he says, his voice tight. "For our family. The economy is in the shitter."

"Are you? Or are you doing it because your parents finally approve of your career?"

He rubs his hand over his face. "Rachel, please. Don't bring them into this."

"Why not? They're the reason you took this job in the first place!" A burst of laughter from the living room makes me lower my voice again. "You were happy before. We were happy."

"We can't all just do whatever makes us happy all the time, Rachel. Sometimes being an adult means making sacrifices. Being a *man* means making sacrifices."

The way he says it—like I'm some naive child who doesn't understand reality—makes something snap inside me.

"Don't you dare lecture me about sacrifices. You want to talk about sacrifices? Fine. Let's talk about how I've sacrificed having any say in our life together. How every decision you make now goes through your mother first. How—"

"For the last time, leave my mother out of this!" His whisper is sharp enough to cut glass. "This isn't about her. This is about providing for our family, about being responsib—"

"No, this is about you being too scared to disappoint Mommy and Daddy!" The words fly out of my mouth like poison darts, but I can't stop myself. "God forbid their precious son works in something as frivolous as video games—"

"You have no idea what you're talking about." His voice has gone deadly quiet. "None."

Chapter 11

Karan

The words leave my mouth before I can stop them, and Rachel's face hardens in response. Part of me wants to reach out, to grab her shoulders and make her understand. But the rest of me is too tired, too wrung out to try.

Mom and Dad were so proud of me when I got this job. The memory of Dad's face lighting up, of Mom hugging me tight—it's seared into my brain. After years of disappointment, of subtle comments about wasting my degree on "children's entertainment," I finally did something right in their eyes.

I can't let them down.

Not again.

There's got to be a way… A way to keep their pride in me and give my wife what she needs. I love her too much to consider the alternative.

"Really?" Rachel crosses her arms, the crack in her voice splitting my heart in two. "Then explain it to me. Help me understand why you'd choose to be miserable."

"I'm no—"

The lie dies in my throat. Because she's right.

I am miserable.

But I have to hope that it's going to improve as I get used to this. It has to.

Because how do you begin to separate from something so deeply ingrained in yourself? Something that's been repeated so many times to you, shown by example, shoved down your throat, so much so that it becomes an inescapable part of who you are?

I don't think I can.

The sound of the twins laughing drifts in from the living room, punctuated by Océane's gentle voice. The normalcy of it punches me in the gut.

When was the last time I made my sons laugh like that?

"And you're not the only one who's miserable," Rachel continues. "You know I had to get the boys early from school again today? And that they called you first?"

"I must have been in a meeting," I say before I can think.

The truth is, the knowledge that the boys are struggling tastes bitter in my mouth. And knowing that I put it all on her again—it's got nausea crawling up my ribcage.

"You know what?" Rachel's shoulders slump. "Never mind. I can't do this right now."

She turns away from me. Something inside me fractures. My wife—my anchor, my home, my everything—feels like she's on another planet. The distance between us stretches wider with each passing day, and I don't know how to bridge it anymore.

I keep saying the wrong thing.

Fuck, I'm too tired to think straight.

My gaze sticks to her as she walks away, her small frame rigid with tension. All I want is to call her back. To tell her that I'm drowning. That every time my boss yells at me, every time I miss bedtime with the boys, every time I see the disappointment in her eyes, I die a little inside.

Instead, the words stay locked in my throat.

"Daddy!" Corey's voice breaks through my spiral of thoughts. "Can you read us a story?"

I look over to find both boys peering around the kitchen doorway, their matching dark eyes hopeful. Behind them, Océane gives me an apologetic look.

"I tried to get them ready for bed," she says softly, "but they insisted on waiting for you."

Something warm blooms in my chest, thawing the edges of the cold weight of my argument with Rachel.

My sons still want me. Still need me.

"Of course I'll read you a story." I force a smile onto my face. "Go brush your teeth and pick out a book. I'll be right there."

They scamper off with pent up excitement. Océane lingers for a moment, her eyes darting between me and the direction Rachel disappeared to.

"I'm sorry about this morning," she says. "With the juice, I mean. I didn't mean to make you late."

"It's fine. Really. Please don't worry about it."

And I do mean that.

Océane's eyes shift downward. "I didn't want to cause a fight."

I sigh heavily and rub Océane's shoulder. "You didn't. It was all me."

My burden to bear.

I head to the boys' room, where they're already in their pajamas and arguing over which book to read. The familiar sight of their matching Star Wars sheets and the glow-in-the-dark stars on their ceiling grounds me somewhat.

The boys end up picking a Bluey book. They settle into their beds, and I sit on the floor between them. As I read, I try to do the voices like I used to, to bring the story alive the way they've always loved.

The boys giggle at my attempts, and for a moment, I feel like myself again. Like the father I want to be.

But even as I read, I can feel tomorrow's meetings looming over me. I hear my boss's voice in my head, listing all the to-dos I have for this week's sprint.

Like every sprint, there's just too much, but we have to sustain this growth, or they'll find someone to replace me who's willing to do it.

I finish the story and kiss both boys goodnight. Before I leave their side, I linger a moment longer than usual, giving each of my sons a long, drawn-out hug. Their sleepy "Good night, Daddy" echoes in my ears as I shut their door, leaving it open just a crack—the way they like it.

The shower calls to me, promising to wash away some of this day's weight. Under the hot spray, I try to sort through the mess in my head. Rachel's words keep playing on repeat:

"Quit that stupid job that's slowly killing you."

She doesn't understand. She can't. Not when she loves what she does, when she's respected in her field. Not when she had the strength to walk away from toxic family relationships.

I once had the strength to do what I wanted, but those were different times, and that was a different me. Before our lives were painted over with the lingering fear of cancer's fatal hands, or the sobering reality of everything it will take to secure my sons' futures.

Rachel does so much. Despite Will being the oldest, she's the one who shoulders the most responsibility—it's why Océane is here—but she's always taken on this burden by choice.

She hasn't been forced under pressure by a father like mine to be the perfect man.

The provider.

The brave, stoic pillar who doesn't need anyone.

When I finally emerge from the bathroom, the condo is quiet. Too quiet. I peek into the guest room. Océane is already asleep, curled up in a tight ball under her blankets.

And across from the hallway…

The master bedroom is dark and empty.

I wander toward the living room, my brow furrowed, and finally find Rachel on the couch. She's curled up on her side with two thick blankets pulled up to her chin. She's not asleep. I can tell by her less than steady breathing. But she's pretending to be.

The sight of her choosing to sleep here instead of our bed hurts as much as a physical blow to my gut.

For a moment, I stand in place, wondering if I should try to talk to her. To explain how, for once in my life, the voices in my head calling me a failure, a terrible son, finally went quiet when I saw the pride shine in Dad's eyes the moment I told him about the job offer. To share how I can't just shoot down Mom, especially because we never know if the cancer is going to come raging back.

I wonder if I should tell her how my knees weaken and my chest burns at the terror of disappointing anyone—my parents, my boss, our boys.

Her.

But I'm so tired. Of everything.

So I turn away and head to our bedroom alone. The bed is massive without her in it.

I grab her pillow and hold it close, breathing in the lingering scent of her strawberry shampoo.

Fourteen years together, and this is the first time we've gone to bed angry like this. The first time she's chosen to sleep somewhere else.

Chapter 12

May 2016

I'm clapping and cheering so hard that both my hands and throat hurt, but I can't stop myself, because my Karan is up on the stage, with his team, accepting his award for Best Prototype in Ubisoft's Game Lab competition.

A lady next to me, who was also clapping along, gives me the side eye, but for once, I don't care what other people think of me.

My heart is too full.

As soon as he gets off the stage, Karan makes a beeline for me. I can't help it; my legs start to run towards him, too.

I leap right into his arms and melt into chest. Karan grips my back and thighs, spinning me around as joyous laughter bubbles out of his chest.

"I knew it," I cry, unable to hold back my tears.

Karan stops spinning, peppering kisses on my hairline. "Couldn't have done it without you."

Refusing to let me go, he lifts my chin and kisses me as if no one's watching. I'm so light I may very well float away.

When he pulls out of the kiss, I'm left gasping for air.

"I've got to go to the networking thing after this," he says, eyes full of stars. "Come with me?"

"No, it's okay." I grab his hand and squeeze. "I'm feeling a bit peopled-out."

Already, though the crowd is thinning, the edge of my skin is too sensitive, and my heart starts speeding up.

"Got it." He kisses me one last time. "See you at home, then."

I make my way out of the building, feeling an odd blend of surreal energy and anxiety. Only once I'm in the safety of our apartment do I sink back down to earth and let the exhaustion of the social event wash over me.

I fall onto the creaky futon in the living room. Well, living room is a bit generous. It's the only room apart from the tiny bedroom behind me. The kitchen area, near the apartment door, is wide enough to accommodate a single person, and the bathroom is the tiniest I've ever had, but I love this place because it's ours.

Mine and Karan's.

I pull my laptop from the small coffee table, with plans to put on a movie and unplug my brain for the night. But first, I open my email, more out of habit than as a thoughtful decision.

My heart leaps in my throat when I read the subject line of the unread email from Océane:

Everything is fucked

I don't wait a single second to open it.

It's seriously hell without you here, Rachel. I wish I could just skip high school and go straight to CEGEP so I could move to the island with you and Karan and finally get out of this fucking place.

I had gym class today, and I wasn't lying when I told Miss Tracey that everything hurt. For real, Rachel, I swear I'm telling the truth. I don't care that I'm twelve and supposed to be young and full of energy or whatever, because that's not how I feel. I'm always so tired, and I don't know why.

She made fun of me in front of the whole class. Then you can guess what Mom and Dad had to say about that. "You need to be more like your sister! You need to try harder! Put in real effort! Blablabla…"

I don't know what I'd do if I didn't have you to talk to, because literally no one except you believes me or understands me.

I love you.

Nausea creeps up my throat, and my heart shatters into tiny pieces for the hundredth time. Nearly every time Océane sends me an email, it hurts to read it.

But I do, because she's right. No one else is there for her. She needs me.

It's my burden to bear.

I type back a thoughtful reply. I have no idea how long it takes for me to complete the whole email, because time ceases to matter when I'm speaking to Océane. All I know is that every single word matters. She's on the verge of a precipice, of completely giving up, and saying the right thing is my only line of defense to keep her from tumbling down.

I validate her feelings and try not to let the seething anger at my parents cloud my judgement.

Why the fuck are they like this with her? How dare they?

My parents were never perfect with me and Will—they were demanding and prone to screaming when angry—but at least, they were on our team. If a teacher had dared to bully us like Miss Tracey is bullying Océane, they would have rallied against them, not resting until we had justice.

I don't understand why they don't believe her. She needs to see a doctor, not get berated.

Just as I hit send, the door of the apartment opens.

I look at Karan in surprise.

"Home already?"

"What do you mean, already?" He shuts the door behind him. "It's pretty late. You've been gone two hours already."

"Oh."

I didn't realize how long I spent ruminating on Océane's email and typing back my reply.

But now that's dealt with, and I can think about how shitty my parents are being later. Because Karan's smile is splitting his face in half.

"How did it go?" I pat the futon next to me.

Karan sets his backpack down next to the door and joins me on the futon. "So, um… Ubisoft offered me a job."

He rubs his hand through his beard.

"Holy shit!" I jump from the futon and hop up and down, fully aware that the downstairs neighbors are going to hate my guts. "Karan, that's amazing!"

A wild look glitters in his eyes. "I know. I'm not going to take it."

I pause and blink. "You're not… what?"

Maybe I heard him wrong.

Karan stands and clasps my shoulders. "I've got an awesome opportunity here. The other guys from the team also got an offer, but they're not taking it. We talked a bit after the event, and we want to expand on this project and start our own studio."

My chest tightens. I should be happy about this. Their prototype really is awesome, and with a lot of time and hard work, I could see this becoming something that's successful on the market.

But…

"What's wrong?" Karan asks. His thumb strokes the side of my shoulder.

"Don't you think it's a bit… risky?" I bite my lip.

"I mean, yeah, a bit. But there are programs to help us get started."

He spouts off about a provincial government assistance program that pays new creative business founders a minimum wage, as well as other funds they can apply for.

It's all making me sick.

"We talked about this," I whisper. "I won't be able to work as many hours once I start grad school. There's no way we can make ends meet if you're stuck on minimum wage. And that's only for a year… what happens if you guys don't get funding by then?"

"We could take contract work. I've talked to other indie studio owners who do that."

"Yeah, but…" I place a hand on his chest, trying to ignore the pit in my stomach.

I hate to do this to him, but this move makes no sense. Not this early, at least.

"Wouldn't it make more sense to get some real life experience in an established company first? You'd get way better odds of getting funding if you can get your name on a few triple A games first, and you'd understand more about the ins and outs of the industry."

It's the sensible thing to do. We're plenty young, and Karan still has so much time in front of him to pursue his dream.

"So…" His smile fades. "You don't think I should do it?"

"I think you should… but not now." I smile at him despite the way my insides are twisting uncomfortably. "I believe in you. And I believe you can create something amazing again, when the time is right."

He swallows. "Yeah… maybe you're right."

I stroke his cheek. "And hey. Once I'm done with grad school and land an actual pharmacist job, I can be the breadwinner while you go off and accomplish your dreams."

Karan's face twists, like he's the one who's going to be sick next. "No, yeah. You're right. I need to take the job."

Silence lingers between us for a long beat before he kisses the top of my head.

"It's the smart move," he adds.

I should feel relief, but instead, there's a nagging sensation beneath my ribs. I want Karan to accomplish everything he could ever dream of. This isn't shutting the door forever.

I hope he sees it that way.

"You okay?" I ask him.

He straightens and smiles. "Absolutely. You don't need to worry about a thing, Rachel. I trust you."

Chapter 13

Karan

"**B**oys!" Rachel's sharp tone cuts through the cacophony of Pierre Elliott Trudeau International Airport. "Stop running around people's luggage!"

She grabs Corey's hand as he's about to dart between a elderly couple's cart.

Understandably, she's on edge. Mom texted five minutes ago to say they got stuck in traffic coming from Pointe-aux-Trembles. We still have plenty of time before our flight to Sydney, but Rachel hates cutting things close.

"But I'm excited!" Corey protests, while Cayce continues to bounce on his toes.

"I know you are, but—" Rachel starts right as my phone chooses that moment to start ringing.

The caller ID makes my stomach drop.

It's my boss.

"I need to take this," I tell Rachel, already stepping away.

Her face tightens, but she nods, turning her attention back to the twins.

"Hello?" I answer, walking a few steps away from my family.

"Karan." My boss's clipped tone immediately sets me on edge. "We have a situation."

"What kind of situation?" I ask, dread already pooling in my stomach.

I turn back to Rachel, who's finally gotten the boys to sit on a nearby bench, watching me with her green eyes narrowed with concern.

"Oliver pushed to live and broke the whole thing." My boss' words hit me like a punch to the gut. "The whole system is down. We need you here."

Fucking Oliver. He means well, but as far as juniors go, he's…

Well, I can't sugarcoat this. He's terrible.

"Wait, what happened at his code review?" I ask with my heart hammering against my chest, still in the bargaining phase.

This isn't happening.

"Who reviewed it?"

My breath quickens, my heart going staccato against my ribs. We have systems in place for this. Everyone, no matter their seniority level, gets their code reviewed by someone else on the team before pushing their changes to the live version.

So Oliver isn't the only who royally fucked up.

"Does it matter?"

"I'm at the airport," I say, my voice coming out steadier than I feel. "I'm literally about to board a flight for Christmas vacation with my family."

"I understand that, but this is an emergency. I'm calling both you and Bianca in. The entire app is unusable for our entire customer base."

I press my fingers against my temple, a headache building. "Can't someone else handle it?"

Bianca is a solid developer. Surely, she can figure it out if she's paired with someone who's at least mediocre.

"You know as well as I do that you're the best on the team, Karan." He pauses. "Look, the company will cover your rebooking fees. Just get here as soon as you can."

The line goes dead before I can respond. I stand motionless for a moment, phone still pressed to my ear.

The ambient sound of the airport rings in my ears as I try to figure out how to tell Rachel.

"Karan?" Her voice is soft. Worried.

I turn to find her standing right behind me.

"What's wrong?"

"Shit went down at work." The words taste like ash in my mouth. "The whole app is down. I need to go back and fix it."

Rachel's face goes through a series of emotions—concern, understanding, and then, finally, anger.

"No," she says firmly. "No way."

"Rachel—"

"We're about to board a plane. Then the ferry." Her voice rises slightly, and she glances at the boys before lowering it again. "They can't seriously expect you t—"

"They'll cover my rebooking fees."

"*Your* rebooking fees?" She takes a step back, her eyes widening. "What about us? What about the boys?"

I swallow hard. "They'll only cover mine."

"Of course they will." The bitterness in her voice cuts deep. "So what? I'm supposed to handle the boys alone on a ferry crossing? While your parents hover and question every parenting decision I make?"

The mixture of rage and despair in her voice sends me stumbling back.

"Rachel…" I try to catch her hand, but she pulls away. "I'm stuck between a rock and a hard place here. Trust me, I don't *want* to go."

She lowers her voice again. "You're seriously going to leave me alone?"

"My parents will be here to help—"

"That's not the point!" She runs a hand through her chestnut hair in frustration. "The point is that you're choosing that fucking job over your family. Again."

A choked back sob tears at the back of my throat. "I'm doing this for our family. Please, Rachel—"

"For our family?" She scoffs. "Please. I can't even rely on you anymore. At all."

Her words hit their mark with devastating accuracy, hooking into my heart like a thousand tiny daggers. For a moment, I can't breathe.

All I ever wanted was to be the boulder on which the people I love most can rely on. Solid. Unmovable. Yet, I've failed at this one thing.

But if I don't go, I'll lose my job. And how can my family rely on me then?

"Rachel, I—"

"Go," she says, stepping back. "Your boss is waiting."

"I'll be there before Christmas Eve. I swear." I reach for her, pulling her close despite her resistance. "One day. Two max. I'll just need to catch up."

She doesn't fight the embrace, but she doesn't melt into it like she used to either. "The boys are going to be devastated."

"I know." I press my forehead against hers, breathing in her familiar strawberry scent. "I'm sorry. I'm so sorry."

"Are you?" She pulls back just enough to look into my eyes. "Because sometimes I think you're so afraid of disappointing literally everyone else in your life—your parents, your fucking boss— that the kids and I don't even factor into your equation."

***

Rachel's words still echo through my brain when I make it to my desk several hours later. I can't shake them off because I can't convince myself that she's wrong.

"It's about time!" my boss, Antoine, nearly screams when he sees me take a seat.

"I took the first flight back I could."

"Stop explaining and just start fixing this thing." He smashes his hand against my desk, shocking me and Bianca to our feet as we flinch back. "Someone leaked my phone number, and now angry customers are blowing me up, as if I could personally fix this."

Of course he can't. Antoine co-founded True Keys with an actual developer. He brought the business and marketing brain, while the developer built the minimum viable version of the app. But when they had a falling out, Antoine bought out the developer and became the sole head of the company.

"We're on it," Bianca says to placate him. "I already found out what Oliver did wrong, so now it's just a matter of Karan and me fixing it."

"God damn it," Antoine nearly screams again. "Is it so hard to do things right?"

My blood goes cold.

Is it so hard to do things right?

I can't count the number of times my father screamed those exact words to me. I always had good grades, but there were times that I came home with a few Bs instead of straight As. The anger and disappointment in his eyes still burns into my chest.

I swallow back the primitive fear wreaking havoc on my nervous system.

I'm safe. I'm safe. I'm safe.

I run the familiar chant through my mind like a spell, desperately casting it to banish the panic clawing at my insides. I'm not sure if I'll ever believe it, but for now, I've got to claw my way back to the surface.

For Rachel. For Cayce and Corey.

If there's one thing I don't want for them, it's for them to feel fear. I don't want them to ever feel unsafe. Not just because of me, but because of the world around them. The game is rigged against us, and the harder I work, the more I can tip the scales back in their favour, because they deserve the world.

So I bury it all and get to work.

Chapter 14

Rachel

've never felt more alone than I have now as the ferry cuts through the dark waters of the Cabot Strait.

The metal railing is cold under my hands as I lean against it, watching the December sun sink toward the horizon. The wind whips my hair around my face, carrying the sharp scent of salt and diesel. A few other passengers brave the cold on the deck, but they keep their distance, leaving me alone with my thoughts.

Which is probably for the best, because right now, my thoughts are ugly things.

They spew out of me like poison, infecting every thought with decay.

I imagine Karan sitting in his ergonomic chair at the office, surrounded by his three monitors, trying to fix whatever crisis emerged this time, and I want nothing more than to wring his neck.

To let the poison spill out of me and into him.

Is he even thinking about us? Does he care?

Probably not. He's probably too focused on making his boss happy.

On being the good employee. The perfect son.

When did that become more important than being a good husband and father?

The deck vibrates beneath my feet as the engines push us further from Nova Scotia. I'd been dreading this crossing even before Karan bailed. Seventeen hours is a long time to be trapped on a boat with two energetic five-year-olds.

But now, with Martine's constant hovering and Surinder's disapproving looks every time I try to set a boundary with the boys, it feels like an eternity.

"You're too strict with them," Martine said earlier when I tried to limit their screen time. "They're on vacation. Let them have fun!"

So now my sons are below deck, probably still glued to whatever shows Martine downloaded on her tablet. I was too tired to argue. Too tired to explain again why we try to limit screens or why we have routines, even on vacation.

A gust of wind hits me, and I pull my coat tighter around myself. The sun, uninhibited by the continents out in the open sea, continues its slow descent, painting the sky in shades of orange and pink. It would be beautiful if I weren't so angry.

Angry at Karan for leaving.

Angry at his stupid boss.

Angry at his parents for enabling him.

Angry at myself for letting it get this far.

A family comes out onto the deck. It's a mom, dad, and two kids around Cayce and Corey's age. They're all bundled up against the cold, laughing as they make their way to the railing about twenty feet from where I stand. The father lifts one of the children onto his shoulders and points at something in the distance while the mother takes pictures.

The sight makes my chest ache. That should be us. Karan should be here, letting the boys sit on his broad shoulders, making up stories about sea monsters lurking in the dark waters below. We should be making memories together.

Instead, I'm standing here alone while my in-laws do their best to erase every parenting boundary I've ever set.

My phone buzzes in my pocket. For a moment, hope flares—maybe it's Karan, telling me he fixed the problem and he's already on his way. But it's only Sophie, checking in.

Sophie

How's the crossing going so far? Not planning to throw yourself overboard yet?

I start typing, then delete it. Start again.

I haven't told her that Karan went back to Montréal, and I don't know how to get the words out. How do I explain that I'm hiding on the deck because I can't fucking breathe?

I settle on keeping it simple.

It's fine. And cold. And pretty.

I shove the phone back in my pocket before she can respond. Sophie means well, and she's one of my favourite people on this Earth, but right now, her concern would just make me cry.

And I'm tired of crying over this marriage.

With a second thought, I take my phone out. I know who I need to call.

Océane answers within a single ring.

"Weren't you just texting Sophie?" she asks instead of saying hello like a normal person. "Why are you calling me?"

"Want to play Wish They Were My Parents?"

For a moment, Océane is silent on the other end, and the only sound through the phone comes from Sophie's kids screeching. Sophie and Will agreed to have Océane stay with them while we're gone.

"Okay, sure," Océane answers. "You okay?"

"There's this sweet family on the deck here. The parents look like they're enjoying themselves even more than the kids. I wish they were our parents."

"Ha." Océane pauses. "Mine's going to be easy. It hasn't even been twenty-four hours, but I see the way Sophie is with her kids. So patient. Firm, but kind. Imagine if we'd grown up with that kind of discipline. I wish she were our mom."

"Same, girl, same."

The happy family is still there, now all huddled together taking selfies. The mother's laugh carries over the sound of the engines and the wind, bright and carefree. Her husband pulls her close, pressing a kiss to her temple, and something inside me breaks.

When was the last time Karan held me like that? When was the last time we laughed together, really laughed, deep from our bellies, with hardly anything to worry about?

"Mommy?"

I turn to find Corey standing near me, his cheeks red from

the cold wind. He's wearing his coat, but it's unzipped—something Martine must have overlooked in her hurry to let him follow me.

"Give me a sec, Océane." I lower the phone from my ear as I kneel down to zip up his coat. "What are you doing out here, sweetie? Where's your brother?"

"Still watching shows with Grandma." I'm shocked they're apart and not panicking, but I don't say anything to avoid calling attention to it as he lets me fuss with his zipper. "But I got bored. And I missed you."

The simple honesty in his voice makes my throat tight.

"I'll call you later," I tell Océane, and we say a quick goodbye right before I pull my son into a hug.

He smells like the candy Martine gave him earlier.

"I missed you too, sweetie." I pull back and manage a smile. "Want to watch the sunset with me?"

He nods, and I lift him up to settle him on my hip. He's getting so big, and soon, I won't be able to do this anymore.

Together, we watch the sun slowly disappear over the horizon.

"Is Daddy really coming for Christmas?" Corey asks after a while, his voice small.

"He said he would."

The words taste bitter in my mouth.

"But what if he doesn't?"

I close my eyes briefly as another spike of anger surges through me. It's one thing to hurt me. It's another to hurt our sons. To make them doubt his devotion to them.

"Then we'll still have Christmas," I say finally. "We'll still have fun with Grandma and Grandpa, your aunts and uncle, and your cousins."

"It won't be the same," he mumbles into my shoulder.

"I know, sweetie." I press a kiss to his temple. "I know."

We stand outside until Corey starts to shiver. The happy family has gone back inside, leaving us alone with the dying light and the endless expanse of dark water.

"Let's go find your brother." I set him down. "Then we can all go have dinner."

He takes my hand as we head back inside. The ferry's fluorescent lights feel harsh after the soft sunset. We find Martine, Surinder, and Cayce exactly where I left them—huddled around Martine's tablet in the lounge area. Cayce doesn't look up as we approach.

"Oh, there you are!" Martine's voice carries across the space, making several other passengers look our way. "Rachel, I was about to text you. The boys need dinner."

"I know," I say, keeping my voice level. "Let's head to the restaurant."

Over dinner, which is comprised of overpriced ferry food that the boys barely touch, Martine chatters about all the activities she has planned for us in Newfoundland. I hear snippets about ice fishing and sledding, but I'm not really listening.

Honestly, I don't care what we do. I just want Karan to be with us.

I push my food around my plate. Next to me, the boys are getting cranky. And no wonder, too. They got too much screen time, too much sugar, too little structure. But when I suggest it's time to try and sleep in our cabin, Martine waves me off.

"Let them stay up a little longer," she says. "They're on vacation!"

I stand up abruptly, my chair scraping against the floor. "I need some air."

Back on the deck, the sun is completely gone now. Stars speckle the black sky, their light reflecting off the darker water.

I pull out my phone and open my text thread with Karan. His last message stares back at me:

Karan

I'm sorry. I'll make it up to you. I love you.

But he won't. He can't. Because I'm not angry over one missed trip or one broken promise.

I think about the boys growing up watching their father prioritize work over family. About them learning that it's normal to be absent, to let your wife shoulder everything alone, to live for other people's approval.

The thought crystallizes in my mind, clear and sharp as the winter air around me: when the holidays are over, I'm asking Karan for a divorce.

The realization doesn't hurt as much as I expected it to. Part of me has known for a while now that we were heading here. That all the love in the world can't save a marriage when one person has stopped trying.

I look out at the dark horizon, where the stars meet the sea, and let the tears finally fall.

Chapter 15

Rachel

February 2019

When my phone rings and I see Océane's name on the screen, I know something's deeply wrong. *She never calls.*

By any other means, it should have been a perfect Saturday. A romantic walk through the indoor section of Montréal's botanical gardens, hot chocolate at our favourite cafe, and nothing urgent on our to-do list. We were headed back to our apartment to prepare ourselves a nice home-cooked meal, Karan holding my hand, as if we were a brand new couple.

I stop in the middle of the busy downtown sidewalk and pick up. "Océane?"

On the other end are the heart-wrenching sounds of my sister's sobs.

"Océane, hey. I'm here." I step aside with Karan, who cradles my shoulders as if to protect me, but he can't protect me from this. "Tell me what's wrong."

"Rachel, I'm scared," my sister manages to say through her sobs.

My blood goes ice cold. "Okay. Tell me what happened."

"Mom freaked out. I brought a failed essay home because I had to get it signed, and she and Dad, you know how they are, they started arguing with me over it, but it got worse, way worse, because I was sick of it this time, and I…I…oh my God, I—"

"Breathe." I calmly help Océane through a few breaths, though I'm boiling on the inside.

"They were screaming so loud, and so I wanted to head to my room, and then Mom threw a soda can at my head, but I didn't know what it was at first, all I know is that it surprised me and I slipped down the stairs, and now everything hurts, Rachel…"

Fuck.

My hands tremble against my phone. Although Karan still holds onto me, it's like he's on an entirely different planet. I float inches away from my own body, but I have to focus, I have to fucking focus—

"Okay, Océane? Listen to me." I peer up at Karan, my steady rock. "Stay in your room. Pack your stuff, only what you really need. We're going to come get you."

"What? Ho—"

"Don't worry about it. Just… hold on, okay? Karan and I are on our way."

***

A day later, my sister is safely tucked away in Karan and my's bedroom, sleeping away the pain while I try to forget the screaming match I had with my parents as I took my sister away.

Try to forget the hateful things they said. The hateful things *I* said.

Karan came up with the idea to give Océane our room until we find a better solution. With her recent diagnosis of fibromyalgia, I don't dare make her sleep on our creaky futon.

So when Karan's parents arrive all the way from Val-d'Or with a trailer hitched to their car and a spare bed and mattress that we can place near the futon just for her, the facade I've been working hard to keep up for the sake of my sister crumbles.

Martine is the first through our apartment door. I run to her, and, without hesitation, she takes me in her arms as I let my tears pour out.

A vicious blend of guilt, horror, anger, and heartbreak spills out of every inch of me. It took me too long to get Océane out of that house. Away from *them*.

I was too focused on my own little life, on moving up the ladder at the pharmacy, on my relationship with Karan, to truly face the fact that my own parents could hurt my sister like this.

Now, they're gone.

Out of our lives.

Out of my life.

I made it clear when I walked out that they would never see us again.

Océane is alive. Her sprained wrist will heal.

And we no longer have parents.

I'm on my own.

Martine strokes my hair with a soft touch, holding me through the sobs that rack my body.

"It's okay," she whispers to me. "I'm here for you always, you know that, right?"

Oh. That's right. I'm not quite on my own.

In that moment, I love Martine so much it hurts.

I grip her tighter, and I try to form the words that I want to say to her, to thank her for showing up, but at that very moment, there's simply too much to feel all at once.

But she doesn't let me go.

***

Karan

February 2019

If I didn't know Océane was moving out of our place a month from now, I'd be worried about Rachel.

For the past week or so, she hasn't been… quite herself. I can understand her worries. Will came through and found a room for Océane that he's willing to pay for. The roommate who was looking to fill the room seems nice enough.

Still, it must be nerve-wracking to let her sister go.

Luckily, I've been keeping a surprise from her, and this might be the perfect thing to cheer her up. I know how much she's been encouraging me to keep working on game concepts outside work, and how it makes her smile to see me deeply lost in my passion.

So now that I've got a minimum viable product to show her, I have no doubt she'll be excited.

Sitting at the tiny desk near Océane's bed, I open the folder containing the executable file I've compiled, and wait. I rotate the chair to peer around; Océane is sitting on her bed, a book in hand. The door to the bathroom is closed. That's where my wife must be.

When Rachel comes out, she seems to be in a much better mood. A hint of that beautiful smile that I love appears on her lush pink lips.

"Hey," I call out to her, immediately grabbing her attention. "There's something I need to show you."

"Oh." Her smile deepens. "Okay, awesome. Then there's something I need to show you, too."

It's a good day for surprises, or what?

Rachel comes to stand next to me, and I double click the executable file. I'm so giddy that my hands start to shake.

"I've finally got something, honey."

"Can I look, too?" Océane asks, her eyes bright.

"Of course." I shift my chair slightly to give both Rachel and Océane enough room to see what I'm doing, grabbing my controller as the file loads and opens.

The next five minutes are pure joy. I play through the core game loop of my concept, which is part farm sim, part space exploration and survival, then hand the controller over to Rachel and Océane for them to try it out.

Their exclamations of surprise and fun mean everything to me. It's one thing to make a game mechanic *work*, but it's quite another to make it *fun*. You only get to find out if it's fun when someone else plays it and tells you.

"Karan, this is awesome," Rachel says. She leans over for a quick kiss, her eyes crinkled with happiness.

"I'm glad you think so," I start. "Because that's not all I wanted to show you."

I close the game, then pull out a few text documents. On the surface, these seem much more boring compared to the prototype, but they could change everything.

"I've already filled out all the paperwork, Rachel. I think it's finally time for me to do it. You're doing so well at the pharmacy, and I've got two strong projects under my belt at Ubisoft, and the down payment for the place we've been looking at is something we can afford even if I'm only making minimum wage for a year or so, and so…"

I trail off when I turn only to be confronted by Rachel's crumpled face.

The image of her with humid eyes and a trembling bottom lip is not the reaction I had in mind at all.

"What's wrong?" I stand and cradle her cheek.

Océane moves away, sensing we're going to need space.

"I was going to tell you right after this," Rachel says, her voice sounding so small.

"What is it, Rachel?"

"Karan…" She takes in a deep breath. "I'm pregnant."

The world collapses beneath my feet.

I'm… going to be a father?

I always wanted to be a father. And I can feel it, deep in my bones—the unbridled joy that's about to come out and obliterate everything else in its path. The joy that will make me pick up my wife in my arms and have us dance in our apartment, even with no music.

But in the fraction of a second that comes before that joy, my dream dies.

The world is not what I thought it would be when I first dreamed of becoming a father.

Everything is harder. More expensive. More competitive.

In these conditions, with a child, there's no way I can quit my job at Ubisoft and take the risk I wanted to take just five seconds ago.

Not if I want to be the provider I need to be.

The provider my father taught me to be.

I'm safe. I'm safe. I'm safe.

I don't know if my current job will be enough. Only time will tell, but one thing is certain:

I'll never start my own indie game studio now.

Chapter 16

I barely manage to grab Cayce before his small fingers reach the dancing flames. My heart slams against my ribs as I pull him away from the cast iron fire stove nestled in the corner of Jocelyne's cabin living room.

"Hot," he protests, squirming in my arms. "I just wanted to see—"

"No touching." I press my face into his dark hair, breathing in the familiar scent of his shampoo mixed with the sharp winter air still clinging to him. "Yes, it's hot. That's why you can't touch fire, baby."

Around us, the cabin buzzes with the controlled chaos of arrival. Bags crowd the entryway like sleeping animals, winter boots leaving dark puddles on the wooden floors. Martine's voice carries from the kitchen, directing Surinder about proper placement of the groceries.

Of course, the way I placed stuff wasn't good enough.

Anjali's kids—or should I say, her adults—are loudly catching up with Jocelyne, sharing news from CEGEP and university.

And I stand here, clutching my son, trying to remember how to breathe.

"But Daddy says I'm brave," Cayce argues, still fixated on the flames. "Like a dragon."

The mention of Karan sends a fresh wave of anger through me. He should be here, helping me wrangle our adventure-seeking son. Instead, he's probably still hunched over his computer in Montréal fixing someone else's mistakes.

"Even dragons can get burned." I set Cayce down but keep hold of his hand. "Why don't you help me unpack? Then maybe we can make hot chocolate."

His face lights up at the suggestion. Those happy eyes remind me so much of Karan that it hurts. Both twins inherited their father's expressive brown eyes, the way they crinkle at the corners when they smile. Usually, these similarities warm my heart.

Today, they sting like tiny daggers.

"Can I have marshmallows?"

"Three," I say firmly, already anticipating Martine's protest that he should have more *because it's Christmas*.

If Martine had her way, my sons would walk away from this cabin with diabetes and insomnia.

We head toward our bags, and Corey appears from wherever he was hiding, drawn by the mention of hot chocolate. Both boys start pulling things from their backpacks, which creates more chaos, but I can't bring myself to stop them. Their excitement, their pure joy at being here, is the only thing keeping me from screaming.

The fire crackles behind us, throwing dancing shadows on the walls. Outside, snow falls in thick flakes and coats my rental car. The ferry crossing feels like a distant nightmare, but its effects linger in my tight shoulders and pounding head.

Two weeks. I just have to get through two weeks of this. Two weeks of Martine's hovering, of Surinder's disapproving looks, of pretending everything's fine for the kids.

Two weeks until I can ask their father for a divorce.

The cabin's familiar scents of pine and woodsmoke fill my nose as Karan's nineteen-year-old cousin Aisha sits on the couch near the fire stove.

"How's my favourite baby cousin?" she asks Cayce, who is all too happy to rush toward her to play.

"Rachel, honey." Martine's voice carries from the kitchen. "Where are you putting the boys' snacks? They should be somewhere accessible."

I close my eyes briefly and count to five in my head. "The blue basket on the counter, like at home."

"Oh, but wouldn't the top cabinet be better? Then they won't be tempted all day."

Before I can respond and argue that she literally just said the snacks should be accessible, she's already rearranging everything. The sound of containers being shifted makes my jaw clench.

"Mommy, look!" Corey holds up a framed photo he's found, his small fingers smudging the glass. "Is that you and Daddy?"

My throat tightens as I look at the image. Karan and me, maybe six years ago, standing in front of this very fireplace. His arms are wrapped around me from behind, his chin resting on my head. We're both laughing at something off-camera. Our joy shines, even through the slightly faded photograph.

I was pregnant in that picture, though the bump was hardly visible. Our smiles held all our hopes and dreams.

"Yes, baby." I take the photo from him gently. "That's us."

"Daddy looks different," Cayce observes, peering at the picture. "His tummy was bigger."

Karan did lose some weight this year. I never cared about his weight, but now, it's yet another worry on my shoulders. Another sign that this job is leeching the life out of him.

A loud crash from the kitchen saves me from responding. Anjali has dropped a pot while unpacking with her husband Suresh.

"Sorry!" she calls out, but she's giggling. Suresh joins in while Aisha rolls her eyes at her mother's clumsiness.

"Auntie Anjali has butter fingers," Aisha tells my boys, and soon their laughter mingles with everyone else's, turning the cabin into a symphony of joy I wish I could join.

"Children should help in the kitchen," Surinder comments from his perch by the window, his tone heavy with meaning. "It teaches responsibility."

I bite back a retort about how my children are five and already dealing with enough changes. Instead, I focus on unpacking their clothes, knowing Martine will probably rearrange those too when I'm not looking.

The snow falls harder outside, thick flakes obscuring the view of the bay of beautiful Cull's Harbour. Somewhere out there, a ferry cuts through dark waters, carrying more holiday travelers toward their own complicated family gatherings.

I wonder if any of them are also planning to end their marriage when it's all over.

***

A day and a half crawls by in a blur of forced smiles and careful navigation around Martine's 'helpful' suggestions. The twins' excitement grows with each passing hour, their questions about Daddy's arrival becoming more frequent, more urgent.

When I finally hear the crunch of tires on snow, my whole body tenses.

The boys freeze mid-play, their heads snapping toward the sound like synchronized puppets. Then Cayce drops his toy dragon, and Corey abandons his puzzle.

"Daddy!" They bolt for the door as it swings open.

A blast of frigid air sweeps in, carrying snowflakes and the scent of winter. And there he is, filling the doorframe. Snow dusts his dark hair wrapped in a bun and catches in his beard, his cheeks red from the wind.

Our eyes meet over the boys' heads as he scoops them both up, one in each arm. Despite everything, my breath catches. He looks exhausted, dark circles shadowing his eyes, but he's still heartbreakingly handsome.

Still the man who's owned my heart since I first laid eyes on him.

"Oh, my boys… I missed you so much!" His voice is rough with emotion as he hugs our sons close.

They cling to him like little monkeys, talking over each other in their excitement to tell him everything he's missed.

"The ferry was huge!"

"We saw whales!"

"Grandma let us have chocolate for breakfast!"

That last one makes Karan's eyes find mine again. A question forms in them, an acknowledgment of how much has happened in his absence. I look away first.

"Rachel." He sets the boys down but keeps his hands on their shoulders. "I'm so sorry, again. I hope I can—"

"Your bags are still in the car?" I cut him off, unable to handle his apologies right now.

Not when I can smell his cologne—the same one I gave him for our anniversary—mixed with cold air and something uniquely him.

It's going to distract me from what I have resolved to do.

He nods, and I grab my coat from the hook. "I'll help you bring them in."

"Oh, I can—"

"It's fine." I'm already moving past him, careful not to brush against him in the narrow entryway. "The boys need to finish their puzzle anyway, so you can help them with that."

The cold hits me like a slap, but it's better than staying inside. Better than watching him with our children and remembering all the reasons I fell in love with him. Better than seeing how easily he fits into this family gathering, like he never left us stranded at the airport.

Because of course his family is proud of him for being a hard worker.

The snow crunches under my boots as I make my way to his rental car. Behind me, the door slams shut, then his familiar footsteps sound out as he follows me into the gathering dusk.

Once back inside, the stairway to the guest rooms is impossibly narrow. It forces us closer together than I've been to Karan in weeks as we carry his luggage to our room. His suitcase bumps against each step as I back up the stairs, guiding it while he lifts from below.

"Careful," he murmurs when I stumble slightly, his hand

brushing mine on the handle and sending an electric shock through my system.

The touch catapults me back fourteen years, to our first Christmas here. We'd snuck up these same stairs after everyone was asleep, giggling and drunk on cheap wine and youth. Karan had pressed me against this wall, his kisses tasting of peppermint, the fire for him burning deep in my belly.

Now, the memory sits like lead in my stomach.

We reach the landing, and I step aside to let him maneuver the suitcase into our room.

Our room.

The words feel wrong now, like trying to squeeze into clothes you've outgrown.

The space is exactly as I remember it. A queen bed is pushed against the wall, handmade quilt in shades of blue and grey, a small window overlooking the bay. And nothing was wrong with the room for the last two nights I've slept in it.

But now, seeing Karan set his bag next to mine, everything feels different.

Smaller. More confining.

My wedding ring catches the late afternoon light streaming through the window. A shiver runs down my spine.

"Rachel." Karan's voice is soft, hesitant. "Can we talk?"

Before I can answer, thundering footsteps on the stairs announce the arrival of our sons. They burst into the room like a tornado, climbing over the bed and each other to reach their father.

"Daddy! Come see the fort we made!"

"No, first you have to see my drawing!"

"But you promised to read us a story!"

Karan laughs; that deep, rich sound that still gives me goosebumps. A sound I haven't heard enough over the last year.

"I'll come and look at everything, I promise. I'm just placing my stuff, okay?"

The boys pout but agree. They race back downstairs with the same energy they came up with. I pretend to look through my own luggage while Karan places his own stuff on his side of the bed, but after a single minute of silence, I can no longer breathe.

"We should head down," I say, already moving toward the door. "Your mother's making dinner."

"Rachel, please." He reaches for me but stops short of actually touching me. "Just... five minutes?"

I look at him then, really look at him. At the worry lines creasing his forehead, the way his shoulders slump with exhaustion.

"Not now," I finally say. "The boys need you."

I'm not ready to talk. Plus, I'm not lying. His boys need him more than I do.

I leave him there, surrounded by our matching luggage and shared memories, all the words I can't say yet heavy on my tongue.

After dinner, comes bedtime, which is a carefully orchestrated dance we've perfected over five years of parenting. Even with the tension between us, our bodies remember the choreography.

Karan gets their pajamas while I supervise teeth brushing. I fetch fresh water while he checks for monsters under the unfamiliar bed. Together, we tuck them into the queen bed they share, our hands occasionally brushing as we smooth the blankets.

"One more story?" Cayce pleads, his dark eyes wide and hopeful.

"You've already had three," I remind him, but Karan's already reaching for another book.

"It's their Christmas vacation," he says softly, and for a moment, he sounds so much like his mother that I have to bite back a snarl.

I should argue. Should maintain the routines we've worked so hard to establish. But watching him settle between our two sons on the bed, his deep voice bringing the story alive with different characters and sound effects, I can't bring myself to interrupt.

By the time he finishes, both boys are fighting to keep their eyes open. We kiss them goodnight and leave the door cracked just the way they like it.

The hallway of the second floor feels smaller than ever as we stand in it, listening to their breathing even out. The sounds of the family downstairs have quieted; everyone is starting to settle in for the night after a long day of cooking and catching up.

"They missed you," I whisper, because it's safer than saying I missed him too.

"I know." His voice cracks slightly. "Rachel, I—"

"We should get ready for bed too," I cut him off, already moving toward our room. "It's been a long day."

He follows me silently, and soon we're engaged in another familiar dance. Taking turns in the small upstairs bathroom. Carefully avoiding each other's eyes as we change in our guest room. The bed seems to shrink with each passing moment, the space between us growing impossibly wide even as we're forced to share such intimate quarters.

I slip under the covers first and immediately turn to face the wall. The mattress dips as Karan joins me, his warmth radiating across the careful distance we maintain. This is the same bed where we've spent so many Christmas nights. Where we've shared whispers, whimpers, and moans alike.

Where we now lie like strangers.

I'm almost asleep when his hand brushes my shoulder. The touch is so light I could pretend I didn't feel it, could let myself drift off into the safety of unconsciousness.

But my body betrays me. It leans into his warmth like a flower seeking sunlight.

God damnit, why do I still crave him so much?

"Rachel." My name on his lips is barely a whisper. "Please look at me."

I shouldn't. Everything I've planned, everything I've decided—it all depends on maintaining this distance.

But fourteen years of loving him wins out, and I turn over.

In the dim moonlight filtering through the window, his eyes are impossibly dark. His hair is loose around his shoulders—he must have taken it down while I was facing the wall—and my fingers itch with the muscle memory of running through it.

His hand cups my cheek, thumb brushing across my skin with aching tenderness. I should stop this. Should remind him of all the reasons we're broken.

Instead, I let him draw me closer.

The first brush of his lips against mine is hesitant. When I don't pull away, he kisses me properly, and fuck, it's like coming home. He tastes the same—like peppermint and something else that I can only describe as undeniably Karan—and his beard scratches my skin in a way that sends shivers down my spine.

My body responds without conscious thought, pressing closer, hands sliding into his hair. His arm wraps around my waist, pulling me against him, and I gasp softly at the familiar heat of his body against mine.

Hot need rushes through my body. And, for a moment, I let myself forget.

It's a painfully short moment.

The memories crash back like a wave and take my breath away. Not in a good way. I wrench out of his grasp, breathing hard.

"I can't." My voice shakes. "I can't do this."

"Rachel, please—" He reaches for me again, but I'm already scrambling out of bed.

"No." The word comes out sharper than I intended. "I just…"

I let my voice drift away just like he's been drifting away from me. From his sons.

In the silvery moonlight streaming through the window, I watch his face crumple. The hurt in his eyes makes me want to take it all back, to crawl back into his arms and pretend everything's fine.

Instead, I grab my robe and flee the room.

Chapter 17

Karan

can't move from the bed.

The phantom warmth of Rachel's body lingers on the sheets, her scent lingering on the pillow beside me. The kiss replays in my mind. I miss the softness of her lips, the way she melted against me for that brief, perfect moment before everything shattered.

Her footsteps echo on the wooden stairs, each one driving the knife deeper into my chest. The finality in her voice when she said "I can't" feels like a door closing.

And I have no fucking idea how I'm going to open that door again.

I have to.

When I can finally make myself move, I follow her path to the top of the stairs. Through the railing, I can see her curled into herself on the worn couch by the fire. The flames of the open fire stove cast shifting shadows across her face, highlighting the tension in her shoulders, the way her hands twist nervously in her lap.

Years ago, I would have known *exactly* what to do. I would have gone to her, wrapped her in my arms, whispered the right words to make everything okay. Because I still had her trust.

Now, I stand frozen, watching the woman I love suffer alone.

And I'm completely helpless to fix it.

A soft sound from the boys' room draws me away. Their door creaks slightly as I push it open, letting the soft hallway light spill across their sleeping forms. Cayce has kicked off his side of the blanket again. He's always been a restless sleeper, like his mother. Corey's arm dangles off his side of the bed, his favorite stuffed dragon clutched loosely in his other arm.

I move carefully into the room to adjust blankets and tuck limbs back onto the mattress. Their peaceful breathing fills the space. In the dim light, I can see Rachel in their features. I see her in their slightly upturned nose, the arch of their lips.

The sight makes my chest ache.

Instead of returning to the empty bedroom, I find myself carefully crawling to the center of their shared bed. They shift instinctively, making room for me the way they always have. Corey immediately curls into my side, while Cayce throws an arm across my chest in his sleep.

The trust in their unconscious movements breaks something inside me. How many moments like this have I sacrificed for a job that's stripping away at my soul?

The wind whistles outside, echoing in the silence of the cabin. I wonder if Rachel is thinking about our kiss and replaying it over and over like I am.

Corey stirs against my side, mumbling something incomprehensible. I run my fingers through his hair and try to remember the last time I was awake and aware enough to do this. To simply lie here and watch them sleep, to be not only physically but mentally present for these small, precious moments.

I can't remember. It's like the last several months are a complete haze in my brain.

No wonder Rachel left me standing at the airport without a kiss goodbye. No wonder she flinched away from my touch tonight. I've been slowly disappearing from their lives, piece by piece, and somehow I convinced myself it was for them. That the higher pay would give them a better life.

But lying here, with the solid weight of my sons against me, all I can think about is where that "better life" is headed. I've been trying to convince myself that it's going to get better.

But will it?

Startups like True Keys don't ever let up. They chase growth at all costs.

Fuck, what have I done?

The memory of Rachel's kiss haunts me. The way she responded initially, like muscle memory taking over, before reality crashed back into her brain, loops through my head. I can still taste her chapstick, still feel the silk of her hair between my fingers, still see the moment her eyes changed from warm to wounded.

Sleep tugs at the edges of my consciousness, but I fight it. Maybe staying awake could somehow freeze this moment, keep the morning from coming and let me just be with my sons, with nothing else to worry about.

But my eyes grow heavy despite my resistance, and my last thought before drifting off is of Rachel. Of the growing fear that I'm losing her.

Of the terrifying possibility that I already have

Chapter 18

Rachel

August 2020

Twins. It just *had* to be twins.

Sitting in my bed, both babies cradled in each arm so they can properly latch onto me for breastfeeding, I've never felt less like a person. I'm a husk, a whispered memory of what it's like to be human, hidden underneath stretch marks and pelvic pain and sore nipples and the constant, bone-deep fatigue.

Corey is latched on without an issue, but Cayce is struggling again. By now, after six weeks, you'd think the three of us would have mastered this breastfeeding thing.

Apparently not.

He starts fussing, then erupts into cries, and because it's all too much, I start crying too.

Karan bursts into the room, two bottles of formula in hand. My chest tightens at the sight of them, and I take a breath to stop myself from crying.

"I'm fine," I lie.

"Rachel." Karan sits onto the bed. "Once in a while isn't going to hurt them. You need to rest. Let me."

"But nipple confusio—"

"Rachel." Karan puts the bottles down on the night table and places both hands on my knees, his gaze cutting through me like a knife. "I know how much breastfeeding them means to you. I don't want to discount that. But, please…"

Now both babies are crying in sync, Corey having unlatched at the sound of his brother's cries. My hormones are screaming at me to soothe them at any cost.

"Having you this exhausted won't help them."

My bottom lip quivers as I look down at my babies. I've tried so hard to do everything perfectly. Everything so they could have the best of the best. But maybe Karan is right. How can I be the best mom I can be if I'm constantly melting down?

"A bath would be nice," I whisper.

Karan smiles in relief, lifting both babies from my arms. "Then go. I've got them. Take as long as you need. And then make sure to get some sleep."

I run myself a bath and step into the tub before it's full. The sensation is heaven. All the tension in my muscles start to loosen up, and I can finally breathe again.

To keep myself from falling asleep, I grab my phone and start scrolling through social media. The water is hot and soothes my tired bones. Karan is right; I need a nap after this.

As I scroll, I don't really pay attention to the text and photos I'm moving past.

Not until I see *it*.

My heart stops. I scroll back up. The photo I just quickly scrolled past will surely show me a couple who only *looks* like them. It's not actually them.

But the second I lay eyes on the photo again, I can't deny the truth. Nor can I stop the icy dread from spreading across my veins.

The photo looks innocent enough. If I'd seen it under any other circumstances, I might have been just fine. But seeing my parents' smiling faces glaring back at me—a photo shared by a cousin of mine—is all it takes for me to snap.

I scream then. A blood-curling scream that rattles every bone in my body.

They're not *here*

They *should* be here

I'm losing my mind, when will this end

I need my mommy and daddy I need them I NEED THEM NOW

Please, oh God, make it stop, I need help, I need HELP!

"I've got you."

He's…

Yes, he's got me in his arms…

I can feel the warmth of him seeping through my skin. He's here. But he's drowning, too. I know that, I can sense it when I look in his eyes and see the heavy shadows, and when I notice how pale his skin has gotten.

The words keep pouring out of me on repeat:

"I need help, I need help, I need help…"

And Karan, my husband… I love him even more than before when he finally responds:

"It's okay, I'm going to get us help."

***

I'm calm and dry in my bed, lost in a dreamless sleep, when Martine finally arrives from her long drive down from Val-d'Or. I only awaken to pump my milk so I don't disrupt my supply, then sink right back into sleep as soon as my head hits the pillow.

When I awaken again, Karan's familiar shape is cocooned around my back. His chest rises and falls steadily against me. So he's asleep, too.

I smile as I close my eyes. Good. He desperately needed the rest, too.

The past six weeks have been a complete fever dream. For both of us.

No wonder I had a complete meltdown.

When I was little and imagined myself becoming a mom, it was always very clear that I would do so with my parents in the picture. I imagined my mother giving me breastfeeding advice, or my father, rarely a calm man, softly rocking my baby to sleep.

Their actions have robbed us all of that reality. And now, I'm left grieving for people who are still alive… for moments I never got to have, and never will.

Soft music flows from the living room. Martine must have put on a lullaby to soothe the twins. Already, despite the heavy fatigue that still weighs on my frame, a tug at my chest pulls me towards them.

Because they're mine.

I pull away from Karan, careful not to awaken him, and step out into the hallway. Martine's happy humming mixes in with the lullaby. But when I arrive in the living room, the vision I had in my head doesn't align with the sight in front of me.

My babies are propped on their tummy on a soft blanket lying on the floor, their gazes fixed forward. In front of them is a propped up smartphone, the screen blaring out the lullaby along with quick successions of bright images and colours.

Martine is there, too, but she's sitting on the couch as she hums, her hands busy folding laundry that I haven't had time to get to.

My throat constricts. Two conflicting waves rise against each other in my mind:

Martine is here to help. Thanks to her being here, both Karan and I got to catch up on some much needed sleep. Earlier, I had nothing left to give to my babies, and without her help, I don't know what we would have done.

But I've read enough research and studies on screen time for babies under two years old to know how bad this is for them. They're six weeks old, for crying out loud. No matter how much the guilt chokes me up at saying something to Martine when she has given us this help, I can't let this fly.

Martine sees me standing at the doorway and smiles. "You look a lot better, sweetie."

"I feel better." I walk over to my babies and kneel next to them, taking the phone away. "Listen, Martine…"

"That's been helping them last longer in tummy time," Martine interrupts. "And get some much needed cleaning done around here. You two are definitely in the thick of it. I'm so glad Karan called me."

I stand and hand the phone back to her. Her brow furrows as I go back to my twins, who start fussing a little.

"I understand that," I say as I pick up and cradle both my babies. "And I appreciate all your help. I really do. I'd just like to ask you not to use screens or TVs. Music is fine, but no screens. Not until they're at least a year old."

Martine purses her lips. "Karan watched TV when he was a baby, and he turned out just fine. More than fine, if you ask me."

"I know he turned out fine," I argue, doing my best to keep my tone friendly. "But there's still a risk for their development. We know more about the way screens affect young kids now than we did before."

I hope she can understand I'm not criticizing her parenting choices.

We do the best with the information we have and the resources we're given.

Unfortunately, that's not how Martine takes it. At all.

She raises her eyebrows. "So you think I was a bad mom for putting Karan at risk?"

"What? No." I focus on the sensation of my babies against the bare skin of my arms to help me stay settled down. "I think you did the best you could with the information you had at the time."

"Whatever." She stands, pockets her phone, and heads towards the hallway. "I won't dare to turn on that dangerous screen again."

With that, she's gone.

I taste something sour in my mouth. Martine has never, ever taken that tone with me. Never.

But maybe it's because I've never truly disagreed with her before.

Chapter 19

Karan

The kitchen feels impossibly crowded this morning. Rachel stands at the far counter, carefully angled away from where I'm getting coffee. When I reach past her for the sugar, she shifts subtly to maintain the careful bubble of space around herself.

My mother notices. Of course she does. I catch her exchanging worried looks with Dad as she serves up another round of pancakes.

But she says nothing. Instead, she adds extra blueberries to Rachel's plate the way she always has when she thinks one of us needs cheering up.

Only the boys seem oblivious to the tension. All their attention is on my cousins as they happily chat away about the ice fishing we'll be doing today. Ajay, the eldest of the two, demonstrates proper fishing technique with his fork while both Cayce and Corey hang on every word, eyes wide with anticipation for their first real ice fishing experience.

"And then you have to be really quiet," Ajay explains seriously, "or you'll scare all the fish away."

"Like this?" Corey whispers, making himself so small in his chair that we all can't help but laugh.

The sound of Rachel's laughter mingles with mine for a moment before she catches herself. The joy disappears from her face, turning to ash.

She busies herself with clearing plates and turns away before I can catch her eye.

"Everyone bundle up properly," Mom calls as we start to disperse. "It's freezing out there."

Rachel helps the boys with their snow gear while I pull on my own winter clothes. When Corey struggles with his zipper, I step forward to help, but she's already there, fingers deftly fixing the problem.

The message is clear. She doesn't need me.

Instead, I get a head start on helping Dad carry the fishing rods out to the hut on the ice.

Outside, the morning air burns my lungs in the best way. Fresh snow blankets everything, transforming the seaside mountain landscape into something magical. The frozen bay stretches out before us, enveloped by the cozy wall of trees and mountains.

My cousin Aisha, Auntie Anjali, and Aunt Jocelyne are already outside, visible as colorful dots against the snow as they set up equipment near the fishing huts. Before Dad and I have time to reach them, the door of the cabin opens behind us, and my kids woosh past me at a speed I would have thought impossible if I hadn't witnessed it with my own eyes.

"Careful!" Rachel and I call out simultaneously.

I look back, and our eyes meet for a second before she looks away.

She adjusts her scarf higher around her face.

The walk to the fishing spots gives me time to think, each crunching step on the packed snow giving me an opportunity to stay grounded. Last night's kiss plays on repeat in my mind. The moment of connection. The crushing rejection that followed.

The way she fled rather than stay and fight.

Setting up the ice fishing huts has always been a family affair, but today the usual camaraderie feels forced. I work with Dad and Ajay to drill holes and secure lines, trying to lose myself in the physical labor.

Across the ice, Rachel struggles with a piece of equipment, but catches herself before asking for help.

We used to be a team at this. The first time I brought her ice fishing, she'd pressed close against me as I showed her how to set up the gear. Her cheeks were pink from the cold, her laugh echoing across the ice as she deliberately missed steps just to keep my arms around her longer.

"You're thinking too loud." Ajay's voice breaks through my memories as he hands me another anchor, dark eyes studying my face. "Want to talk about it?"

"Nothing to talk about." The lie tastes bitter on my tongue.

"Right." He looks pointedly between Rachel and me.

With the gusts of wind and the distance between us, it's unlikely that she can overhear.

"That's why you two are acting like... well, whatever this is."

"Ajay—"

"No, listen." He secures his end of the line before continuing. "I remember the first time you brought Rachel to a family event as vividly as I remember last night's Kozhukattai."

We both wince. His father, my uncle Suresh, who's originally from South India, tried his hand at the dumpling recipe his own mother used to make him.

Calling him 'not a great cook' would be a compliment.

"Was the dough even cooked?" I chuckle.

"I don't think so. I—hey, wait, that's not the point." Ajay points at me with a wooden rod. "What I'm saying is, the sight is seared in the back of my brain."

"Damn. You were, what, five years old?"

"Yeah, but it marked me." He shakes his head. "I always thought my parents loved each other, but you two? You were something else."

I sigh.

Ajay remains quiet for a long moment while he assembles another fishing rod. "And this year, it's like, I don't know… you guys don't even seem like you're married."

The truth of it strikes like a physical blow. The fact that other people are taking notice is alarming.

I watch Rachel across the ice, the familiar way she tucks escaped strands of hair under her hat. Even now, with this distance between us, my heart responds to her smallest movements.

Seven years of marriage, fourteen years of loving her, and somehow I let it come to this.

Across the vast white expanse of the frozen bay, Aunt Jocelyne shows Corey how to spoon slush out of the holes to prevent the ice from forming back, while Cayce hovers nearby, pretending he already knows everything there is to know about ice fishing.

Despite not wanting kids of her own, she's always been great with them. She catches my eye and gives me a meaningful look, tilting her head toward Rachel.

The morning light catches on Rachel's hair where it escapes her wool hat. She's working with Aisha now, the two of them setting up some camping chairs around the fishing hut. Even from here, I can see the tension in her shoulders, the careful way she holds herself apart from the family's usual easy affection.

It's like she's already starting to detach herself from them. From me.

Mom and Dad are sharing worried glances again. They've known Rachel since she was seventeen—watched her grow from the shy, reserved girl into the accomplished woman and mother she is today.

They were at every CEGEP and university graduation with us. They celebrated her first official pharmacist job with as much excitement as we did.

To them, she's not just daughter-in-law; she's the daughter they never had.

Aunt Jocelyne approaches Rachel with a thermos of what's probably her famous hot chocolate. I observe as she coaxes a small smile from my wife. The two of them have always shared a special bond, Rachel once telling me she admired how Jocelyne never apologized for choosing a life that made her happy, even when it didn't fit others' expectations.

The irony of that conversation isn't lost on me now.

"You know," Ajay says, "staring at her isn't going to fix anything."

"I'm not—"

"Save it." He cuts me off with blunt honesty. "Look, you might still see me as a kid, and you might have more life experience than me, but even I can see you're screwing this up. Rachel's not the type to wait around forever while you figure out your priorities."

His words hit harder coming from him. Ajay, who used to follow me around when we were kids—or rather, when he was a kid and I was a teenager—who looked up to me as the cousin who had life all figured out.

Now he's looking at me with something like disappointment.

"I know my priorities," I say, but the words ring hollow even to me.

The issue isn't that I don't know. It's that I may have figured it out too late.

And the last thing I want is to hash it out and ruin Christmas for the entire family.

Ajay raises an eyebrow. "If you say so…"

But I can tell he doesn't believe me, and truthfully, I don't know that I truly believe myself.

Chapter 20

Karan

The tension in the air as we sit at my parents' dinner table is palpable. I swallow a bite of Mom's roast chicken, hardly taking the time to savour the juicy meat.

It's not that it's quiet. Not at all. The boys, sat at their mismatched high chairs my parents found at a garage sale, are babbling and knocking things over and not quite eating as much as we'd like. Mom's the one feeding them; she insisted, saying she didn't mind eating her own plate after.

There's something else, and I can't put my finger on it. Rachel seems to be doing fine. I know some of Mom's comments have begun to grate on her, but we're leaving in just a few days, and she told me she's okay.

Dad is quiet, but he always is during dinner. Still, I keep an eye on the lines of his shoulders for flashes of upset. Or rage.

Old habit.

And is that tension I see in Mom's shoulders, or is that from the awkward angle she's contorting her body in to feed the twins?

I continue to eat in silence, the weight of it threatening to crush me.

When it's clear neither Cayce or Corey will inhale another bite, Mom sighs. From the corner of my eye, I spot Dad tensing. Instead of starting to eat her own plate, Mom leans forward, forearms on the table, fingertips pressed together in a fragile steeple. Her gaze drops, then lifts up again to look straight at me.

"Karan, Rachel," she starts, the grave tone of her voice immediately sending my heart lurching in my chest. "We have something we've been meaning to tell you."

Time stands still. I don't dare breathe. A second passes, but to me, eternity and terror stretch this moment into an endless abyss.

Mom takes a deep breath and drops the bomb onto me. "I have ovarian cancer."

My ears ring; whatever words come after those four, I don't hear them. They loop on repeat in my head, jabbing me in painful pricks, and when Rachel grabs hold of my hand, I hardly feel it.

Not Mom. She's so young still. It doesn't make sense. She was fine. She was doing *just* fine. How could she have cancer?

This doesn't happen to us. Not to my family. Not to those I love.

But it just did.

I think of every unspoken word. Every dream she's still holding on to. It seemed like she still had so many years—decades, even—in front of her. But now that those decades have been put in jeopardy…

Will my mother die before I can prove to her that I'm the son she always wanted me to be?

Have I made a huge mistake by chasing a career she and Dad never wanted for me?

Oh, God…

"Karan?" Dad's voice echoes through the fog.

I stir out of the nightmare fuel that are my thoughts only to see him looking back at me with concern etched onto his features.

He, too, looks so fragile now.

"Beta, do you understand?"

"Yes."

I repeat back the words he and Mom just spoke out, as if on autopilot, not really digesting them; words like prognosis and radio and chemo and other terms I never thought I'd be uttering at this table.

Not about my mother.

All the while, Rachel doesn't let my hand go. I hone in on the sensation of her soft skin against mine to keep myself grounded.

"If you think about it, I'm quite lucky," Mom says, though the tremble in her voice betrays her fear. "They caught it early. I'm otherwise in good health. I think, all things considered, we don't have too much to worry about."

She fiddles at her braid of silver hair.

Hair that she's going to lose.

I can't lose her. I'm not ready.

"When's your next appointment?" I blurt out.

"Tomorrow," Mom answers.

"I want to be there."

Unlike Mom, my own voice stays steady.

"I want to be there, too," Rachel echoes as she squeezes my hand. "And to help in any way either of you need."

Rachel shoots my parents a reassuring smile, and a surge of love for my wife rips through me.

What would I do without her? How would I move forward and face this mountain alone?

I pray I never find out.

The rest of dinner eases into small comforts now that the truth is out in the open. I spend most of the rest of the evening asking Mom questions about her diagnosis and putting up a hopeful front, making sure to reassure her that she is, in fact, going to be okay.

Rachel handles bedtime for the boys while I help Dad with the dishes, and Mom takes a moment to rest, running a quick hand through my long hair like she did when I was young.

Only when Rachel and I are alone, the boys breathing steadily in their sleep in the two cribs next to our bed, do I allow myself to fall apart in her arms and cry.

Chapter 21

Rachel

Everyone else seems to be having fun while I'm stewing in my despair. That's the thought that keeps circling in my mind as I watch the family spread out across the frozen expanse.

I've been wandering aimlessly, but I need to keep my mind occupied. My boots crunch against the snow-dusted ice as I make my way toward where Aisha is setting up one of the smaller fishing huts. She gives me a tentative smile as I approach.

"Need help?" I ask, honestly happy for any task that will keep my hands busy and distract me from my mess of a mind.

"Sure," she says, then adds hesitantly, "Actually, can I tell you something?"

I nod, then help her secure one of the hut's corners against the wind. The fabric snaps in the cold breeze.

"When I was little, maybe six or seven, Karan used to read to me whenever our families got together." Her voice is soft, almost lost in the wind. "He'd do all these different voices for the characters, though sometimes he'd start coughing from grating his throat a bit too much. He never quit in the middle of a story though, no matter how bad it got."

The image hits me hard—a younger Karan, all long limbs and messy hair, stuck in a coughing fit yet determined to finish a story for his little cousin. It's so perfectly him. That dedication is one of the things I love most about him.

But why is she telling me this? Where is this coming from?

Reality crashes into me once again as a glimpse of last year trickles into my brain. That same dedication drove him to ignore my pleas for him to rest last year when his flu developed into pneumonia. He'd rather work through a life-threatening illness than let down his boss.

The same dedication that I love so much from him has been slowly killing our marriage.

"He's always been like that," I say, surprised by the thickness in my throat. "Never knowing when to stop."

"Yeah." Aisha meets my eyes. "But I just feel like you used to be the one who could make him pause. Take a breath."

Before I can respond, let alone fully digest what she's telling me, Corey's voice rings out across the ice. "Mommy! I think I got something!"

I start moving before I can think about it. My maternal instinct takes the wheel in moments like these. Out of the corner of my eye, I see Karan heading our way too, but I reach Corey first.

Unfortunately for my excited son, it's only a snag. The line caught on something beneath the ice. I can feel Karan hovering behind me as I help Corey free it, my shoulders tensing at his proximity.

Our son's excitement dims as he glances between us, and guilt twists in my stomach. The boys have been picking up on the tension. Of course they have. They're five years old. It's that weird age between early childhood and full lucidity.

They're awake enough to understand and communicate, and still completely unjaded, still untainted by some of the harsh realities of the world.

It makes them so intuitive.

I straighten up and avoid Karan's gaze, then move away to work on my own line. The wind is picking up, carrying snippets of conversation across the ice. Aisha is telling some story that has Martine and Anjali laughing, while Surinder and Suresh debate the best spots to make the next few holes.

A beautiful day, by any other metric than my own.

The fishing line tangles in my hands. I yank at it in frustration, but it only makes it worse. Someone—I think it's Anjali—offers help, but I wave them off. I don't need help. I don't need anyone to see how badly I'm failing at even this simple task.

The thought of failure ambushes me, sending a tremor through my hands that makes the tangled line worse. Tears threaten to escape from my eyes. Ridiculous. I'm not going to cry over a stupid fishing line.

I blink hard against the cold wind.

I'm stronger than this.

The crunch of boots on ice resonates behind me, and I can tell it's my husband before he speaks. After fourteen years, I know the sound of his footsteps, the pattern of his breathing, the way the air changes when he's near. It's muscle memory, bone-deep knowledge will likely be in my DNA until the day I die.

"Let me help," he says, his voice soft in a way that makes my chest ache.

I keep my eyes on the tangled line. "I've got it."

"Rach." The old nickname hits me like a physical blow. "Please."

That *please* undoes me somehow. It's not just about the fishing line. We both know that. And suddenly, I'm too tired to keep fighting.

My hands still as he steps closer, and I breathe in the familiar scent of him—coffee and wool and that same cologne he's worn since college. My body remembers this, remembers him, even as my mind screams at me to maintain the distance I've so carefully built.

His fingers brush mine as he takes the tangled line, and even through two layers of gloves, the contact sends a jolt through my system. I catch my breath, hoping he doesn't notice, but of course he does. Karan has always noticed everything about me, except when it matters most.

"Remember the first time we came here?" His voice is low, meant only for me as he works on the knots. "You told me ice fishing was the most ridiculous way to spend a vacation."

Despite everything, my lips curve up slightly. "It is ridiculous."

"But you came back. Every time, you came with me."

"I didn't come for the fishing." The words slip out before I can stop them.

His fingers pause on the line, and I watch them, these hands I know so well. Hands that used to cup my face when we kissed, that cradled our boys when they were newborns, that now spend more time typing code than touching anything real.

"I know I haven't been here lately," he says. "Not really here, even when I was physically present."

I look up at him then, really look, for the first time since our fight last night. His eyes are the same deep brown that made me forget my lecture notes that first day I caught a glimpse of him in that CEGEP humanities class, but something in them appears different now.

"Karan…" I start, not sure what I'm going to say.

"I want to be here now," he cuts in, his voice urgent. "Not just for this vacation. For all of it. For the ridiculous ice fishing trips and the quiet mornings and the chaos of getting the boys ready for school. For you."

A gust of wind whips my hair across my face, and before I can react, his hand is there, tucking it back under my hat. It's such a familiar gesture, one he's performed countless times over the years, and my throat tightens at the muscle memory of it.

This time, I don't pull away.

"Words are easy," I say softly, but I can hear the waver in my own voice, sense the crack forming in the walls I've built.

"Then let me show you." The tangled line falls forgotten between us as he takes my hands in his. "Give me the chance to show you."

Around us, the family continues their ice fishing. Corey's excited chatter echoes to my ears, along with Cayce's dramatic retelling of some weird dream he's supposedly had to his cousins, and Jocelyne calling out that lunch will be ready soon. But in this moment, all I can focus on is the warmth of Karan's hands around mine, the earnest plea in his eyes, the weight of fourteen years between us.

I look down at our joined hands, then back up at him.

The man I fell in love with along the shores of the Saint Lawrence river. The father of my children. The stranger he became. The person standing before me now, asking for another chance.

And slowly, standing on the edge of something both terrifying and hopeful, I nod.

Chapter 22

Karan

"Who wants to help me with lunch?"

Auntie Anjali hasn't stripped out of her snow suit yet, and she's already thinking about food. I can't help but smile. Though my situation with Rachel is precarious at best, being surrounded by the known comforts of my family is a relief.

"I will." Rachel's voice hits me straight in the sternum.

Since I took over helping the twins out of their suits, Rachel is already out of hers, now dragging her wet outdoor clothes towards the fire stove to hang them to dry.

I look up, but her back is to me while she hangs her stuff. I wish I could see what was going on inside that pretty head of hers.

Her volunteering to help Anjali with dinner has got to be a good sign, right? Since I've stepped foot in this cabin, all I've noticed was how disconnected Rachel seems, floating around like a ghost.

Disengaged.

As if she's got one foot out the door already.

Does this signal a change, or is she volunteering simply to be polite?

I know Rachel. The last thing she wants is to be a burden to others. She'll always find a way to be as helpful as possible and uplift the people around her. It's the same reason she's invited Océane to live with us.

"Wonderful!" Auntie Anjali squeals before turning to me. "You're helping, too."

"What?" Air leaves my chest, and I freeze in an awkward position, all bent over from trying to remove my boot.

"We're making Aloo Wadiyan for eleven people. And we don't have any rotis, so we need to make those, too." Anjali smirks at me. "And I know for a fact that you make better rotis than Rachel."

"It's not lack of effort," Rachel calls out.

She's still by the fire stove, now hanging our sons' snow clothes.

"They're made with love, but they're ugly." The words come out of my mouth before I've had time to think them through.

I love to joke around with Rachel. It's part of our love language.

At least, it used to be. I'm not sure joking around right now is the best move.

But my heart leaps in my throat when Rachel bursts out laughing. A tingle of warmth spreads across my body in the most comforting way. It's been too long since I've heard her laugh like this.

I missed that sound.

For a moment, our eyes meet. I lose myself in the green forest of her irises. In that short moment, I can read so much from her expression, but I don't know if I can trust my judgement. Trust what I'm detecting.

A glimmer of a chance.

Her gaze falls when Corey comes up to her with a leg hug attack. I take that opportunity to turn to Anjali.

"Fine, Auntie. I'll save the family from the scourge of Rachel's rotis."

Anjali claps her hands happily. "Good! Get going then."

Mom is already distracting the twins with what seems to be a card game, so we should be able to cook unbothered.

Anjali turns to Rachel, who's now making her way towards her, having freed herself from the leg hug. "Can you start on the onions and potatoes while I crush the wadi?"

Rachel nods in a small, shy motion. She's no longer laughing, but a tiny, shy smile remains on her lips. I pick a spot on the counter and start grabbing everything I need to make the roti—whole wheat flour, a large mixing bowl, a measuring cup of water, and a rolling pin—while Rachel starts scavenging the fridge and pantry for her ingredients.

Though she's far away, the skin of my body prickles, longing to have her near me.

I almost sigh with relief when Rachel places herself next to me. We're far apart enough that I've got enough space to make my dough, and she's got enough space to place Aunt Jocelyne's huge wooden cutting board. But, given my size, our elbows brush when she reaches to grab the chef's knife hanging on the magnetic blade holder.

Is it my imagination, or did she shiver at our contact?

Both of us get to work while Anjali preps the wadi and grates ginger and garlic. It's anything but a calm moment.

Around us, the cacophony of the cabin is in full force—the roaring of the fire within the wood stove, Aisha's phone blaring as she lounges on the old couch scrolling through videos, the twins at the table laughing with Mom, Dad and Suresh deep in conversation about the merits of coffee versus tea, and Jocelyne asking Ajay about his recent trip to Chennai to visit his grandparents on his father's side.

It's a full house for sure.

For the first time, the thought crosses my mind that maybe Rachel didn't want this. With everything that's been going on with us, maybe throwing us into the pandemonium that is my family wasn't a great idea for Christmas this year.

I watch her out of the corner of my eye. Her knife skills are impeccable, the potatoes and onions neatly diced. No surprise. Rachel somehow excels at everything she touches. Everything except roti, it seems. I'd say it's unfair, but I love her so much that I don't care.

Suddenly, she looks up from the cutting board, catching me looking at her.

"You're staring." A ghost of a grin threatens to spread on her plush lips.

"Can you blame me?" I try to keep my tone light, but my heart is pounding in my chest.

This is the closest we've been to a real connection in what feels like months. Even closer than the imperceptible nod she gave me earlier this morning.

Rachel rolls her eyes, but it's playful. I can tell the difference.

"Mom!" Aisha shouts, waving her phone in the air from

the couch. "Nani wants to talk to you."

"Why'd she call you, then, Beta?" Anjali leans her fist against her ample hips.

"Because you didn't pick up, duh."

"I'm busy working some magic here!"

Despite her argument, my aunt wipes her hands on a towel and strides over to speak to her mother—my grandmother—on Aisha's phone.

This leaves me alone with Rachel. Well, as alone as we'll be on this open-plan first floor of the cabin. Still working the dough on the rotis, I search for something to say that won't ruin the tentative peace we found only a short moment earlier.

"You know," I start, kneading the dough with more enthusiasm than necessary, "I was thinking…"

Rachel raises an eyebrow, her silence urging me to continue.

"That maybe we could use more getaways like this." I try to sound casual but hopeful.

"With your family?" Her voice is guarded now.

I'm on thin ice.

"No. Just us." I swallow hard, then gesture to her and back to me. "More moments like these, I mean. Maybe we should make a habit of leaving town from time to time."

Her knife pauses mid-slice. The air shifts again, and that familiar disconnect threatens to creep back in.

"I'd like that." She resumes her chopping, and from her vanished smile, I fear I'm losing more ground. "But it's not going to happen, is it?"

"What do you mean?"

She halts her chopping again, this time boring her green eyes deep into me. "The last thing I want is for us to plan something nice, and then get disappointed when your boss inevitably calls you in for whatever emergency or fire you need to put out."

My heart sinks all the way to my feet, but before I can respond, Auntie Anjali comes strolling back.

"Maa wanted to make sure I puree the tomatoes. It's the way she's always made it, and she never skips the opportunity to remind me."

I laugh to myself, but it's short-lived when I remember what Rachel just told me.

Anjali gestures to the food. "Focus, team. People will be hungry soon."

Rachel and I exchange a look. I frown, trying to communicate everything I want to tell her in a single glance. After spending nearly half of our lives together, I have to trust that she'll know what I'm trying to say.

I want to do better. I will do better. Just give me a chance to show you.

As I roll out each roti, I glance at Rachel beside me. Her hands move quickly yet gracefully, and my heart does little flips with every brush of our elbows. I've missed being this close to her. So much so that I have to actively focus to keep it together and not trigger a hard-on while my entire family chills in the background.

Now that Auntie Anjali has gotten the stove going, the area near the kitchen is starting to warm up, despite the cold trying to seep in from outside. Rachel brushes a strand of hair from her forehead with the back of her hand in an effort to cool down.

The sight triggers a memory from our earlier days. When we met, we both lived in the dorms of John Abbott College on the west end of the island of Montréal. The dorms were small apartments with two bedrooms each, with two people to each bedroom.

My roommate Eric and I, both with new girlfriends, had a deal. *If there's a tie on the bedroom doorknob, you don't go in.* So when Rachel and I had rushed to my bedroom in giggles, only to fall across a tie on the doorknob, we'd decided to cook together instead.

But I can't overstate how shitty the tiny kitchens in the dorms really were. As was our hand-me-down equipment. Twenty minutes later, the curry I was lovingly teaching Rachel to make was on fire.

"Remember that time we nearly burnt down the dorms in our first year at John Abbott?" I ask Rachel as I start to cook the rotis, my voice hopeful.

Rachel sets down her knife and hands her bowl of chopped veggies to Anjali. "Oh my God. No. I blocked that from my memory."

A… joke? Is Rachel really joking with me?

"No one was more traumatized than Eric and Tracey," I add.

"I was pretty traumatized at traumatizing them." Rachel's eyes go wide as she speaks. "Imagine if the roles had been reversed. I would have been mortified."

We'd managed to put out the fire, but not before we triggered the dorm-wide fire alarm, forcing everyone outside… including Eric and Tracey, who were still in the middle of whatever they were doing in the room.

I scoff. Rachel looks at me in surprise.

"The roles would never have been reversed," I explain. "Those two never touched the kitchen with a ten-foot pole."

A laugh erupts out of Rachel—a real laugh. Something

tight insight of me finally unwinds. That bubbly sound is more soothing, more healing, than any drug. It's almost distracting enough to make me burn the roti, but I'm of sound enough mind to flip it just in time.

We finish up as Anjali rushes to our side to inspect our progress. She beams at us like a proud parent and nods approval at my perfectly rounded rotis.

"Perfect!" she declares, sweeping the finished rotis into a basket. "Everyone, dinner's ready!"

A chorus of voices echoes back, and suddenly the cabin is filled with a scramble of feet and a tangle of arms reaching for food. The small dining table is overcrowded with the basket of rotis, the steaming pot of Aloo Wadiyan, and bowls, glasses, and utensils for everyone.

Rachel and I barely make it to our seats before the onslaught begins. The twins argue over one specific roti—because, of course, they can't just each decide to grab another one—while Surinder defends his samosa-hating position against Jocelyne's playful insistence that he's no brother-in-law of hers.

In the middle of it all, Rachel eats quietly, looking down at her bowl without making eye contact with anyone else. Our knees briefly bump against each other under the table when we both reach for a roti. She freezes, then smiles to herself and keeps eating.

As lunch unfolds, my mind works at a hundred miles an hour. I've got to find something… some way to show her how much she means to me.

And I can't wait until we're back home. An idea sparks in my my brain. I'm not sure if it'll work, but suddenly, I can't wait to find out.

Chapter 23

Karan

As the family disperses after lunch, Martine pulls me aside with a concerned look that immediately makes my stomach churn.

"I was hoping I could talk to you," she says.

I'm watching the twins as they race around the snow with Surinder, Jocelyne, and the cousins. They didn't waste a second getting dressed to go back outside after lunch. Their laughter echoes through the windows, and it almost makes me want to join them instead of facing whatever Martine has in store for me.

"Uh, sure," I say, trying to sound less reluctant than I actually am.

The sound fades as I follow her upstairs towards the bedrooms, my pulse a deafening metronome in my ears. Martine holds the door to her bedroom open for me and gestures with an open palm, like she's inviting me to enter a therapist's office instead of a small guest bedroom with no seating except for a bed.

"Everything okay, sweetie?" she asks as I walk past her.

Her voice is softer now, but I know better than to be fooled by it.

I plaster on another smile. "Yeah! Absolutely! Why wouldn't I be?"

"Oh, I don't know …" She draws out the words and plays with her salmon-coloured headscarf. "Well, I do know, but I didn't want to say anything at first."

She sits on the bed and taps the spot next to hers in an invitation.

An invitation I really don't want to take.

But I promised myself I wouldn't rock the boat while I was here, so I sit. And I try to remember that once upon a time, this woman and I were closer than I've ever been with my own mother.

"It's just that…" Martine pinches her lips. "Well, you seemed a bit distant today."

"Did I?"

I know I did.

"Is everything all right with you and Karan?"

"Yes, everything's fine." The lie tastes bitter on my tongue.

"You know…" She looks towards the door, as if she's worried someone might walk in and overhear. "Karan is a bit like his father."

I think about how Karan's helping with the dishes, and how I doubt Surinder even knows how to turn the dishwasher on.

I keep this thought to myself.

"Oh?"

"Yes. He can be such a workaholic sometimes!" She laughs a little, shaking her head like she's just said something charming and self-deprecating. "It can be difficult to find time together when he's so focused on other things."

"Yeah, it is difficult."

Martine squeezes my hand. "But after thirty five years of marriage, I'll tell you this… sometimes you have to compromise."

I take a deep breath to resist the urge to pull my hand away. Or scream.

"I know."

"Especially in interracial families who come from different cultures. It's all about understanding each other's needs. I remember how hard it was to make our lives fit at first, but compromise led us where we are today. One of those compromises was accepting his need to be a provider. And him being a provider also meant his work was important."

I want to roll my eyes. Martine may be Québécoise like me, but from what I know of her family, they were a lot more traditional than your average Québécois family. She was all too happy to be the nurturing homemaker who submits to her husband and his parents. She was all too happy to get married.

It wasn't the same for me. I didn't care either way about marriage, like many Québécois. We got married because Karan proposed. And I happily went along with his parents' plan for a hybrid Québécois-Hindu ceremony because I love all sides of Karan, and had no special attachment to the white wedding dress so many North American women dream of.

All that mattered was that I married the love of my life, so I was all too glad to adorn the beautiful red and gold Lehenga.

But Karan was never the work-obsessed man he is today. That man was born from the parental pressures Martine and Surinder have put him under. He's not the man I married.

Or was he always there somewhere, hidden underneath the surface?

"Women these days have so much to deal with," Martine continues. "So many expectations. It's like society expects you to take on the role of husband *and* wife."

She smiles with her teeth, causing me to brace myself for the blow I knew was coming next.

"Have you considered… quitting your job?"

My jaw falls to the floor.

"Excuse me?"

"Oh, don't look so offended. It was only a suggestion."

Martine thinking that me quitting my job would fix everything is laughable. No matter how many times I've lovingly talked about my work during family dinners, she and Surinder just don't seem to get it.

I became a pharmacist because I want to help people. Because my brain is wired in a way that makes it easy for me to do this work. Plus, Karan and I make almost exactly the same salary. Me quitting my job would halve our income.

And how would I support my little sister then?

"Yeah, no, I'm definitely keeping my job, Martine."

"In that case, you just need to be patient, sweetie. Karan will come around if you give him the support he needs."

I'm not going to argue about the fact that I've been giving Karan all the support he needs to thrive at his stupid job. I'm the one who's been holding down the fort. The one who's been taking time off work to pick up our sons when they have a bad day at school.

Instead, I grit out, "Yeah."

I stand from the bed, sick to my stomach.

"I'm gonna go lie down for a bit, okay? I think I ate a bit too much."

Martine stands with me and pulls me into a hug. "Of course, sweetie. Take care of yourself, too. It's all good."

I stumble out of the room and go straight to mine, then let myself collapse on the unmade double bed. The air is thick and heavy. I let out a shaky sigh and hope Martine doesn't hear me through my door.

Her voice still resonates in my head, almost like she's right next to me still. I turn on my back and grab my phone from my pocket to start scrolling through social media to distract myself.

Martine came right out with it, didn't she? She might as well have told me I should try harder and that it's all my fault. The weight of her words sit on my chest. I don't always see eye to eye with my mother-in-law, especially since the birth of the twins, but she never, ever gave me the impression I wasn't good enough for her son.

Until now.

I slam my eyes shut to keep the tears at bay.

I hate that she's making me feel like this.

Fuck.

Thoughts of my own mother swirl in my head. Even before she and my father began their outright emotional abuse of my sister, which eventually escalated to physical abuse, they were never really a safe place for us. I always had the feeling that their love was conditional on my success.

I just never understood how true that was until Océane failed to achieve the level of success Will and I did.

Martine, despite all her flaws, always made me feel like I

deserved to be loved no matter what.

Maybe I'm overthinking this. What I really need right now is to talk this out.

I dial Sophie's number, and she picks up on the second ring.

"Hey!" she calls out in her bright, familiar voice.

"Sophie," I say, my voice sounding small and desperate.

"Rachel, you okay?"

A rush of gratitude pours through my veins like warm water.

"No."

I mean it to come out as a joke, but it sounds too raw.

"Hey, what happened?" The concern in her tone is immediate.

This woman has been in life for only just over a year, but I cherish her so much.

"It's just…" I start, but my voice threatens to unravel. "It's been a day."

"Want to talk about it?"

"Yeah."

Without hesitation, I spew out everything that's happened over the last few days. Karan joining us late. The desperation that's been hanging out in my bones. Today's confrontation with Karan—and Martine.

"Wow," Sophie breathes out. "The audacity of that woman."

"She means well," I say, immediately jumping to Martine's defense and hating myself a bit for it.

Why do I always do that? Why do I always downplay my emotions when it comes to Karan's family?

"But I don't know how long I can keep doing this."

"Whether she means well or not, your relationship with her son is none of her damn business. Seriously, if I ever become that kind of boy mom with Julian, just go ahead and shoot me." Sophie takes a deep breath. "But I'm getting ahead of myself. What do you mean, how long you can keep doing this? You mean staying at the chalet?"

"I mean, my marriage."

Sophie falls quiet.

The tears I've been holding back start to fall, thick and hot against my cold cheeks.

"Karan says he wants to do better, but I've been asking him to do better for nearly a year now, and nothing. What if the guy I married isn't there anymore? What if we're too different? I just…" I look up at the wooden beams of the ceiling. "I'm so tired."

"Rachel," Sophie whispers. "I didn't know it was this bad."

"I didn't either." I press my hand to my mouth, like I can take the words back. "But it is. I think about it all the time."

"It?"

I swallow hard. "Divorce."

"Oh, Rachel." Sophie lets out a long breath, and more tears come flooding out of me.

"It sounds crazy, right?" I wipe at my eyes with the back of my hand. "I never in a million years thought I'd ever say that word."

Not about Karan and me.

"You don't sound crazy," Sophie reassures me. "You sound like you're in pain. And listen, I'm not going to tell you divorce is the way to go, because it's some serious shit, but please know that I'm on your team, and I'm here for you."

"What is Will going to think?"

He's so close with Karan. He'd be losing a brother.

"Fuck what he thinks." She chuckles. "Well, not really. I love him and all, blah, blah, blah, but you shouldn't base your life decisions on what your brother thinks. And if you do, I'm going to throttle you."

I laugh a little bit before I fade into silence. Sophie stays on the other end of the line, remaining quiet as well. A hint of guilt starts to creep into my bones when I remember that she probably has better things to do than sit around and listen to my sulking.

"How's my sister?" I ask to break the silence.

Despite her seeming fine the last time I spoke to her, I have to make sure she's actually okay. That she's not lying to me about how she's truly doing only to make me feel better about abandoning her for two weeks.

"Oh, she's actually doing amazing. She's had a good couple of days so far, and the kids love having their aunt with them."

Relief floods into my veins. There's that, at least. As guilty as I felt about leaving Océane behind for the holidays, I'm now more confident that she's in good hands with Sophie and Will. And why wouldn't she be?

It's only that hardly over a year ago, Will could barely bring himself to speak to our sister. Not because he didn't love her, oh no. But because he was ashamed of his freeze response when our parents' abuse towards Océane escalated.

I was the one who got her out of that house. Who confronted our parents and screamed so loudly I lost my voice for three days after. So, for the longest time, he helped her out with money and not much else, in an effort to avoid his own guilt.

Thankfully, it's gotten a lot better over the last year. Will's in therapy, and the three of us hang out all the time. He hangs out with Océane alone, too. I think his relationship with Sophie has a lot to do with it.

She gives him the courage he always needed to show up as the big brother Océane wanted so desperately.

"Actually, why don't you just ask her yourself?" Sophie asks right before shuffling echoes through the phone. "She overheard me and wants to talk to you, now."

"Oh. Uh, sure."

I barely finish my sentence before shuffling echoes on the other end of the line. I guess Sophie wasn't asking for my permission.

"Rachel!" my sister exclaims in the most upbeat tone I've heard from her in a long time.

"Hey, honey." I try to steady my voice.

Océane already has a shit ton to deal with in her own personal life. The last thing I want to do is burden her with my marital problems.

But how much did she overhear Sophie?

"So, how crazy is it out there?" she asks, a bright, curious tone illuminating her voice. "I was picturing something that could go well with Yakety Sax playing in the background."

A laugh rips out of me without permission. "I mean, almost. But it's not that bad. It's fine. I'm fine."

"Are you?" This time, Océane's tone isn't so peppy. "Typically, when I'm fine, I don't have to repeat it out loud so many times."

Of course my baby sister would know how to call me out on my bullshit.

I rub my face with my hand. "Okay. Yeah. I'm kind of falling apart out here. But that's not your responsibility. I just want you to focus on taking care of you, okay?"

"Rachel?"

"What?"

"Why are you dumb?"

I straighten up out of shock. "Excuse me?"

"You're so smart, yet you can be so dense sometimes. I just don't get it."

Océane's voice is so light and unbothered that I have to double check that we're actually having the conversation I think we're having.

I'm so confused.

"What the hell are you talking about?"

She sighs on the other end of the line. "You know I'm a full grown adult, right?"

"Uh, yeah? Bu—"

"And yeah, I'm disabled. I know that. Does that mean I can only focus on myself and never help or support anyone else? Even my sister?"

I let the silence on the line grow. Heat creeps up my neck. Finally, I find the words.

"I'm not saying you *can't*. I'm saying it's not your responsibility. I'm sorry I offended you."

"You didn't offend me, Rach. You're just really frustrating me because I want to be there for you, and you're making it really hard for me to be a sister to you."

"You're my baby siste—"

"Rach, you're not my mom." Océane takes a deep breath.

"And that's the thing… you and Karan are the same in that way."

"What?"

Now I've truly lost the thread of this conversation.

"Both of you spend so much energy catering to other people's needs. You're all over me and always making sure I'm okay, and he's obsessed with catering to his parents' every whim. Then, add the fact that you have twin boys to that mix, and where does that leave what the two of you need?"

Her words hit me like a ton of bricks.

"Is any of what I'm saying making sense?"

"Uh, yeah." I blink a few times and attempt to ground myself to the conversation instead of floating away in the turmoil of thoughts my sister brought up. "But that's what being an adult means."

It means you're never the priority. Your needs can't come first, because others will always rely on you. Especially those who can't fend for themselves.

It's different for Karan. He prioritizes whatever his boss wants, then his parents. In both of these cases, these people can fend for themselves. That's miles away from what I'm doing.

We are *not* the same. Not anymore.

"I mean, you can keep telling yourself that," Océane says.

Oh, shit. Did I say all of that out loud?

"Yeah, you did."

Gah. I did it again.

"But it is different," I argue.

"In your head, maybe it is," she continues. "But do me a favour, Rach. Don't use me as an excuse for why you can't fix your marriage."

"I never said tha—"

"You didn't need to say it. And I overheard enough from Sophie to understand what's going on. I'm not a child, Rach." She's starting to sound frustrated. "Please. What you and Karan have is something that some people will go a lifetime looking for and never find. Don't give it up so fast."

My gaze drifts to the bedroom window. I stand and make my way to the glass, taking a moment to look outside. There, below my line of sight, is Karan, playing in the snow with our boys.

My heart swells, both a painful and sweet sensation. The man who's laughing in the snow, whom I'm looking at now, hasn't shown up in months. Yet, there he is, right in front of me.

Is he still there? Is there a chance?

Chapter 24

Karan

"**D**ad, I need to pee!"

Cayce pulls me out of my staring daze. I blink a few times, then look down at my son, who's jumping up and down in the snow, a pained expression on his face.

"Well, go pee," I tell him with a smile right before turning back to the second floor window where I thought I caught a glimpse of Rachel looking down at us.

But she's already gone.

"I need help with the zipper!" Cayce exclaims, more urgently this time. "Can you come with me, please?"

Oh. Right. This might be the kind of thing I'd be more aware of if I didn't spend so much time at work. I know winter only just set in this year, but still, today is the first time I'm playing in the snow with my boys this year.

Guilt gnaws at my insides. Would they still love me as much if I gave up the job that's building them a better future? Or would they hold it against me when they're older? Would they harbour resentment for not having every option laid out for them?

I don't know. I *can't* know.

We grew up in different times, a different place. In the nineties and early aughts, growing up in a mining town like Val-d'Or, there were opportunities aplenty for the men who were willing and able to work hard. Even an entry-level job like helper at a diamond drill represented enough money to raise a family with several kids on a single salary. That's what my father did.

He quickly made his way through the ranks and into upper management while my mother stayed home to raise me. Sure, he worked long hours sometimes, but I never missed out on anything because my mother was fully focused on me.

Things are different today, especially living in the city, where living costs are so much higher than in Val-d'Or. I would have to double my current salary if Rachel were to stop working and spend more time with the boys.

Not that I want that for her. She always made it clear to me that her career is vital to her. But it does mean that my boys are growing up in a completely different reality than me.

I never grew to resent my father for his career. He worked hard, yes, but I never felt lonely.

But what about my boys? Are they already growing distant from me as I spend fewer and fewer family dinners with them, attend fewer and fewer bedtimes? Or would it be worse if I sacrificed their secure futures?

Those haunting thoughts swirl through my mind as I take Cayce inside for his bathroom break. They fester while I wait outside the bathroom door, while I zip Cayce back up into his snow suit.

Only her familiar footsteps pull me out of the nightmare.

I don't have to turn around to know it's Rachel coming down the stairs. I'd know her cadence anywhere. A deep-set instinct to turn around, grab her by the hips, and lift her up to kiss her senseless takes over my body, but I resist.

That's not what she wants from me right now. If she wants anything at all anymore.

Still, I have to turn and look at her. And God, she's such a sight. She's in loose black joggers and a forest green knit sweater that brings out the green of her eyes. Her long, thick brown hair cascades over her shoulders, reflecting the overhead lights.

That sweater of hers hangs low enough that I get a peek at one of her collarbones, and I picture myself kissing her there, the way she likes it; how I'd savour her soft gasps, the involuntary shift of her hips, the taste of that silky skin…

Cool it, Karan.

Though the thick snow suit I'm wearing can probably hide any evidence of my daydreaming, I'm not going to take any chances.

"Are you two going back outside?" Rachel asks, making her way to us.

She kneels to my right, her eyes locked on our son, and gives him a kiss on the one part of his cheek that isn't covered by his neck warmer.

"Seems like you guys were having fun out there."

"Yes, I just needed to pee!" Cayce exclaims. "Are you going to come play with us, Mommy?"

I look at Rachel, trying to read her expression, but she doesn't look away from Cayce.

"Absolutely, I will," she says with a grin, right before

booping Cayce's nose. "Go back outside with Daddy and I'll come join you guys."

"You don't have to," I say as Rachel straightens back up, the smile on her face vanishing as soon as we lock eyes. "You can rest if you want. I've got it."

"No, I want to." She gives me a small smile. "I'll be out in ten."

As she walks away, I can't help but wonder the reason behind her joining us in this way. Is it to spend time with me, or only to play with the boys?

Or maybe a little of both?

***

The snowmobile was a *bad* idea.

It'll be fun, I thought. *We'll make awesome family memories*, I convinced myself, even once I realized the particular model my aunt owns is much smaller than what I initially believed.

The boys?

They positively freaked out.

Sitting in the large sled attached to the snowmobile, they had the wind in their faces and adrenaline pumping through their blood while we zoomed across the frozen bay and through the forest trails. I know they're going to rave about this to their city friends at school once we're back from the Christmas break.

What I didn't anticipate was what having Rachel so close would do to me.

Having grown up in Val-d'Or, this wasn't my first time on a snowmobile. Nearly everyone who works in the mining industry in that town owns at least one of these bad boys, if not more. I mean, what else are you going to do during the endless winters in a place with zero mountains?

But, as I said earlier, my aunt's model is much smaller than what I'm used to. And I'm a big guy. This left hardly any space for Rachel, and gave her no choice but to hold onto me for dear life.

The heat of her at my back, her arms tightly wrapped around my chest, her lean legs stuck to mine…

It was pure torture.

It's been so long since the two of us held each other close like that. And having her so close, gripping me so tightly, just gave me a taste of what I'm missing.

And it's only not about sex. Yeah, of course, I want my wife, so much so that it makes me dizzy at times, but it's that closeness, that intimacy that I miss most.

Holding her safe in my arms because I'm the one she trusts the most. Hearing her most secret thoughts whispered in my ears and no one else's because I'm her confidant.

Part of me wishes I could whisk Rachel and my boys away, to a cabin not dissimilar to this one, away from the expectations of the world. When it's the four of us and no one else, everything feels so simple. So effortless. We could live off the land, pave our own way.

But that's not how the world works. Rachel has her sister. I have my parents. And we have to provide.

I have to provide.

Still, the idea that sparked in my mind after lunch is still very much active. There's still a way I could show Rachel just how good we are together. How much her happiness matters to me.

So, as we come back inside with the rest of my extended family and strip off our winter gear, that spark of an idea starts to form into a real plan.

First things first, I need to get away from Rachel's prying eyes. I can't tell her what I have in mind, because I know she'll refuse outright. This needs to be a surprise. It's not a good rule of thumb to ask for forgiveness instead of permission in a marriage, but desperate times call for desperate measures.

"You look exhausted," I tell her while she helps Auntie Anjali hang snow gear next to the firestove. "Why don't you go take a nap before dinner?"

Rachel looks over at me and bites her lip. "You sure? You don't need a break?" she asks, gesturing to our two boys, who are already running around the cabin's main room like two banshees.

I shrug. "No way. I'm good. You go rest, okay?"

She hugs her arms; Anjali nudges her shoulder with a teasing smile.

"I'd take him up on that if I were you," she tells Rachel. "In fact, I think I'm going to head up for a nap myself."

Rachel nods, her face blank. "Hmm. A nap does sound good."

Relief washes through me.

Yes.

Now I can move forward with my plan.

I wait a good ten minutes after Rachel heads to our bedroom upstairs before cornering my cousins Ajay and Aisha, who are both doom scrolling on their phones on opposite sides of the couch.

"On a scale of one to ten, how bored are you two?" I ask, feigning innocence.

Both of them frown before looking at each other with suspicion.

"Why are you being weird?" Aisha asks first.

"I'm not being weird."

"Yeah, man, you kind of are," Ajay confirms.

"What do you want?" Aisha continues.

"What? Nothing!"

"Really?" Aisha narrows her eyes.

I rub my beard nervously. "Okay, fine, I want something."

That earns me a good-natured eye roll from both of them.

"Could you watch the boys for me for, like…" I take out my phone to look at the time. "An hour? Hour and a half at most?"

Normally, I'd ask Mom, but she's got her hands full with dinner.

Both their faces light up.

"Say less," Aisha says as she nearly jumps from the couch. "I could eat those boys up."

"Okay, cool." I rub my hands together.

Ajay stands, but with less enthusiasm than his sister, raising a single eyebrow. "Dude, what are you up to, exactly?"

I sigh and rub my mouth. "You'll find out soon enough."

I grab my coat and sprint towards our rental car before they can change their minds.

Chapter 25

The scent of something like meat pie pulls me from a deep sleep. I have to blink several times to clear the blurriness from my eyes and wipe the edge of my chin to remove what seems to be drool.

Wow. I didn't know I could fall so deeply asleep during a simple nap.

I make my way downstairs, still in a daze, and offer to Martine and Jocelyne to start setting the table while they're putting the finishing touches on what seems to be an amazing feast of a dinner. Right as I'm placing utensils on the table, Suresh strolls from the living area to the table and grabs plates to help me out with a smile.

"That nap did you some good?" Suresh asks, sweeping a strand of salt and pepper hair behind his ear.

"I think so."

"We should meet up more often." He chuckles, pointing to the living area, where Ajay and Aisha are sprawled on the floor next to the wood stove, playing Hungry Hungry Hippos with my boys. "Watching your kids is making my kids more responsible. And they haven't touched their phones in a full hour."

I stop mid-movement, almost dropping the fork I'm in the middle of setting down. My gaze darts from one corner of the cabin to the other, scanning for my husband.

He's nowhere in sight.

"Wait," I breathe out. "Why are Ajay and Aisha watching them? Where's Karan?"

Suresh shrugs, not looking too bothered. "He went on an errand somewhere, but he said he'd be back for dinner."

An errand? What kind of errand could he possibly go on? This cabin is nestled deep into a peninsula, at least a good 45 minutes away from the next major town, Gander. For this reason, Jocelyne keeps this place well-stocked, especially when she has company over.

A touch of anger seeps into my bones. There he goes again, leaving me. For all I know, he drove to Gander to find a cafe with faster Internet than we have at this cabin because his *boss* needs him to fix some other bullshit.

I take a breath through my nose to keep myself grounded. There's no reason for me to freak out. I have no idea what Karan went out to do. No proof that he's out doing something for his boss.

If I'm going to start imagining faults where there are none, then we truly have no chance of saving this marriage.

Right on cue, the door slams open, revealing Karan's gigantic frame. He's covered with a dusting of snow, including his beard. A huge smile splits his face in half.

My heart skips a beat at the sight of him. Even now, with all the doubts swirling in my head, I can't deny what this man does to me.

If only that were enough.

In isolation, our story is the 'perfect' love story. If the curtain had fallen on us that night he texted me to join him in the stairway for our first kiss—if that had been the end of our story—it would have been so easy. Or even if that same curtain had fallen that day in the hospital, when I gave birth to our boys, it would still have been a happy ending.

But that's not how life works. There is no 'ending'. Well, I mean, there is, but I don't want to go so dark. Even if we were to divorce, our story doesn't end.

It only gets a lot harder. And lonelier.

Karan's dark brown eyes fixate on me right as he closes the door.

"When did it start snowing?" Surinder asks from his seat on the couch, looking up from the newspaper he'd been reading. "Looks like you got dipped in a snowbank, Beta."

Despite his father's comment, Karan doesn't shift his focus away from me. He pats snow off his shoulders and starts undressing himself, painfully slowly. First comes off the hat, liberating his silky black hair tied back in his usual bun. I picture myself running my fingers through it. A shiver runs down my spine.

Next, he shrugs off his winter jacket. The way his shoulders ripple through his shirt… is obscene.

What is even happening?

I blink and look around, double-checking to make sure that we really are at this cabin with his family, and that I'm not having a mental breakdown. But when I look back at my husband, there's nothing obscene about the way he's unlacing his boots.

Well. Not on the surface.

Damn. We haven't had sex in a long time, but I hadn't realized the impact this dry spell was having on me. Here I am, in broad daylight—or rather, broad moonlight—salivating over Karan like a college girl.

A hand waves in front of my face.

"Earth to Rachel," Suresh says.

"Huh?" I break away from staring at Karan and turn to Suresh. "Sorry, did you say something?"

He points at my feet with a chuckle. "You dropped the cutlery."

Shit. I look down at my feet and see the evidence sprawled on the floor.

Wow. What is wrong with me?

"Still recovering from your nap?" Karan asks, immediately making his way over to me.

Before I have a chance to bend over and pick up the stray forks and knives I dropped, there's my husband, on his knees.

Just how I like him.

Snap out of it!

The heat from his gigantic body radiates to my shins. I swallow and watch him pick up my mess.

"I could have done that," I say with a voice less steady than what I hoped.

He looks up at me, his thick lips twisted into a crooked smile. "I know. But you don't have to do everything."

Before I have a chance to reply, he stands, towering over me. "I'll get clean ones."

My gaze follows him as he walks over to the sink, dumps the utensils I dropped, and grabs fresh ones from the drawer.

He holds me in a daze.

***

I make it through dinner without too much trouble, though I'm still partly in a daze. Somehow, I manage to do a good job of blending in, participating in conversation where I can without too much mental effort.

Dinner is followed up by game night, where we play a series of board games ranging from trivia to card games. It's loud and overwhelming, but if I zoom out of my own head, it's actually quite a lot of fun.

And I've got to admit that seeing my husband laugh and enjoy himself is a rare sight I didn't even know I missed.

There is no time for game night at our house. Not anymore. I fondly remember the days before Karan took on his new job, when we'd both horse around with the boys until bedtime, then followed that up with anything from long-winded discussions about the state of the gaming industry or whatever drama had occurred at the pharmacy, to movie nights cuddled on the couch together under a blanket.

Before William was with Sophie, we'd invite him over solo for game night from time to time, but there was also a brief and joyous overlap when she came into his life before Karan left his job. They'd both tag along when they could find a sitter, Océane also joining them from time to time.

Needles prick at my heart at those memories. I'd do anything to get that sliver of life back.

We take a quick pause in our games to go put Cayce and Corey to bed, and then we're back at it, this time taking out *L'Osti de jeu*—a Québécois version of *Cards Against Humanity*.

Though I'm having fun and getting sore ribs from laughter alone, I'm the first to bow out for bed.

"Wait," Karan says when I stand from the table, rising to stand with me. "I want to show you something."

"Ew, get a room," Aisha snorts.

"Aisha, that's inappropriate," Martine scolds her niece.

Odd of her to say when we've just been playing a saucy game, but maybe she doesn't like to imagine what's in her son's pants.

Trust me—I've been trying not to think about that, either.

"Is it going to take long?" I sigh. "I'm really tired."

Karan gives me a reassuring smile. "Literally two minutes."

I nod without a sound, then look around the table to make eye contact with every family member. "Well, good night, all."

Everyone wishes me good night, and I turn to head upstairs, followed by Karan's heavy footsteps.

My breath becomes shallow, my mouth dry. The last thing I want to do tonight is fight. I don't have the energy for it, and I'm terrified of what the outcome would be.

Of the things I could potentially say and never take back.

Karan is patient with me and sits on our bed while I occupy the upstairs bathroom to brush my teeth, comb my hair, and wash my face. The entire time, dread has me hostage, setting up shop in the cavity of my chest. Even the cold water I use to rinse my face isn't enough to stop the beads of anxiety sweat from forming all around my nape.

Finally, and not without hesitation, I make my way back to the bedroom and sit on the bed, a good two feet away from Karan. I steady myself by clasping the edge of the bed with my hands.

"Hey." Karan touches the edge of my chin with his index, putting soft pressure to turn my head towards him. "Rachel. Look, I'm not blind. I know we're…"

Something vulnerable flashes through his eyes, and he looks downward.

"Well, we've had better days."

I scoff. "That's one way to put it."

"I know." He takes a deep breath. "Rachel, I love you so much."

"Don't." I clench my jaw and fight against the burning behind my eyes.

I don't want to fight. Not tonight. I don't want to unleash the rant I've been holding inside me. The one that wants to tell him that his words mean nothing if he can't show me.

This is a fight I refuse to have here. Not with his family surrounding us, front row witnesses to our downfall. We have to make it through this holiday and sit pretty until we're back home.

Then, we can hash it out.

"I know what you're thinking." Karan strokes my jaw with his thumb.

It's a gesture I want to lean into. But I stay put.

"I can hear those thoughts swirling around in that pretty head of yours. You want to tell me I'm full of shit."

I laugh despite myself.

"Did I get it about right?" he asks with a bittersweet smile.

"Yeah." My voice is barely more than a whisper.

"I'm not here to argue or fight, love." I close my eyes to put up a stronger fight against the tears that desperately want to escape. "Like I said downstairs, I want to show you something."

I shrug. "Okay. What?"

Karan drops his hand away and pulls out his phone, tapping and scrolling for a bit before he turns the screen over to me.

"On Boxing day, this is where we're going. Just you and me." My eyes go wide. "We'll be back here by New Year's. I already checked with my family for Cayce and Corey. Everyone's happy to share babysitting duties."

I open my mouth, but only a strangled sound makes it out. My gaze darts from Karan's face to the image of the gorgeous A-frame cabin on his phone. It takes a while for my brain to put two and two together and understand what he's telling me.

"You booked us another cabin?" I finally ask.

"Yeah. It's not far from here. That's where I went while you were taking a nap."

My brows furrow, so Karan clarifies. "I wanted to go see it in person. Make sure it was perfect."

"This…" I scratch my neck with a nervous energy. "If you think a few days on a romantic getaway is going to fix—"

"Rachel." Karan lowers his head to be in line with mine. "I know. I can see you're struggling and overwhelmed, and this is to get you out of here. We can take some time and talk."

At the quivering of my chin, he sighs deeply.

"I really want to try, Rachel. Please. Say yes."

It's tempting. It really is. The fact that Karan is willing to sacrifice time with his family to spend it with me alone says a lot, but still. It all feels like too little, too late.

At the same time, what harm can this do? At least, if we fight, we won't be surrounded by his family. I won't be in enemy territory while he has his entire clan to support him.

This could make or break us, but at least, at long last, this hell I've been living in would be over.

I gather all of my breath and courage before I respond: "Okay."

Chapter 26

Rachel

February 2022

"**M**ommy's home!" I exclaim before shutting the door behind me.

The callout has its desired effect, and before I can start to take off my coat and boots, my two boys come running from the living room in my direction.

"Mommy!" they both squeal.

I pull them into my arms.

I love my job, and I love helping my patients, but there's nothing quite like seeing my little boys after a long day. Or, in the case of a last-minute weekend morning shift like this one, a long morning.

"Mommy, Mommy, come see," Cayce insists as soon as I let them both go.

"Oh yeah, you have to see this, Mommy!" Corey chimes in.

"See what?" I remove my coat and bend over to untie my boots, and feel my breath leave my lungs as soon as I stand back up.

Karan stands in the hallway, one shoulder leaning against the wall. A shy smile I don't recognize sits on his face, but that's not all I don't recognize. The long locks he's so proud of, that he loves to put back in a bun, are gone. Instead, his hair is now about two inches long and combed back.

"Look at Daddy's hair!" Cayce says, pointing to his father.

Corey imitates his brother, but right now, all my attention is on their father.

"Karan…"

Nothing else will come out of my throat.

"Not my favourite," he starts, weaving a hand through his now shortened hair, "but you've got to admit it makes me look a bit more… distinguished?"

"But… you loved your hair." I manage to take a step forward, then mentally curse myself.

Be supportive.

"You do look great, Karan."

"I did love it." He closes the distance between us, enveloping me in his arms and kissing my forehead while the boys attach themselves to his feet and squeal. "But I thought this would make me look more professional. It'll grow back, so it's okay."

"What for?"

He swallows, and I watch his Adam's apple bob.

"I'm applying for a new job."

"What?" My stomach lurches. "But you love your job!"

"I know." He kisses my forehead again. "Listen, I was just waiting for you to come home, but I'm meeting Will downtown."

"Why?"

"He's going to go over my resume to improve my chances."

"But—"

"I really gotta go. I'll explain it all later." He peers down at his feet. "Okay, boys, stay with your mom. I need to go."

"Boo!" both twins cry out as they're forced to let go of their father's legs.

I watch Karan put on his jacket and boots, still trying to make sense of everything he's dumped on me. I barely register his goodbye before he shuts the door.

The only time Karan ever thought of changing jobs was the day we both found out I was pregnant. And back then, he hadn't been thinking of changing *jobs*, really. He'd been thinking of finally pursuing his own thing. It was only a mishap of circumstances that I happened to get pregnant at the same time.

I've been patiently waiting for him to show interest in such a project again. The boys are starting kindergarten next year, and things have been much easier since they've slowly grown out of toddlerhood. If we wanted to, we'd have the resources for him to go for it.

But he hasn't brought that conversation back.

For a while, I thought it was because of Martine's cancer. Of course, it didn't make sense to start a company while his mother was undergoing treatment and frequently needed us to travel to Val-d'Or to give them a hand.

But she's getting so much better now. The cancer is shrinking. She's responding well.

Things ought to get better from now on, no?

So why this sudden change? This desire to appear more "professional?" If anything, he's moving away from his dream.

It's giving me a bad feeling, but I can't put my finger on why.

Chapter 27

"Let me get that for you."

"No, I've got it."

I give up this one battle, which is sure to be only the first of many, letting Rachel grab her own suitcase from the trunk of our rental car while I focus on my own.

We roll the luggage through the freshly fallen snow on the long path up to the A-frame cabin nestled high up in the mountains. It's late afternoon, and the sun has already begun to set, but I can still see the puff of steam escape her mouth as Rachel breathes heavily during our ascent.

Not that I'm faring any better. With my current job, I haven't been able to spend as much time at the gym as I'd like, and I can tell. A five-minute walk up to a cabin shouldn't get me winded like this.

But the gym is the least of my worries. Right now, I need to fix what's wrong with me and Rachel. The rest can come later.

"I swear," I say with a huff, trying to force a smile. "The view from the cabin… is worth it."

"I hope we didn't forget anything in the car, because I'm not going back down for it." Rachel turns her head back towards the car, then shrugs. "Yeah, nope."

"I think we got everything. I can go back if we forgot something."

"How noble of you."

"Well, I did pick the place."

"Fair point."

Finally, we make it to the cabin. This time, I don't ask before I grab Rachel's suitcase to lug both mine and hers up the wooden porch stairs.

"I was doing fine," Rachel argues, placing a hand on her hip.

"I know. I want to help because I love you, Rachel."

She parts her lips but doesn't say anything as I make my way up the stairs, type in the door's passcode, and open the door for her. She lowers her head with a shy smile and walks inside.

The place is stunning. At this hour, there's minimal natural light making its way through the floor-to-ceiling windows of the A-frame, but the dark wooden floor and walls are still bathed in a golden glow.

A spiral staircase leads to a mezzanine where I know we'll find a cozy sleeping area. The downstairs area is fully open concept, with the kitchen area underneath the mezzanine and a living area furnished with a plush, cream-coloured couch I can already imagine sinking into with Rachel in my arms.

"Wow," Rachel utters, her green eyes wide.

She squints and looks toward the kitchen area, where more large windows showcase the patio with a stunning mountain view.

"That's where the hot tub is, right?"

"Yup." I lift my eyebrows and smile at her. "I knew you'd zero in on that first."

Rachel and hot water are an inseparable duo. When shopping for our condo in the city, a large bathtub was on our list of must-haves.

Part of the reason I drove to see the place in person before booking it a few days earlier was to make sure the hot tub was functional, as advertised. I wasn't about to risk telling Rachel about it only for her to be disappointed upon our arrival.

I've disappointed her enough.

I could tell she was anxious about this getaway—in a good and bad way. Christmas Eve and Christmas Day at Aunt Jocelyne's cabin both went by without a hitch, but Rachel did keep to herself more than usual. I guess that's to be expected, considering everything that must be weighing on her.

"Hmmm." Rachel removes her boots and coat, then takes a few careful steps around the cabin.

That elation from seeing the place has already drained from her, leaving an edgy, nervous version of my wife in its stead.

I remove the large cooler backpack containing the food we'll be eating for the next few days. "Why don't you go in for a soak right now? I'll get dinner started."

She turns to me like a deer in headlights. "Like, right now, now?"

"Why not?"

"I…" Rachel's hand goes to her throat.

"Hey." I take one large stride to close the gap between us. "You go relax. We'll have a nice French onion soup, just the way you like it, and we'll talk after. Okay?"

Her jaw clenches, but she nods.

"Okay. Yeah."

A warm flow of relief seeps through my skin.

It's not that I think a soak in the hot tub and a nice, warm bowl of onion soup will fix everything. I'm not an idiot. But I do want her at ease. Or, at least, as much at ease as she can be.

I settle myself at the counter and start slicing the onions while Rachel changes into her swimsuit upstairs. Even with the harsh clang of the chef's knife hitting the wooden cutting board, I can still make out the sounds of cloth hitting the floor of the mezzanine.

At this exact moment, Rachel is straight above me. Taking off her clothes. Letting the cool air caress her soft, kissable skin.

The knife bites into my thumbnail, and I groan out an expletive in a muffled voice. If my nail had been any shorter, the blade would have sliced my skin.

I need to focus.

I fully hone in on what I'm doing, trying to ignore the sounds of silky fabric sliding against Rachel's skin as she slips on her swimsuit.

Slice. Slice. Slice. Drop onions in a bowl. Grab another onion. Slice. Slice. Slice.

The stairs creak, and gentle footsteps echo all the way to my ears. I resist the urge to turn and stare at what I know must be a breathtaking sight. I don't need to. She's going to pass right by me to reach the porch and slip into the scalding water. Water that will make her cheeks red, that will make her skin glisten in the moonlight.

Fucking hell.

I follow the sound of her footsteps right until I know she's about to enter my field of vision. Instead of looking, I avert my eyes. Still, from my peripheral vision, I catch glimpses of her lean legs and have to grit my teeth.

The patio door opens. A cold draft sweeps inside, and I can only imagine the goosebumps scattering across Rachel's creamy skin in the short time it will take her to make it to the hot tub. But I keep slicing, slicing, slicing.

Until I look at my bowl of onions and realize I've made way too much.

I push the bowl of onions aside and head to the fridge, where I've already stored our food. In between a carton of eggs and a block of cheese is a bottle of white wine; I grab it and immediately pour Rachel a glass.

By now, she's probably in the hot tub, and if I'm lucky, she will have turned on the jets so that I don't get tempted to bask in her beauty.

I head to the patio, hardly feeling the cold. Rachel's eyes are closed, and to my relief, the jets are turned on. Her long chestnut hair is tied back into a messy bun. I don't want to make her jump, so I clear my throat to get her attention.

"Huh?" Her eyes burst open, her brows furrowing when she sees what I'm holding. "Trying to soften me up with wine?"

I chuckle nervously. "I just want you to enjoy yourself as much as you can."

She frowns. "Getting me all relaxed isn't going to make me go easy on you, Karan."

"I know." I bend and extend my arm towards her. "But you deserve this."

She sighs, then slips an arm out of the hot water to grab the wine glass. Her eyes narrow at me, but a hint of a smile ghosts her lips.

"Thank you." She closes her eyes and takes a sip. "This is actually really nice."

"Good." I linger for a moment, then go back inside, now fully feeling the effects of the cold.

I go through the motions of caramelizing the onions and preparing the flavourful broth Rachel taught me to make back in our college days. Now that our inevitable showdown is slowly inching closer, an unsettling terror begins to gnaw at my insides.

To be honest, I still have no idea what I'm going to do. Or say. I've shown Rachel that I'm willing to set time aside for her, to work out what we have to work out, but how do we even move forward?

I can't quit my job. The disappointment I'd have to live up to in front of my parents—the shame—threatens to send me spiraling back into panic. The thought of it alone quickens my breath.

They're finally starting to see me as the provider they know I can be. I can't fail in my duties as a son, either.

I can negotiate with Rachel, tell her I'll put her first more often, but I can't completely put my responsibilities as a son aside. Especially not given my mom's health.

But Rachel understands. Of course she does. She's plagued with her own familial responsibilities that she can't abandon

After all, she invited her sister to live with us. Without asking me first.

Not that I mind. Océane is a wonderful girl. The twins love having her around. And we weren't using that guest room anymore, not since my parents moved closer to us.

Still… would it have hurt to ask? To trust that I understand what it means to be there for your family?

This isn't about Océane, I remind myself, violently pressing some cheese through the grater.

I wince when the edge of my finger catches against the grater. Damn, this really isn't my best cooking day.

Right as I slide the cheese-covered bowls of onion soup into the oven for a nice broil, the back door opens. I straighten in time to find Rachel, wrapped in a fluffy white towel, her skin flushed and glistening. Her almond-shaped eyes seem a bit heavier than before—more relaxed, maybe?

I run my gaze down her neck to her narrow shoulders. They're definitely not hiked up to her ears like they have been for the last couple of days, but they're not as relaxed as I'd like them to be.

I'll have to work on that.

Rachel shuts the door and closes her eyes, inhaling deeply. "Oooh. It smells so good in here."

Her raspy voice sends a shiver down my spine.

"It's almost ready." I lean one hand against the oven's handle. "Take your time to change, and I'll set everything up."

She peers at me through her eyelashes, which are still wet from the hot tub. She shoots me a small smile. I treasure it like the gift that it is.

"Okay," she says, hardly louder than a whisper.

Ten minutes later, we're both sitting at the small mahogany dining table, across from each other like we do at home. If I were to say that out loud, Rachel would call me out about the fact that I haven't been at a family dinner in forever.

But tonight, I'm here. I've refilled Rachel's wine glass and gotten my own, and our respective bowls of onion soup are still way too hot to touch.

"I should have called you to the table later," I say, scratching the back of my neck awkwardly.

Rachel pinches her lips. Both of her hands lay under the table on her lap. "It's fine. I'm really hungry, anyway."

"Yeah, but you can't eat."

"I might just try anyway."

"I don't want you burning your tongue, Rach."

She smirks. "Wouldn't you?"

"Never." I understand her joke, but I want to make my stance clear with her. "The last thing I ever want is for you to get hurt. You have to know that."

Rachel's nostrils flare. "Maybe that's what you want, Karan. But it doesn't matter what you intend when your actions hurt people."

She slips her right hand from under the table, picks up her spoon, and digs through the broiled cheese layer to get a nice, steaming spoonful of soup.

"Rach—"

She pops the spoon in her mouth and winces, then proceeds to blow out of her mouth like she's trying to ventilate it. She swallows, puts down the spoon, and looks deep into my eyes.

"I'm your wife. Nah, fuck that—I'm your partner. Married or not, I would have learned to trust you in exactly the same way over the years. So you can whine all you want about what you want or intend, but keep this one thing in mind.

"I trusted you. I've been through it all with you, thick and thin. And I've followed you through everything, trusting you'd make the right choices for us. For our boys. Just like I trusted you to feed me onion soup that wouldn't burn me. And look, it's not all bad."

She gestures to the soup, a sharp motion of her arm that conveys her frustration loud and clear.

"Yeah, it's scalding hot, but it's fucking good. So I'm not saying it's all bad, Karan. But…"

She bites her lip and looks away.

Trusted me.

Past tense.

Fuck.

I resist the urge to lean over the table and lift her chin. "Come on. Talk to me, Rach."

I need her to stop talking in metaphors. This has nothing to do with onion soup, and we both know it.

Her eyes well up with tears when she looks back at me. "I'm sick and tired of you choosing to be away from us. Away from me."

She smacks her chest with her palm. A tear escapes down her cheek, and my heart sinks all the way to my feet.

"I begged you not to go back to the office when we were at the airport. Begged you, Karan. But you left me alone."

"I didn't have a choice. It was my job on the line, and I—"

"You always have a choice!" Rachel shrieks, her voice breaking. "Stop with the bullshit, or I'm done."

My heart pounds violently against my ribs, and my vision tunnels. She can't be serious, can she?

"Rachel…"

"No more excuses, Karan, please." She places both hands

on the table, as if gripping on to them for dear life, and maybe she is. "Can you honestly tell me, without an ounce of exaggeration, that you didn't have a choice back then? What, did your boss have a hitman with a sniper aiming at you, ready to shoot if you were to say no? He wouldn't really have fired one of his *best* software engineers on the spot, would he?"

Her eyes are wild.

I swallow past the lump in my throat and take a deep breath.

She'll forgive me if I can make her understand. Then everything will be fine. I can fix this.

"Maybe not on the spot…" I straighten my spine. "But I'm trying to build something for us, Rach. I took this job specifically for the pay bump, and there's no way for me to get to the next level if I refuse to be all in."

"You're trying to build something for us, huh?" Rachel leans back against her chair and crosses her arms. "Karan, we don't *need* more money. We were doing perfectly fine before you switched jobs."

"I don't want to be doing *just* fine." I grit my teeth, the constant, ever-whispering hint of terror weighing down my shoulders and laughing in my ear. "This world is going to shit, Rach. House prices are insane. Everything's getting more expensive.

"If we don't want our boys to struggle—if we want them to be able to own a house someday and actually thrive—we have to be proactive and save much, *much* more than we have been for them."

"I don't get it." Rachel shakes her head. "We've been saving plenty. The boys will be fine—more than fine."

Her eyes narrow. Her arms are no longer crossed, and she's moving them frantically now.

"It's about more than that, isn't it? This whole charade, this whole forcing yourself to be something you're not with this stupid job… don't tell me you're doing it only for us. You're doing this to impress your parents."

The last word comes out like poison.

"Of course I am!" The words come out much louder than I intend them to. "Yes, that's part of it, and what's wrong with that? Are you going to fault me for wanting my parents to be proud of me, Rach? Really?"

Shut up, Karan. Don't go too far.

"Yes, I'm going to fault you for that if it comes at the expense of *our* family." She's seething now. "The boys miss you. *I* miss you. All so you can go on some crusade to get approval from mommy and daddy, really?"

"You don't get it."

Don't say it. Don't say it.

"Maybe it was easy for you to scrub your parents out of your life, but I'm not built like that."

Regret clings to me like a growing vine on my spine as soon as the words are out in the open. Shock registers on Rachel's face, and for the first time since this argument started, she's silent.

"Shit." I drop my head in my hands, leaning my elbows against the table. "Rachel, I'm sorry."

"That," she starts, her voice fragile like glass, "was the hardest thing I ever had to do."

"I know. I didn't mean it." I raise my eyes to get a glimpse of her, expecting seething fury.

What I see is so much worse.

Her shoulders slump like they're carrying a weight too heavy to bear. The faintest tremor runs through her fingers as she rubs at her temples, her eyes rimmed red and glassy, like she hasn't slept in days.

"And you know what?" she asks with a shrug. "I'm beginning to think that this…" She gestures to me and then back to her. "Whatever this has become is going to be even harder. I'm tired of fighting you and trying to convince you to spend time with me or the boys. It's breaking my heart every time you decide not to choose us. Choose me."

She looks straight through me, her chin wobbling.

"And so maybe, at this point, the easier choice would be for me to leave."

I stand as if stuck by lightning, Rachel flinching from the motion. Every muscle in my body is tensed up, ready to pounce.

"I don't believe you."

I am *not* losing her.

It's Rachel's turn to stand. "I said no bullshit, remember? I mean every word, Karan. It would be *so much easier* for me to just give up on us!"

She's not serious. Letting go of everything we've built… of the love that I know still blooms in her heart for me, because she wouldn't be here if it weren't the case… it wouldn't be that easy.

"No, Rachel. I don't believe it—not one bit. The two of us, you can't just pull out these roots that easily. You can't snuff out our love like it means nothing."

Her eyes go narrow with defiance. "Watch me."

And she begins to turn, away from the table, away from me, and…

A possessive hunger takes over me all at once; as if driven by an otherworldly force, I close the space between us in a single stride and grab her wrist.

"No."

She turns to face me, and everything else falls away. A roaring tidal wave swallows everything in its path, leaving only the uncontrollable love I have for this woman.

My wife.

Her pupils are blown. I may be much, much bigger than she is, but not an ounce of fear floats in her eyes. She knows I would never, ever hurt her.

No, what I see in those emerald eyes is a spark.

I knew it. She can't leave me that easily, and I can read that all over her face, over the way her body has rotated to face me instead of trying to pull away.

"You're not going anywhere." With a careful force—assertive yet gentle—I grab her by the hips and lift her up, rotating her so I can press her up against the wall. "You're mine, Rachel."

And I show her just how much I mean it by pressing my mouth against hers.

Chapter 28

Karan's mouth on mine stokes the dying embers scattered all across my spine. Whatever was running through my head instants before—whatever was pushing me to leave—falls away to dust.

Before now, Karan has always been a gentle man. He knows how to get rough from time to time, but his kind, patient nature makes it so that he likes to take his time with me.

That patience is out the window now as he kisses me more fiercely than he ever has.

The way his tongue claims my mouth, how our teeth collide, the breathless gasps that escape both of our lips as he presses me up against the wall… It sweeps me up in a tornado of desire. Karan's hand finds my hip and grips me, hard enough to elicit a whimper from me.

If this were our first time, I know he'd pause, back away, and ask if this is okay.

But this is far from our first time. He knows me, knows my sounds, knows what makes me tick. And he knows that whimper is begging him for more.

The long fingers of his free hand grab the back of my head and tilts me up to give him better access. I'm drowning in the clean taste of him, and as he moves closer up against me to pin me completely against the wall, I gasp at the delicious pressure of his hips and the rock-hard length between them. My lower belly coils, winding up tight.

"You're mine," he repeats, his voice husky and ragged as he pulls away from the kiss just long enough to press our foreheads together. "You hear that, Rach? You're mine, and you're worth fighting for. Let me show you just how much."

He trails kisses down my jaw and into the hollow of my throat, and I revel in the soft yet prickly sensation of his beard scraping against my sensitive skin.

I didn't expect this. Not at all. When I got up from that chair, ready to leave this place, I was certain Karan was going to let me go. I'd imagined that maybe he would argue with me, using his words and his words alone. Only in my wildest dreams did I imagine that he'd truly fight for me like this.

Now, I've never wanted him more.

My hands weave through his hair, loosening the bun holding it in place; an obscene sound escapes Karan's lips when I run my nails along his scalp. As he kisses, sucks, and pulls his way down my shoulders and into my collarbone, his palms squeeze my hip on one side and my ass on the other.

I want to cry out in protest when the heat of his hands move away, but I resist when I feel him use those hands to lift the hem of my sweater.

"Karan," I gasp against the scrape of his teeth between my breasts.

"Baby," he sighs, right before wrapping his mouth around my left nipple, his thumb flicking the other in sync with the roll of his tongue.

The sensations pulse through me like shocks of electricity, zapping straight to my lower belly. My hips buck in a frantic effort to relieve the pressure there.

"God, your skin," he whispers against my breast. "You drive me wild, Rach."

He looks up at me, those warm eyes now hooded and darkened.

"But imagining you leaving, and someone else having you…"

I raise an eyebrow. "Jealous, are you?"

"Understatement of the century."

He kisses his way down my belly, and the anticipation at knowing exactly where he's going is killing me.

It's been so long since he's touched me like this, and every scrape of his beard, every flicker of his tongue against my skin, feels like heaven.

"I'm going to remind you how good I can make you feel; how loud I can make you scream my name, and no one else's."

"Oh…"

The gasp is involuntary, as is the way my fingers fist his hair. Karan groans in response, but doesn't stop his path downward.

When his fingers hook against the waistband of my sweatpants and underwear, I clench my thighs and hold my breath. Painfully slowly, Karan drags the fabric down my legs, exposing me to the cool ambient air.

After fourteen years together, I shouldn't be shy at being laid bare to him like this. Still, after so long, my breath hitches and my legs tense up.

Karan immediately notices the shift in my energy and

stops. He looks up at me, his eyes now softened with worry.

"Rach. Is this okay? You want me to stop?"

"Fuck, no. Please don't stop. I'm just…" I knock my head back against the wall and look skyward.

"Hey." He grips my hips, but his thumbs run gentle circles against my skin. "Baby, look at me."

With a careful breath, I obey and meet his gaze again.

"You don't have to be shy with me. You know that."

I laugh nervously. "It's just been so long."

"I know. And that's on me. It's all on me. And what an idiot I am, Rach. Because… fuck, just look at you." He parts me delicately and moans under his breath. "You're so beautiful, absolutely everywhere. You deserve to feel good, baby." One hand grips my ass to press me closer to him while the other hand keeps me parted.

"Karan," I whimper.

Having his hot mouth so close to where I need him most is torture.

"You're so wet already, Rach." He slides his thumb through my center, and although I sigh at the sensation, it's far from enough. "Is that all for me?"

"Mmm-hmm." I have to bite my lip to stop myself from crying out from the unrelieved pressure.

He's going to make me pass out.

"Look at you, all wound up. Again, that's my fault." He presses his lips against my inner thigh, so close yet so far. "I'm sorry I haven't made you come like you need. Because you need this, don't you?"

I only hum in response.

"Tell me you want it, Rach."

"Yes."

"What do you want?"

"Touch me, Karan?"

"With my hand?"

His thumb gives my clit a gentle flick, and I let out another whimper.

"Yes—no—I mean—"

"Tell me what you want, baby, and I'll give it to you."

"I want your mouth!" I scream. "Your tongue. Please, Karan."

I don't know how much more of this I can take.

Karan's response is immediate; his fingers dig even deeper into the skin of my ass, and he rewards my vocal demand with a long swipe of his tongue, sending goosebumps across every inch of my body.

"Oh my God," I gasp, gripping his hair for dear life.

"That's not my name." He looks up at me and slips two fingers inside me, the gentle stretching makes me see stars.

"Karan, please!"

With an animalistic groan, he presses his tongue against me again, continuing to stroke me gently with his fingers. The sensations build up at the base of my spine, in the muscle of my thighs, and right at my center.

Karan makes right on this promise, his tongue flicking and lapping expertly in all the right places. Right now, everything else—his job, his family, the despair I've been feeling around our future—falls away, scattering to the ether like dust. There's only room for him, the delicious friction of his beard, his fingers and tongue pulling ragged gasps and moans from my throat.

A pressure builds up not only at my core, but in my heart, too, as it swells and fills like I didn't think was possible anymore. When I'm right along the edge, everything in me tenses, and just as I knew he would, Karan reads me like an open book and begins to slow down his movements, opting to give me slow, deep thrusts of his fingers as he sucks down on my clit.

It's exactly what I need, and I fall.

I fall, without an ounce of fear in me, the freedom of the flight spreading through my body in waves of ecstasy. Karan's moans vibrate against my center, and I hold on to that as I ride the fall. For a brief moment in time, I am nothing but light, soaring across the sky, held safely by Karan's reverent touch.

I don't realize Karan has stopped moving and is now cradling me until he whispers in my ear. "You did so good, baby."

When I come to, we're both on the floor, my knees having buckled from my release.

I still can't feel my toes.

"Holy shit," I whisper, my voice hoarse.

I must have been screaming by the end.

My legs are still shaking, so I wrap my arms around Karan's neck and bury my face in his chest, inhaling his scent as I attempt to catch my breath.

Karan strokes my hair, his caresses so gentle that he doesn't seem like the same man he was a few minutes ago. The man who nearly slammed me against the wall and possessed my mouth like he would die if he couldn't have me.

This doesn't fix everything. Of course it doesn't. But it feels so fucking good to be close to him like this. And to have him actively doing something to keep me in his vicinity.

The desire he lit in my belly isn't gone. The scent of him is intoxicating, and I grip onto his shirt, trying to pull it up to reveal the skin underneath. Confronted with his bare chest—so large, soft, yet strong, and covered with thick black hair I want to lose myself in—my breath hitches before I press my lips to him.

"Rachel." Karan groans as he grabs onto my shoulder to stop my movements. "Baby. We're not doing that tonight."

"What?" I look up at him and see the desire reflected in his eyes.

Fuck, it's hot to see him at my mercy like this, so why won't he let me reciprocate?

"This was just for you." He strokes my jaw with his thumb and gives me a small smile. "You deserve it."

"But…" My gaze looks him up and down, and I bite my lip. "Karan, I want to."

One corner of his lips turns up. "You'll just have to wait."

He stands, helping me up along with him, and to my chagrin, the fabric of his shirt falls back down with our movements.

"I think the onion soup should be cool enough to eat by now."

"Really?" I cross my arms and pout. "You want to go straight back to dinner? And leave you like this?"

I point to the very obvious bulge in his pants.

Karan scoops my neck with one hand and kisses my forehead. "I'm sure you're starving."

I am… but not for soup.

Seems like there's no persuading him, because he's already by the table, moving the bowls and chairs around. When he's done, the two bowls and our chairs are now side by side instead of facing each other.

Karan pulls out my chair and gestures for me to sit. "Come on. Humour me, will you?"

I roll my eyes and make my way to my seat. "Okay, okay. But only because you worked so hard on this meal."

Now, sitting at his side, I have to admit this seating arrangement works much better for me. We've still got hard things to talk about, but we no longer seem oceans apart.

Still. I eat my soup—which is insanely good—but all I can think about is the throbbing sensation that's already back between my legs. Karan's hand rests on my thigh while he eats, and the heat of it through my sweatpants is driving me nearly insane.

Karan always knew how to make me feel good. That was never an issue for us. But I'm still replaying the moment I came undone in my mind, obsessed with wanting to see him fall apart in the same way.

He's the one to break the silence in between two spoonfuls of soup.

"So," he starts, giving my thigh a light squeeze. "I know we still need to talk. I only want to acknowledge that I know I can't cunnilingus my way out of this."

I snort, a sudden burning sensation overtaking my nasal cavity as I begin to cough violently. Karan taps my back while I go through the coughing fit.

"Don't make me laugh while I'm eating soup!" I utter at him, giving him a playful smack in his ribs.

"Sorry, Rach. I swear I wasn't trying to make you laugh." He's pressing his lips together as if trying not to laugh himself. "But I meant what I said. I made you feel good to make you feel good, not to win an argument."

"Well, it did stop me from leaving."

"Thank fuck for that."

"But you're right."

I know he's right, but the thing is, I don't want to fight. I'm so tired of it all. And now, blissed out by what Karan did to me, all I want is one night away from all the bullshit. I lean into him and close my eyes in a soft sigh.

"We'll talk more tomorrow, okay?"

"Are you sure?"

"One hundred percent."

Chapter 29

Karan

April 2025

I've never been prouder of the work I do, but I've got to admit, it feels nice to take a break away from it all.

I swallow a bite of fluffy omelette and take in the sugar shack's cozy, whimsical atmosphere. Tania's family runs the place, and since she's been friends with Sophie for quite a while, Sophie thought it was about time we meet her. That, and I truly needed to cross off "visit a sugar shack" from my bucket list.

Rachel, on the other hand, isn't as excited as I am. She's enjoying the food, but I would have expected her to hum along to the folk music playing in the background, or be a bit more chatty with all of her friends.

"So, you two are married?" Nolan asks me, pointing to me and Rachel.

A warm feeling of pride radiates from my chest.

"Yes," I reply. "Married seven years, been together for fourteen."

"That's amazing. And you're from Montréal too, or…"

"Oh, no. Well, Rachel grew up in Mascouche, which isn't technically in the city, but for someone like me, it still counts." I chuckle. "I'm from Val-d'Or."

"Oh, wow." Nolan raises his eyebrows in surprise. "Do you miss it sometimes?"

"I used to, but not as much anymore. My parents actually moved to the city back in January."

With Mom's cancer, and Dad nearing retirement anyway, it made sense for Dad to retire early and for them to move closer to me. Plus, there are better healthcare options in the city for Mom.

Nolan nods along. "So, Val-d'Or... are you Cree?"

"My father's Punjab, actually."

"Ah, right, I wasn't sure."

"Are you Cree?"

"Nah, Mohawk. I'm from here, but my extended family's from Kahnawà:ke."

"Oh, cool. And are you..." I lower my voice, then glance over at Tania, who's gleefully lost in conversation with Avery and Logan. "There's something between you two, isn't there?"

The way they keep stealing glances at each other, all smiles and blushes, says everything I need to know.

"Oh." Nolan smirks. "No, we're just having fun."

I raise an eyebrow. "Really."

"Definitely. I'm happy staying unattached."

Somehow, I doubt it, but I don't know Nolan enough to keep arguing over it. Instead, I keep the conversation going, and before long, hours have gone by with this group, like a gust of wind.

"What do you think's going on between Tania and

Nolan?" I ask Rachel once we're back in our hotel room.

She's fresh out of the shower, in which she rushed as soon as we arrived, without a single word to me.

She furrows her brow, then sits on the bed—specifically, the bed I'm not sitting on. Still wrapped in a towel, her skin glistens, still slightly red from the heat of the shower.

"I really don't think that's any of our business."

Her bitter tone takes me aback. "Hey, I'm just trying to make conversation."

"Hmm." She starts combing her fingers through her wet hair to break up the tangles.

"Did I do something wrong?" I ask as I stand to join her on the other bed. "I feel like you've been icing me out all day."

Rachel stiffens at my proximity. But she doesn't answer me, opting to bite her bottom lip instead.

What's going on inside my wife's head?

"It's just…" She lowers her head. "It's the first time in months I've seen you this happy."

"Well, today was a good day, wasn't it?"

"I know." She still won't look at me. "I'm not upset that we had a good day. I'm upset that it's the first good day in months."

My heart sinks. It's true that there has been a lot going on. Mom's still getting treatment, and though her cancer has shrunk, she's not out of the woods quite yet. But it's mostly the new job that's taking up most of my time. I want to make a good impression, so when my boss asks me to stay a bit later to help him with something, I don't dare refuse.

Just then, my phone starts ringing. My thoughts immediately

go to Mom. I fish the phone out of my pocket and see Mom's name on the screen, only reaffirming my first fear.

"Mom?" I say as soon as I answer.

"Karan, honey!" she chimes in response. "How was your day at the sugar shack?"

Next to me, Rachel's concerned gaze hovers.

Is she okay? she mouths to me.

I nod in response and focus back on the conversation. Mom proceeds to tell me all about the fun activities that she, Dad, and Avery's mother did with all of the group's kids at the biodome today, and I share our day's highlights in response.

Only when I hang up do I realize Rachel's no longer in the room.

I rush outside, and there she is, in her pajamas, leaning against the small balcony in the freezing air.

"What are you doing out here? Your hair is going to freeze," I tell her.

"I needed some air."

"What's wrong?"

"Really?" She pivots to me, and that's when I see the anger in her eyes. "I have to spell it out for you, Karan?"

I've never been this confused in my life.

"Apparently, I do." Rachel takes a breath through her nose. "We were just having a conversation. You and me. Then, your mom calls, and I understand why you'd pick up; she's sick, and she's got our kids, so there could be an emergency, right?"

She laughs without humour. "Only, there is no emergency, and she's only calling to chat, and that takes precedence over our conversation. Because fuck me, right?"

"Where is this coming from?" I pass a hand through my hair in a nervous gesture. "I didn't want to be rude and hang up…"

"Then why don't you go and join her, then?"

My chest tightens, and all of a sudden, the past months' exhaustion catches up to me. I thought this would be a nice moment to reconnect with Rachel. But evidently, she needs space. Or a fight.

And I'm too tired to fight.

"Maybe I will," I reply.

Her jaw ticks. "Fine."

"Fine."

Despite the cold, Rachel stays on the balcony while I pack my stuff.

This is fine. She's allowed to want space. Whatever this is, I'm sure she'll feel better when we're both back home.

I swallow my pride and leave the hotel room without a second thought.

Chapter 30

Karan

Rachel is a sight to behold on the couch. Against the sound of the crackling fire and the muffled quiet of winter, she's completely blissed out for the first time in ages.

And my stomach fills with butterflies at the knowledge that I'm the one responsible.

After we finished our soups and brushed our teeth earlier, I helped Rachel get cozy on the couch by laying a blanket over her and folding the end of it over and under her feet, the way she likes it. I brought her the paperback she packed for the trip, and while she started to immerse herself in it, I brewed her a cup of chamomile tea and started a fire in the fire stove near the couch.

Through the window, a soft snowfall made up of thick, fluffy snowflakes that float through the air like pixie dust reflect the moon's gentle glow.

It's a good thing she was too tired to fight, because there was no way I was going to let her do the dishes, or anything else for that matter. I meant what I said about tonight being all about her. Once I'm done with the dishes, I'm thinking of giving her a nice foot massage, then, if she's receptive to it, I long to taste every inch of her again.

But first, I need to take care of myself.

Resisting Rachel's advances earlier took all of my willpower. Seeing her come undone against my tongue nearly destroyed me right on the spot, especially since it's been so many months since we've been together in this way.

And if I'm to hold myself accountable and continue to make her feel good tonight, I've got to at least relieve some of the pressure.

I approach my beautiful wife, who's deeply engrossed in her book and cozied up in her blanket. I love the slight movement of her eyebrows as her eyes move up and down the page, revealing every little hint of emotion she's going through while reading. It's almost a shame to pull her from her focus, because I could keep watching her like this for hours on end.

Instead, I lean over to kiss her forehead. She looks up with a startled expression, then smiles.

"Coming to cuddle me at last?" she asks in a hopeful tone.

"Almost. I'm just headed for a quick shower."

She pouts. "Okay, then."

She watches me head to the bathroom, and when I shut the door behind me, her gaze burns on my back.

I waste no time getting undressed and turning on the hot water. As soon as the spray hits my back, I grip myself firmly and grit my teeth as I begin to stroke, pressing my other hand to the glass pane of the shower to support myself.

Tingles of pleasure make their way from my core down my spine, all the way to my toes. The sight of Rachel overwhelms every inch of my mind; her flushed cheeks, her soft whimpers and hitched breath, the way she writhed against my mouth as I tasted the sweetness of her.

A grunt nearly escapes me, but I need to be quiet. The last thing I want is to alert her to what I'm doing and pull her from her blissed out moment of relaxation.

But that hope turns out to be in vain when I hear the door open.

Rachel stands in the doorway, her gaze immediately going down to where I'm gripping onto myself. Her pretty mouth falls open, and I stop my stroking.

"Rachel." I'm panting.

A mischievous grin paints itself on Rachel's face. "I knew it."

She shuts the door behind her with her foot and grabs at the hem of her shirt, beginning to pull it over her head.

"Wait, what are you doing?" I ask, my breath hitching at the sight of her bare chest, her dark pink nipples pebbling up from the cool air, which hasn't warmed up yet from the steam of the shower.

Rachel slips out of her sweatpants and underwear, and what a sight she is, completely bare like this.

"I'm joining you. What do you think I'm doing?"

"Rachel."

I hold the door of the shower shut, as much as my body wishes she would slip inside with me. How sinfully decadent it would be to grab onto those soft hips, to sink deep into her, to feel her flutter around me while she comes.

"Tonight was supposed to be about you."

She grabs the shower door in defiance.

"I know, I know. But, Karan…" She looks up at me, her emerald eyes glowing as she bites her lip. "Please. Let me watch. I want to see what I do to you."

"Fuck, Rachel." I shut my eyes and lean my forehead against the glass, trying to keep my focus.

But there's no way I can refuse the goddess right behind that glass wall literally begging me to let her in.

"You can't behave, can you?" I chide.

She smirks, pressing her breasts up against the glass.

Damn this woman.

"Come on. Let me in."

I grunt in despair and let go of the door, backing up to give her space to enter.

"You go there, and don't you dare move." I point to a corner of the shower and use every ounce of willpower in me to stop myself from touching her.

Rachel obeys and goes to her corner, biting her lip again. The hot water soaks her hair and plasters it to the side of her face.

Before I have a chance to grip myself again, she presses her hands to her breasts and begins to pinch her nipples.

"Touch yourself, Karan."

My God, she's such a sight. When I see her like this, her face slightly scrunched up with the pleasure I know she's giving herself, I see more than the most beautiful woman in the world.

I see my sweet Rachel, the woman who's selfless to the point of nearly caring too much about others. I see the woman who can make me laugh, think, smile, cry, and everything in between. I see the woman who, despite my bullshit, is still here, willing to fight with me.

I grip myself again without letting my gaze stray away from her. When I utter a pained groan and start stroking, she bites her lip and looks downward.

"Eyes up here," I say, my voice strained with the pleasure coursing through my veins.

She obeys and licks her lips. Then, she falls to her knees.

I pause my movement, the sight of her on her knees sending a shockwave through my spine. "Baby, I told you not to move."

"I didn't move. I stayed right here, Karan." She smiles up at me, all innocence and bliss, biting that pretty bottom lip of hers again. "But while you're touching yourself… do me a favour and just imagine what it would feel like to have my lips around you."

My knees nearly buckle under me. Almost against my will, I resume the hard strokes, chasing friction that I secretly wish she were giving me.

"Fuck… baby…"

"It'd be so much better, wouldn't it?"

Still on her knees, Rachel moves one inch closer to me. I'm about to argue, but she's faster than I am.

"I'm not touching you. I'll obey. But picture it, Karan. You already know how nice and warm my mouth is."

I don't know how much longer I can resist my wife. Especially when her words bring back memories of things I've done to her.

Multiple times.

"And it's not only for you." Rachel scoots again, her mouth now so close to me that I can feel her hot breath against my sensitive head. "This would be for me, too, Karan. You know how much I want this? How much I want you to fuck my face?"

I groan in agony, watching her as she slips one hand between her legs. "You could touch me there and find out how much I crave you, Karan."

All self-control snaps; I let go of myself and grab a fistful of my wife's hair instead. Rachel looks up at me with a teasing smile, then wraps one arm around my hip to grab me by the ass for purchase.

"You'll be the death of me," I tell her, my voice full of gravel, right before she slips her lips over me.

Fuck, her mouth is heaven.

Why did I spend so much time fighting her? Why did I spend so long in a daze, going through the motions, trying to please everything in my life but her?

As I grip her hair tighter and groan at the delicious vibration of her humming against me, it occurs to me that this right here—this blissful sense of total control—feels oddly foreign. It wraps around my limbs, flowers through my ribs, and takes hold of me like a second skin. A new surge of power flows through me, and the elation makes me weightless.

I look down at my beautiful wife just as she swirls her tongue in that way she knows I love; I grit my teeth to hold back, then pull my hips back, away from her hot mouth. She looks up at me with big, disappointed eyes.

"Rach," I groan, my fist still deadlocked around her silky hair. "Were you serious when you said you wanted me to fuck your face?"

"Never more serious." A glint of desire passes through her emerald eyes.

"Tap me twice if it's too much." I give her hand—the one still gripping my ass—a light tap to clarify what I mean.

She nods once more, and this time, it's me who pushes my hips forward to take her mouth.

Both her hands grip me behind my thighs for dear life as I begin to rock into her, slowly at first, still gripping her hair like a madman. I know, deep down, that she's the one in control; at the first sign of her having too much or at the first hint of a tap on my legs, I'm stopping immediately.

But still…

The firm hold of my fist against her hair. The sounds her mouth is making as she's looking up at me from her knees. The way I'm slowly able to increase the speed of my hips. I've never felt so powerful. So in control.

And she's the one gifting it to me.

When have I truly been in control? Not when I caved under my parents' pressure to change jobs. Not when they hounded me over and over again to ask her to marry me, despite me knowing she didn't particularly care about the idea of marriage.

Even falling in love with Rachel, this sweet angel, was completely out of my control.

"Oh, fuck… You good, baby?" I grunt to her, picking up speed.

She simply nods and moans against me, bringing me over the edge instantly.

White-hot flames set me ablaze, from my toes to my center, as I finally spill into her, my hips jerking involuntarily.

The relief of it takes my breath away, and only when Rachel is back on her feet with her head against my chest do I remember where I am.

At Rachel's short gasp, I remember I have legs, as shaky as they may be. My wife is partially holding me up, and at my height and weight, there's no way she can keep that up for very long.

"Baby," I whisper, stroking the side of her face and pulling her wet hair behind her hair. "Are you okay?"

She smiles up at me, looking sated, though I'm the one who just got off, not her. "Never better."

"Fuck, Rachel. You took me so well."

The image of her—and the way her mouth felt at every thrust of my hips—is going to be forever seared in my brain.

"It's a good thing you gave in, huh?" She drops soft kisses on my chest. "See what happens when you listen to me?"

You're right." I kiss her forehead and close my eyes.

The last five minutes keep replaying in my brain, and I'm still struggling to catch my breath. It's not only about how good she made me feel, but about how freeing, how life-changing it was to hold that sense of control, for once.

For the first time in my life, I begin to think Rachel may be right about more than I gave her credit for.

Chapter 31

Rachel

Karan spends the rest of our shower in a daze, which, if I had to guess, would be my fault. I'm no stranger to giving my husband blowjobs, but what I let him do to me tonight was new.

And it's obvious that he very much loved it.

Hearing him moan with pleasure, and feeling the tremors in his body, gave me a high that I haven't had in a very long time. I'm not sure where the desire to give him this experience came from, but tonight, I'm at peace.

I let that peace sustain me as I wash his hair and he washes mine, as he gently cleans me up with a washcloth and I do the same.

By the time we're both squeaky clean, neither of us has any energy left to do anything but collapse into the cushy king-sized bed in the loft. Karan turns on his side to face me, and I curl into him, breathing in the scent that's as familiar to me as the scent of the seasons.

How could I ever truly walk away?

Karan was right earlier today. There's no way I could leave without trying. Not if he's willing to show up and try with me.

I'm so tired, God am I so damn tired, but I'm not done.

And when I'm nestled against him, my leg over his hip, the heat of his body keeping me warm, I'm only reminded of everything I have to lose.

"I love you," I whisper against his chest.

"I love you, Rachel. So, so much." He grips me closer as a shudder passes through him. "I swear to you, we're going to figure it out. Okay?"

"Okay. But for now…" I crane my neck to look up at him. "Just hold me?"

"Of course, baby." And so he does, and for once, sleep comes easily.

***

I wake up to the spicy smell of Aloo Paratha wafting from downstairs blended with the scent of dark roast coffee. Before I open my eyes, I tap the other side of the bed, only to find it empty and cold.

Karan must hear me stir, calling out to me from downstairs with his rich baritone voice.

"I'm making you breakfast, love!"

I slip on one of Karan's T-shirts, which comes right down to my mid-thighs. Before I make my way downstairs, I grab a fistful of fabric and sniff it to bury myself in his clean scent, if only for a moment.

Today won't be easy. For a brief, magical evening, we were back to who we used to be. But we've got work to do now. There's so much we still have left on the table—literally.

226

We may have finished our soups, but we never finished our conversation.

I can only hope that we find a middle ground. After last night, I don't think I can envision myself losing Karan again. The distance I've built between us in my mind, to prepare myself for what I believed was inevitable...

I want to take it back. Obliterate it.

That thought only becomes stronger when I make my way downstairs and see my husband wearing only grey sweatpants, his black hair loose from its usual bun as he toils in front of the stove. A slight sheen coats his dark skin from the heat, and I want nothing more than to get as close as I can to him.

So I do.

I press myself against his side and sigh when he wraps one arm around me, keeping his other hand on the handle of the pan. He presses his lips on my forehead.

"I haven't seen you sleep so peacefully in a long time," Karan says with a wistful smile.

"Yeah, well, I haven't slept that well in a long time."

"Hungry?"

"Starving." I inhale deeply, my mouth watering at the delectable scents coming from the Aloo. "Thank you for once again feeding me."

"You've kept me fed for the last six months at least, without me deigning to show up on time for dinner, so this hardly makes up for it." Karan's thumb draws lazy circles on my lower back. "You should keep this shirt. It looks much better on you than it does on me."

"I can't keep it! That defeats the whole purpose. It needs to smell like you."

"Then we'll share it. When you give it back, it'll smell like you."

"We will need to wash it at some point, though."

"Boo."

I pull myself away from Karan to let him finish up the Aloo and go pour myself a cup of coffee, then take a seat at the table. As I wait for Karan to serve us, I peer through the large windows to admire the sprawling mountain view.

It's no longer snowing, the sun now reflecting across the white-coated surfaces in its full glory. It's one of those days when you come back indoors and can hardly see anything until your eyes get adjusted again.

We eat in a comfortable silence, although a slight tension permeates the air. We both know what's coming once we're done with Karan's delicious breakfast. I take my time, savouring every bite, sipping my coffee slowly in between mouthfuls of food to drag out this meal a little longer.

All too soon, my plate is empty. Karan stands and takes both our plates, and when our gazes meet, his smile is bittersweet.

"Thanks," I whisper, holding on to my cup of coffee for liquid courage.

Karan drops the dishes in the sink, comes back to his seat at the table, and clasps his hands together, elbows resting on the mahogany surface.

"Okay." He takes a deep breath. "Let's lay it all on the table, Rachel. You start, and I'll listen."

My entire body is a pincushion, needles sticking me from every direction and numbing my skin. My tongue feels too big for my mouth.

But I have to speak. It's now or never.

"Um…"

Why is this so difficult? I had no trouble getting upset at him over the last year, jabbing at him, and making a case for everything he was doing wrong. Even yesterday, I had the words.

Where are those words now?

"Rach." He reaches out across the table and grabs my hands, giving them a gentle squeeze. "It's okay."

The warm trust I see in his eyes gives me the final push I need to break the dam open.

"I've started to resent that I'm no longer your priority." I breathe through my nose, beating back the burning sensation in my chest, the panic that's trying to claw its way out of my lungs. "Neither me or the boys are. Ever since your parents moved to the city, you've been a different man… You cancel your plans with me at their beck and call, all for nonsensical stuff that should never, and I mean never, take precedence over the commitment you gave to me, your wife."

I tap my chest to emphasise my point.

I want to pause and breathe to steady myself, but it all comes pouring out now, with or without my permission.

"You never take my side when your mom tries to plan stuff with the boys without asking us first, or when she makes jabs about our parenting choices. You… fucking hell, Karan, you cut your hair last year, for an interview you didn't want, for a job you hate, all to placate them.

"And now that job is taking you away from us. It's turned you into a shell of yourself. It's like you're a ghost passing through our home, and we're lucky to get a semblance of a whisper from you, when in reality, we should be getting the best of you.

"And you know what's funny? Just the other day, at the cabin, your mom suggested that I stop working and become a homemaker instead."

The shock that registers on his face doesn't escape me, but I keep going, unable to stop the avalanche of grievances now that the slope has given way.

"That was never me. You know that. I love my job. I love you. I love Cayce and Corey. It used to be possible for me to have all of that, but now, I'm stuck picking up the slack from where you've dropped the ball."

"I want you to have it all," Karan interrupts me for the first time. "It was never my intention to make you feel like you had to give up your job, Rach."

"Does your intention matter when this is where we are?" My throat clogs up with unshed tears. "Look, I know how much your parents mean to you. And I'm very aware that you think it was easy for me to cut ties with my parents, but like I said, that was the hardest thing I've ever had to do."

"I don't think it was easy." Karan squeezes my hand again. "What I said yesterday was completely out of line and selfish. I've never regretted words more than those. Rachel, you're so brave that sometimes it scares me."

I only realize I'm crying when Karan reaches out to wipe a tear from my cheek with his thumb.

"But you're right that it's hard to understand," Karan continues. "My dad… ever since I was little, he always drilled one thing more than any other into me: cherish your parents. Respect them. Worship them. And then when my mom got sick…"

His voice trails off, as does his gaze.

"Karan. Look at me." He obeys. "I know your mom's cancer was hard on you. It's terrifying. But… she's healing now. For the time being, she's in great shape. I know nothing is ever guaranteed, and that's the thing…"

I take another breath to steady myself, though the tears keep falling.

"I'm not saying we shouldn't spend time with your parents. I love them too, you know. And it's wonderful that our boys get to be close to their grandparents like this. But…" I look him dead in the eyes. "You cannot keep putting them first. Not if you want to keep me."

Those last words burn my tongue coming out. And inside my mind, I silently beg and plead that Karan sees the light. Giving him up would be like tearing out a part of my soul.

How can anyone ever heal from that?

Karan's nod is painfully slow. "I hear you, Rach. I really do. There are a few things I'd like to add the table, if that's okay."

I nod my permission.

"You're right about me putting my parents first coming at the cost of our own family. I guess I didn't see how intense it was until they moved to the city and it became too easy to get too close." His jaw trembles. "I don't know how, exactly, I'm going to work through that and find balance, but believe me when I say that I want to."

He pauses, and the softness in his eyes takes a sharp edge.

"But." The tone of his voice sends a chill down my spine. "If we're going to be talking about putting other people first, I can't avoid bringing this up. I really, *really* wish you'd talked to me first before inviting Océane to come stay with us."

"Karan, she's disabled."

It's not the same as his parents. Not at all. There will come a day when Karan's parents are older, or one of them becomes sick again. A day when they truly do need us more than they do now. But that day is not today.

"She *needs* me. I'm the only real mother she's truly known."

"I know that, and that's why I would have said yes!" I flinch at Karan's volume, but he instantly reads me and lowers it back down. "But I should have been included in that conversation. Don't you see that? You completely took away my power.

"Maybe out of spite because of the way I am with my parents, maybe not, but still, Rachel. That made me feel weak. And untrustworthy. Like…" His voice nearly breaks. "Less of a man."

A wave of shame and guilt hits me with full force. For a moment, I'm speechless.

As long as I've known him, Karan never showed signs of being fragile in his masculinity. He didn't mope whenever I defeated him at beer pong during our time in the CEGEP dorms at John Abbott.

When we both began our careers and my starting salary was higher than his, he celebrated me instead of feeling intimidated. Any time he got hit on by another man during our outings in the Village, he respectfully turned them down and seemed to feel flattered instead of freaked out.

But I've been taking all of that for granted.

My husband's lack of fragility doesn't mean he's bulletproof.

Of course his lack of control would make him feel weak. He's already conflicted about being under his parents' thumb. How terrifying, how disorienting it must have felt for me to take away his control in our home as well.

I don't remain in my speechless daze for very long, since these thoughts electrocute my mind in the matter of a second. Within the next passing second, I'm out of my chair and nestled in Karan's lap, holding his head against mine, cheek to cheek.

"You're as much of a man as you were when I married you," I whisper to him, feeling a shudder passes through his body as he returns my embrace. "If not more. I'm so sorry, Karan."

"I should have said something earlier, I know, but I was too fucking exhausted from work to even think about getting in a fight with you."

Karan leans back to take my face in his hands. The way he looks at me makes me feel like the most precious thing in the world.

"All I ever wanted was to make you—and our sons—happy."

I chuckle through my tears. "Maybe we both need to work on our boundaries with our families, then."

"Yeah." He strokes my cheek in a reverent motion. "Maybe it's time we talk about going to couple's counseling."

My body goes rigid. Karan senses this, his expression shifting to worry. He knows what I'm going to say before I say it, but still, I've got to say it.

"I don't know if a counselor can help us," I whisper.

"This is different, Rach. It's for the two of us."

"But what if it isn't?"

I've gone through multiple psychologists, therapists, counselors, you name it. There's a lot of shit I needed to work through when I took my sister out of our childhood home and went no contact with our parents. But, in my experience, none of these professionals can ever tell me anything I don't already know myself.

Apparently, I'm too self-aware for therapy.

"Baby. Look at me."

It's only when Karan says this that I realize I've let my gaze fall to the ground. My husband's soft brown eyes remain patient, steadfast.

"Couple's therapy is completely different from going alone. As long as we both go with an open mind, we can make this work."

"I…" My chin trembles. "I don't know."

"Okay." Karan places a hand on my shoulder. "How about we take a break?"

I nearly sob out of relief. "Yeah. Okay."

"I think we're making good progress." Karan presses a soft kiss to my lips. "We're gonna be okay, Rach."

I can only hope, yet, the pit in my stomach remains at the idea that we haven't worked through everything yet. There's still the question of his job. And I don't know if I can trust that he'll truly make an effort with his parents.

"Hey." Karan raises his eyebrows. "How about we go make use of that hot tub?"

My cheeks heat. So does my lower belly.

"I like that idea."

For all that I know, we teleport ourselves to the patio; that's how quickly we make it outside, how much of a blur that moment in between feels. It's cold, but I only sense heat when Karan gently peels my clothing away from my skin. I do the same to him and revel in the delicious warmth emanating from his towering body.

Only once we're fully naked does he pick me up in his arms to walk us both inside the tub. The scalding water wrapping around my body, along with the contrast of the freezing wind against my face and neck, and the heavy pressure of Karan's body against mine, awakens my senses in the best of ways.

"Rachel," Karan gasps against my mouth when the two of us collide. "God, I love you so much."

"I love you, Karan."

This isn't the wild and frantic kiss from yesterday. This time, we go slow, savouring each other, my hands stroking all over his back and weaving into his hair. Just this—kissing him, bathing in all the sensations of him—feels so good that I could remain in this moment forever.

In the quiet of the mountains and the blue skies above, it's only us. Fourteen years of history between us, and all of the love that we've grown like vines entwining us together, creates a bubble that protects us from all the harm we've done to each other.

And when Karan finally pushes into me for the first time in months, a sigh of relief escapes my throat, mingling with his panting breath.

"Oh," I manage to whimper, when there's so much more I want to say.

Oh, Karan, you feel so good.

Oh, God, I've missed having you inside me.

Karan, on the other hand, finds the words. He slides out, painfully slowly, and thrusts back inside me, bringing all of my most sensitive points alive.

"Nothing compares to you, Rachel," he groans against my ear. "This is…"

So sweet. All-encompassing. Transcendent.

"Fuck, you feel good, Rach." The sound of his voice, deep and husky, goes straight to my spine, sending tingles across my entire body.

"Karan." His name comes out in a gasp. "Oh, my God, don't stop."

"Never, baby."

When the tingles culminate into a detonation of sensations, my vision blacks out. The full-body wave of euphoria that takes over me is more than an orgasm; Karan, as promised, doesn't relent, continuing to thrust into me and whispering encouragements in my ear as tears fall from my eyes.

Even when the initial wave subsides and I can breathe again, I'm still floating in euphoria. A laugh bubbles out of me as more tears fall.

Karan kisses them away and slows down. "You okay, baby?"

"More than okay. Oh… It still feels so good, Karan… please don't stop," I pant, tilting my hips to chase more of him.

He grunts in response to my movement, then kisses the hollow of my neck. "I won't stop. But seeing you like this… fuck, Rach, I don't know how long I'll last."

"Give me everything, then," I whimper. "Come for me."

That seems to take him over the edge; Karan grabs my ass to lift me out and sit me on the edge of the tub, his thrusts becoming erratic and deliciously deep. He buries his face in my neck and groans one final time; seeing him come undone like this only makes me float higher, makes everything that much sweeter.

Because there's nothing that could ever compare to the love, the trust, the intimacy we've built.

The one I cannot stand to lose.

Chapter 32

Karan

"**Y**ou seem happier, man."

I nod to Ajay with a smile, shifting the wooden logs I'm carrying to equalize the load between both arms. Rachel and I have been back since earlier this morning, and already, I can tell every member of my family wants to ambush me for details.

"Yeah, I think so."

A gust of cold wind blows through Ajay's shaggy hair. He winces and nearly missteps into the snow. With his frame being much smaller than mine, the fact that he's somehow trying to one-up me in the number of wooden logs he's carrying is a bit ridiculous.

"You're going to hurt yourself," I warn him. "Why don't you set a few of those down?"

We've barely walked ten feet away from the woodshed; he's not going to make it inside the cabin at this rate.

"Nah, I'm good."

As if the universe was listening for those exact words, Ajay suddenly plummets, face-first into the snow.

"You still good?" I put my logs down and offer him a hand, which he takes with an embarrassed smirk.

"Can you pretend this never happened?" Without a beat to take a break, he leans back over to pick up the logs he dropped.

"Only if you stop trying to impress me for whatever dumb reason." I shrug and pick up my own logs with a chuckle.

"Are you laughing at me?" Ajay asks, a look of shock painted on his face.

"Oh. No. Sorry." I rub the back of my neck with another nervous chuckle. "I'm a little bit on edge."

"Oh?" He stops mid-motion and straightens back up without picking up more wood. "So, which is it, man? You happy, or you nervous?"

"What, I can't be both?" I raise an eyebrow at my cousin, who, I've got to remember, is much, much younger than I am.

And much more immature, as young men tend to be.

"So, did it go well or not with Rachel?"

There it is. I knew he'd been itching to ask me that question since Rachel and I came back. He's been circling around me all day, looking for an opportunity to corner me. I should have known something was up when he offered to help me bring firewood inside.

I look around to make sure we're alone. There's nothing around us but snow and trees, no souls separating us from the frozen expanse of the sea. I sigh, resigning myself. I might as well share now and get Ajay off my back so that I can fully focus on being there for my wife.

I drop my logs again and take an awkward seat on my pile.

"It went well," I start.

When Ajay realizes I'm going to share, he also takes a

seat on his own pile of wood. Might as well get semi-comfortable instead of standing stiffly in the snow.

"But it's far from over."

"Oh, yeah?"

"I'm definitely hopeful we can work through this, though."

That's the truth. A new ember has been lit inside my chest ever since Rachel and I fell asleep in each other's arms that first night. She's coming back to me. At least, she wants to.

My wife is no longer out of my reach.

"She agreed to couple's therapy, for one thing."

"Oh, it's that bad, is it?"

"There's no shame in going to therapy, man. We would probably be in better shape if we'd gone before it got this bad."

Ajay looks sheepish. "Sorry. I didn't mean it that way."

"Yeah, no worries." I pause for a moment, letting air slowly escape through my pursed lips. "It's the stuff with my job I'm more nervous about."

"Your job?"

"Rachel made it crystal clear that I can't keep working as much as I have." I lean against my knees and clasp my hands together. "So, the first thing I have to do when I'm back in the city is to tell my boss I won't be doing any more overtime."

The idea of having that conversation alone brings on a wave of nausea.

I've never gone against an authority figure. Ever. The thought of it alone sends me right back to those moments, when I was small, where my father struck me down with pointed words and a terrifying booming voice.

"Uh…" Ajay's face scrunches up in an air of confusion. "That's it? No more overtime? Isn't that… I don't know, reasonable?"

"It absolutely is."

At least, it should be. I understand how much this job—and the ridiculous hours I've been sinking into it—is piling way too much on Rachel's shoulders. But the idea of going directly against what my boss wants from me elicits a quiet terror that gnaws at me from the inside.

Still. That terror is overshadowed by the love I have for my wife—and the hope that we're going to mend what we have.

"It's just…" I look up at Ajay.

Will he understand what I'm going through? Both his parents are Indian, and Auntie Anjali has so much in common with my father, but not only is she much younger, she also has a completely different relationship with her parents. As their youngest daughter, she simply wasn't treated the same as my father.

Suresh is also much, much more chill as a father than my own. While he and Auntie do have strong ties to our culture and traditions, they seem to have raised Ajay and Aisha with a lot less pressure than I was forced to endure.

That, and Ajay is so young. He doesn't have kids. Hell, I'd be surprised if he had a real savings account. How will his attitude change once he has a family to support?

"I have a lot riding on this job," I finally continue. "The pay is great, but if I refuse to do overtime and stick to doing what's in my job description, I know what's going to happen."

My heart speeds up, thumping against my ribs like a rave.

"I'll stay stuck where I am. When a team needs a new lead, I'll get passed over for someone who was willing to give a hundred and ten percent to this company."

"If the pay is great, isn't that enough?"

I drop my face in my hands. "Ugh. I don't know. I… my boys…"

Cayce and Corey's sweet faces appear in my mind. Who knows what life will look like when they're old enough to head off to college? To buy a home?

The idea of disappointing them in any way—of not giving them every possible advantage to thrive and live their best possible lives in this fucked up world—has me staring into a dark abyss, about to teeter over the edge.

The only reason I was able to move to the city and attend the CEGEP and university I wanted was because I worked my ass off in high school. My father made it clear to me that he would help me pay my way and contribute in any way he could, but rent in the city is expensive. While he had that covered, I had to pay the rest.

I don't want Cayce and Corey to have to work that hard. Not if I can help it.

But maybe I can't.

"For what it's worth, Karan, these boys worship you." I don't notice Ajay standing until he places a hand on my shoulder. "Do you know how many stories about you I sat through while you and Rachel were gone?"

I lift my head with furrowed brows. "Oh?"

"Too damn many." Ajay laughs. "You're their hero, man. So, maybe I'm not a dad, but from where I'm standing, it looks like you're doing a hell of a good job."

"Well. We'll see in ten years, won't we?" I stand and start picking up the wood again. "Until then, we need to get this inside before the fire dies."

Ten minutes later, we've placed our logs in a neat pile next to the woodstove indoors. While Ajay is off helping Auntie Anjali with the dishes from breakfast, I kneel next to the firestove and start carefully stacking logs inside.

The sound of Rachel's footsteps resonates in my ears, and I can't help the smile that possesses my lips.

"Hey."

She kneels next to me, bringing with her the scent of strawberries and lifting my mood instantly.

"So, I noticed something, and I know your mom." She's whispering. "There's a lasagna on the counter."

"Okay?" I place another log inside the stove, concentrating on placing it in the optimal position.

"I think it stayed there all night. It looks like your mom's lasagna." I hum to let her know I'm still listening. "She probably let it cool overnight or something, despite me warning her countless times about leaving food out like this."

"Uh-huh?" My log falls, so I grab the fire poker to play around with it.

"Karan." Rachel's hand on my forearm pulls me out of my focus, and I look into her eyes. "I don't give a shit if anyone else feels comfortable eating that lasagna, but I just want to make sure she doesn't try to feed it to the boys for lunch. Okay?"

"Oh. Yeah, okay." I kiss Rachel's forehead, putting the new to-do at the forefront of my mind. "I'll talk to her, okay?"

Rachel gives me a small smile. "Okay. Great."

I don't waste any time once I've filled up the fire stove to my liking and go looking for Mom. She's at the table with Dad, holding his hand and nursing a steaming mug of coffee. Dad's got his nose in a newspaper while Mom is bent over a jigsaw puzzle.

"Need help with that?" I ask as I sit to Mom's left and pick up a piece of the puzzle.

She looks up at me with a sweet smile. "You know I'll never say no to that."

For a few moments, we don't talk, instead focusing on the puzzle. After successfully placing a third piece, I look at my parents' clasped hands.

My heart leaps to my throat at the way my father's thumb gently strokes Mom's palm. So many years together—so many challenges they've had to overcome, thrown at them by the hands of time—and they're still so very much in love.

They made it work. From what Mom has told me, it was far from easy in the beginning of their relationship. Her aunt, her only remaining living family, absolutely abhorred the idea of her niece dating an Indian immigrant. Dad did everything right, showering her aunt with respect and gifts, proving to her that he could provide for her niece, but she could never stop seeing him as an *Other*.

If the two of them made it work with the world rooting against them, there's no reason Rachel and I can't repair what we have. No reason at all.

But I didn't come to the table to admire my parents' showcase of love.

"Hey, Mom," I say, breaking our peaceful silence.

Mom hums in response without looking up from the puzzle, her brows furrowed in concentration.

"Mom, it's actually important."

She lifts her head. Even Dad peers at me from his newspaper for an instant. "What's up, sweetie?" she asks.

I point to the counter, where the lasagna still sits. "Did that stay on the counter all night?"

"Yes, I was letting it cool down," Mom explains, frowning. "Is that your thing that's actually important?"

My mouth goes dry, and my tongue is suddenly too large for my mouth. Dad's pointed gaze makes my heart beat faster.

"Mom. You can't do that. It'll have gone bad now." I don't sound as self-assured as I wish I did.

Mom sighs. "Karan, it's actually fine. I had to let it sit overnight because it was way too hot to put in the fridge before I went to bed."

"Why?"

"It'll go sour if you cover it up while it's still hot," she explains, confidently. "So it's actually less dangerous to leave it on the counter and put it in the fridge after. Speaking of which, I should go do that."

She stands.

"Are you sure about that?"

She certainly sounds sure of herself. And she's been handling food for decades…

Mom pats my shoulder. "Plus, it's vegetarian. It's totally fine, I promise you, sweetie."

She heads off to the counter to put the lasagna away, and I'm left at the table with Dad, dumbstruck.

I lean back against my chair. I'll admit that I'm not the biggest expert on food safety. But Mom has been cooking her entire life. I grew up on her and Dad's food, and not once did I get sick from eating something either of them made.

She's probably right, then.

It's going to be fine.

Chapter 33

Rachel

While Cayce and Corey horse around with their grandfather, I make the most of the opportunity and curl up on the couch in front of the fire stove, a book in hand. I bring up one of the blankets to cover myself up to my chest, then wrap my feet under my legs and allow myself to fall into the pages.

It doesn't take long for Karan to join me. When he does, sliding up against me and wrapping one arm around my shoulder, I close my eyes to savour the moment.

How good it feels to be able to be close to my husband again like this. Reveling in the heat of his body against mine alone is a soothing balm over all of my worries, of which there are plenty. We didn't wrap up everything with a neat little bow when we left the A-frame cabin, and part of me can't help but linger on our unfinished business.

At least we both put everything on the table. There is no longer a heaping pile of worries bubbling up inside me, rotting into resentment. That doesn't mean we're in the clear yet, but at least, I can enjoy a moment of cuddling on the couch without feeling sick to my stomach.

He wants to try. I want to try.

We're going to make it.

I look up from my book and turn my head to look at Karan, who, it turns out, was already looking at me.

"You creep," I whisper with a smile.

"What? I can't help it if you're the most beautiful thing to look at."

"You're happy just sitting here doing nothing and looking at me?"

"Just?" Karan chuckles and kisses my forehead. "Baby, sitting here doing nothing and looking at you is the best gift I could ever ask for."

If nothing else, I know without a doubt that Karan's love for me runs deep and true. How can I doubt it when he speaks words like these?

I only hope it's going to be enough.

The hairs stand at the back of my neck. My pulse stutters. I don't realize why at first—not consciously. But when I turn to look towards the kitchen and spot Martine with my sons, my blood goes cold.

She's taking out the lasagna. Both of my sons are at her heels, almost frothing at the mouth.

What the fuck?

"Karan." I elbow him, and he looks down at me with big eyes, then follows my glare to where I'm looking. "I thought you said you were going to talk to her. Go stop her. Now."

If I don't want to cause drama, it's got to be him. Not me.

Karan's brow lifts in understanding, and he smiles.

Smiles.

"Oh, yeah," he starts, seeming absolutely way too chill for what's going on. "I talked to her. She said it was fine."

A gulf opens at my feet, and I tumble into a free fall with no warning.

All my hopes—the ones I've been carefully nurturing over the past few days—wither and die, leaving only their acrid taste in my mouth. The future I'd dreamed of crumbles down to rubble before my eyes.

They were only words. Stupid words. Useless words.

Words mean nothing. Absolutely nothing.

I can never win. Not against Karan's mother. She'd already won this battle and claimed her territory decades ago.

"Rachel?"

Karan's name on my lips sounds so far away, he might as well be on another planet.

Maybe I'm the idiot. I expected too much. People don't change—not really. Not deep down.

I've set my expectations too high.

And now my heart shatters into a thousand pieces.

But I can break down later. First, I've got to protect my boys.

"Karan." I leave no room for negotiation in my voice. "Go. Fucking. Stop her. *Now.*"

"Bu—"

"She's wrong." My entire body trembles from the white-hot rage burning through every fiber of my being. "I'm a pharmacist, Karan. I think I would know."

I can't believe he still doesn't trust me.

"Go, or I will."

Eyes round with uncertainty, Karan nods and gets up. I don't wait to watch the argument unfold between the two of them.

I need some air.

As Karan heads towards the kitchen, I walk to the door, grab my boots and coat, and run outdoors.

I pace towards the path that leads to the frozen bay, taking deep breaths to keep myself upright. It may be cold, but I'm fuming and can hardly feel the wind against the skin of my face

It's too quiet out here. The world holds its breath around me. Even the frozen bay lies perfectly still, its surface like glass, while inside my chest everything fractures and bleeds.

How can the world be this peaceful when my entire world is falling apart?

I reach the frozen shore and stare out at the horizon, only allowed to stand here for five seconds before I hear him call out my name.

I don't turn.

"Rachel!" he repeats, his panicked voice and the sound of his boots crunching against the snow at breakneck speed the only things disturbing this peaceful tableau. "Rachel, what are you doing out here?"

He really needs to ask?

With all the fury gathered within me, I turn just in time for him to nearly collide into me.

"Why don't you ever believe *me*?"

Karan looks taken aback. Whatever he was expecting, this wasn't it. "What?"

I don't know what makes me more angry; the fact that he

did what he did, or the fact that I have to fucking spell it out for him.

"I told you, Karan. I told you the lasagna wouldn't be safe. Did you think I told you this for fun? Just to make a scene or cause a fight with your mom, or what?"

Karan's mouth gapes open. "You did… but then she said—"

"That!" I gesture with my arms, barely able to control my movements. "That's exactly fucking it, Karan! That, right there, is the problem."

"Wait, wait, wait." Karan shakes his head. "I just went and told her not to feed it to them. It's fine, Rachel. There is no problem."

"The problem isn't the fucking lasagna!"

I should lower my voice if I don't want the people living in the cabins around the bay to peer outside.

But I don't care. Let them stare.

"I told you something, and then you decided to trust your mommy over me. Me. Your. Wife." I point to my chest, poking myself so hard it almost hurts. "The problem, Karan, is that it took me telling you something *twice* before you actually took action and trusted *me* over *her.*"

This time, Karan doesn't interrupt me. He looks at me with full focus, ready to listen.

Too little, too late.

"And you know." I laugh without humour. "You know your mom's judgement is iffy with health stuff. I'm a pharmacist, for fuck's sake."

"I'm sorry," Karan breathes out, his gaze falling to the ground.

I'm sure he is sorry, but right now I couldn't care less. Not with the burning rage scalding my insides.

"I can't fucking believe you."

"Fuck, Rachel, you're right." He rubs the back of his neck and deigns to look at me again. "She seemed so sure. But you're right; I should have trusted you first. And I'm going to from now on—"

"No."

A look of surprise, then confusion sets in his eyes. "What?"

"I said no."

I clench my jaw, determined not to fucking cry. I think I'm too pissed for it, anyway.

"I'm tired, Karan. I'm so fucking tired of fighting her for your approval. We just spent three days talking about this, and then we come back and you do this? No. I'm done."

Hurt flashes in his eyes as his expression crumples. "Rachel, what are you saying?"

"I'm saying I'm done. This is over." I take off like a shot, rage fueling my limbs as I sprint back toward the cabin.

"Rachel, wait!"

But I'm done waiting for him. In the thick snow, Karan's heavyset shape works against him, and I make it to the rental car before he has a chance to catch up to me. By the time he does, I've already locked the doors.

He bangs against the window with an air of panic. "Rachel! Rachel, get out of the car!"

"I'm going into town," I yell through the window so he hears me. "Don't you fucking dare follow me."

Ignoring his pleas, I pull out of the driveway, letting all the tiny pieces of my heart fall like a trail of crumbs behind me.

Chapter 34

Karan

I stand statued in the snow, knuckles bruised from banging on the car window, throat hoarse from the panicked shouting, and the only thing roaring in my mind is that I have no idea what the fuck just happened.

When I turn to face the cabin, the faces of my family stare back at me through the large glass window overlooking the sea and the mountains.

Have they seen everything?

I head back inside in a daze, my scrambled brain unable to process what has happened.

Why am I not panicking? Why am I so calm as I come back inside? How am I not completely falling apart at the seams?

"Beta," my father says as he greets me when I walk back inside.

Everyone else—my uncle, my aunts, my cousins, my mother, and even my sons—stays at a distance, waiting to see how I'm going to react. Identical looks of worries paint all of their faces, except my boys, who seem completely lost.

Oh, how I've failed them.

"Are you all right?" my father asks, placing himself right in front of me so that I can't move forward in my continued daze.

"No." The word comes out without emotion.

"Come here, Beta." Dad clasps my shoulder with one hand and ushers me forward. "Martine, watch the boys for a minute, why don't you?"

"Of course," my mother utters in a voice that nearly breaks.

I let Dad direct me up the stairs without a single argument. When he gives my shoulder a light press to sit me down on my bed, I follow along and stare at the hardwood floor below me.

"What happened out there?" Dad asks once he takes a seat next to me, his gaze burning a hole through me, the weight of his expectation bearing down on me like a mountain.

I don't answer. My mind swirls like a storm.

Rachel.

I am *not* losing my Rachel.

I can't say it out loud. Can't manifest it into reality.

"Karan. Talk to me, Beta."

I know my father is rubbing my back and shoulder, but I can hardly feel it. It's only a superficial sensation, like I'm outside my body looking in.

I can still talk to her. Of course I can. There's no way this tiny mistake—as much as I realize it may have hurt her—is going to sign the death warrant of everything we are.

I vehemently refuse.

"Karan. Come on. I only want to help." I've never heard my father sound so dejected, so desperate. "We all know something's wrong between you and Rachel. If it wasn't obvious in the way she was cold to you before Christmas, it became a near certainty when the two of you went to that getaway."

"Maybe we only wanted some time away from all of his," I finally say, gesturing all around us.

"You don't mean that. You love your family."

Instant guilt claws at my throat.

"I do, Dad."

"So, it was more than just a lover's getaway."

I pause, my hands beginning to tremble as panic continues choking me.

"I can't lose her, Dad."

I still haven't spoken the truth out loud. Haven't admitted how deep this goes. It's still not too late for me to fight for her.

Dad sighs, a deep, full-body breath that seems to rattle him. "You know that no matter what happens, we'll all be here for you, right?"

He wraps an arm around my shoulders—or, at least, he tries to, but struggles to reach all the way around due to my sheer size. Mom always said I got my height and build from her father.

"Maybe I don't tell you enough, but I love you, Karan. And you have to believe me when I say that your mother and I love Rachel with all of our hearts. If something goes wrong, we'll be heartbroken—maybe not as much as you, of course not—but still heartbroken. But…"

He peers into me, the strength of his gaze forcing me to look into his hazel eyes.

"No matter what, you'll always be our son. There's nothing more important to us than you, Karan. And so we'll always be on your side. You won't ever be alone."

My chest caves in. I slam right back into my body and immediately wish I hadn't. My heart is going a thousand miles an hour, ramming against my sternum like it wants out completely. Nausea has taken hold of my stomach, and my limbs feel weakened, impotent.

Everything hurts, and all I want to do is collapse in on myself, but I can't.

Something about what my father said just doesn't sit quite right with me.

There's nothing more important to us than you, Karan.

What son wouldn't be overjoyed to hear something like that? Who wouldn't feel validated and cherished?

Apparently me, because all it does is send me into a complete spiral.

All my life, my father has drilled into me that I must cherish my parents above all else, and I've done it for years. Decades. Never complaining, always answering when they called.

It was easier for me to complete my duties from afar when we lived six hours away. Only when they moved closer did I realize the price I paid to truly live up to that expectation.

I'm expected to put them first. Yet, as their son, they put *me* first.

It's not adding up.

Because who, then, will put my sons first?

The answer comes as clear as day in my brain:

Rachel.

But that's not enough. Though I don't doubt the potency of Rachel's love and care, having been the recipient of that myself for fourteen years, they deserve so much more. They deserve for their father to put them first, too.

Maybe, just maybe, I should have thought of them and

put them first, instead of constantly chasing whatever vision and wishes my parents held for my career.

The excuse I keep using seems laughable from where I'm standing, Rachel's fury making sense to me in a way it never really has before.

Everything I've claimed to do to make my sons' futures better has been nothing but a thin veil for my own feelings of inadequacy, fed by the pressures my parents have been placing on my back.

But I was ready to change it all. I was ready to step down at work and only work my regular hours. I was ready to make an effort and finally put Rachel and the boys first.

I was fucking ready.

There's no way this single misstep is going to cost me my wife. Not when I finally see more clearly than I ever have before.

I won't allow it.

A bone-deep wave of exhaustion sweeps through my body at all of the realizations lighting up in my head at the same time. Suddenly, staying awake becomes unbearable.

I take a short instant to weigh my options. I can't really run after Rachel, no matter how much I want to. Although I could borrow a car from someone in my family, I have no way of knowing where she's headed.

The only thing I do know is that she has to come back. If not for me, for Cayce and Corey. No matter how angry she is at me, she's not going to simply abandon them with me and escape.

My other option is to rest and hope that by the time she comes back, I'm in fighting order. Because I am not going down without a fight.

"I'm going to nap, if that's okay," I tell my father, scooting a few inches away from him to make it clear that this conversation is over. "I'm so exhausted I can't think straight."

"Of course." The corners of his lips lift in a small, worried smile as he stands. "Take the time you need, Beta. We'll be downstairs when you're ready."

I nod in understanding, then let myself fall against my pillow.

The sleep may be restful to my body, but it certainly isn't restful to my mind. I'm pushed and pulled through a series of nightmares that torment my already fragile mind.

I can't hang on to the details of these dreams before they slip from my fingers and move on to another dream. All I can recall is constantly seeing Rachel look up at me with all that burning hurt and anger in her eyes.

That look stabs me like a knife, over and over again…

Until I'm ripped from my slumber by a piercing scream.

Chapter 35

Rachel

In all of my rage, I don't go very far.

I've only been driving for five minutes before I pull over and park to steady myself.

I can't pretend it's safe for me to be driving in this state. And where would I go, anyway? I won't lie to myself and say I can drive to Gander and book a hotel room, because I'm not going to leave Cayce and Corey behind like that without giving them an explanation.

They deserve better from me.

The heat of humiliation creeps up my neck and into my cheeks. Karan's entire family likely knows what happened, if they didn't see it outright. Who knows what they're going to think of me when I go crawling back to that house?

Whatever. It's not my problem anymore.

But, it kind of is. I actually give a fuck about these people. Fourteen years entrenched in Karan's life have allowed me to build unshakable bonds with his family.

Stop it, Rachel.

If I'm to survive the next 24 hours, I can't start thinking about how much I love Karan's family. And, for that matter, I can't keep thinking about how much I still love *Karan*.

Oh, God.

I have no idea how long it takes before the nausea and dizziness pass. An hour, maybe? Two? However much time has passed, I'm nowhere close to being in good shape, but at least I'm able to drive.

I'm going to go back to that cabin. I'm going to have a talk with my boys; they don't need to be privy to all the details, but they do need to understand that I love them so, so much. And that we're going to see each other at home. Mommy's only going away for a few days.

Then, I can camp out in Gander in the first vacant hotel room I find until our flight back home.

I keep running that plan over and over in my head when I park in Jocelyne's driveway and exit the car. But I pause before I head to the door. I still need to think of something to say to the adults in the room. Maybe that I'm sorry, and that I need some space, and that I wish them all a happy new year.

Yeah. That'll work.

My nerves are frayed by the time I make it to the door and come inside. A quick scan of the main room shows me that everyone except Karan and the twins are staring back at me.

Did he already leave? Did he take his own rental car and chase after me with the boys in tow?

No. He would have seen me parked on the side of the road. Or we would have crossed each other if he left in the last five minutes.

My gaze flits to Martine, who's busying herself by wiping down the counters.

"Where are Cayce and Corey?" I ask, doing my best to level my tone and appear normal.

As if any of this is normal.

"Oh, sweetie, are you okay?" she asks, not answering my question.

Jocelyne and Anjali both walk up to me.

"We were worried about you," Anjali purrs. "You know this is still a safe space for you, no matter what's going on, right?"

"Thank you," I quickly reply to address Anjali before immediately turning back to Martine. "My boys?"

"Oh, those boys!" Martine exclaims. "I love them more than the world, but they can certainly be a handful sometimes, won't you agree?"

I narrow my eyes and put myself on guard. "What happened?"

"Oh, nothing too alarming, don't you worry yourself about that, sweetie." Martine waves me off and keeps wiping the counter down. "In fact, I'm pretty proud of myself for how I handled that."

"Martine, where are my sons?"

"Cayce is in Jocelyne's room, and Corey is in mine." Martine smiles up at me. "They just wouldn't stop fighting over one particular toy, so I sent them to timeout separately."

Every instinct in my body screams. The room starts spinning, so I grab hold of the counter to keep myself steady.

My poor boys. They must be going out of their minds right now with anxiety, and no one's with them to help them co-regulate their big feelings.

I breathe through my nose and shut my eyes. This isn't the time to escalate things. Maybe Martine doesn't know how deep their separation anxiety goes. I just need to let her know that this type of punishment isn't acceptable, especially if she's going to be watching over them to help out Karan while I'm not there.

I place both hands against the counter and lean forward, then lift the corners of my mouth to appear as non-threatening as possible. The last thing I want is for Martine to take this personally or hurt her feelings.

"Hey, Martine," I start, attempting to slow down my staccato heart. From its point of view, I'm fighting for my life. "So, isolating the boys like that really isn't ideal."

She stops wiping the counter and looks up. I've got her attention.

"They get really anxious when they're alone, and how are they supposed to deal with their big feelings if they're locked up alone like that?"

Martine's brow furrows. "So how, exactly, would you have had me handle it?"

"Well, typically, I'll see which of the two seems the most upset, and I'll—"

"You know," Martine interrupts, her voice increasing in pitch, "here I was, really proud of myself for figuring this out on my own and handling it without a tantrum."

She throws her rag in the sink and crosses her arms, continuing:

"I really don't appreciate you coming here and attacking me like that."

Thump-thump.

Ice fills my veins. I can hardly feel Jocelyne's comforting hand on my arm. But I can't lose control of this conversation.

I can't lose control of *myself.*

I. Am. Not. Her.

Not my mother.

"Martine, I'm not attacking you." Despite the turmoil storming within me, the words come out relatively calm. "I only want to let you know how we typically handle this with the twins so that you're better equipped next time."

"It's always gotta be done your way, right?" Martine laughs without humour.

"Okay…"

Deep breath. Steady. Focus.

"I can see that I might have come at this the wrong way, and that you're feeling attacked. I'm sorry, Martine."

I'm not sorry, but I have to defuse this, not throw more fuel on the fire.

"So I'd love to do better next time. If there's something I want to address with you about my sons, what would be a better way for me to approach it without hurting your feelings?"

"You could have just told me, 'wow, good job, Martine, you really handled that well.' That would have been just fine."

"But…" I can feel the control slipping through my fingers, pressure building all around my skull and across my limbs. "That's not constructive criticism. I'm asking, how do you want me to give you constructive criticism, Martine?"

"You don't!"

"I don't?" My jaw trembles. "So, you can behave however you want with my sons, and I'm supposed to say nothing? To just let it happen?"

"Rachel," Jocelyne coos, her grip on my arm becoming tighter. "Let it go."

"Let it go?" I forcefully pull away from Jocelyne's grasp and turn to Martine. "Martine, if I can't even have a conversation with you, if I can't…"

Black spots take over my vision. The pressure gets worse. I might as well be trapped in a pressure cooker; there's no air, nowhere for all the rage to simmer out.

If I don't get out now, it's going to boil over.

"You know what, it's time for me and the twins to go."

I turn around and scan the room for Cayce and Corey's things, which are strewn all over the place. Toy trucks, dinosaurs, and pieces of costumes litter the cabin.

I'm doing this. I'm actually doing this. I'm taking the boys and *leaving*.

Still shaking, I stride towards the toys and start picking them up one by one.

"Rachel, what are you doing?" Martine stammers as she trails behind me. "You're not actually leaving with them, are you?"

No one else says a word.

No one else except her gets in my space.

My already cramped, under-pressure space.

"Leave me alone, please," I beg Martine, keeping my eyes on the items I'm trying to pick up.

My mind is going miles an hour, thinking of everything I need to grab.

Fuck, the boys are going to be so disappointed. I'm going to break their hearts.

But I'm not leaving them here with *her*.

"Don't you think you're being a little bit overdramatic here?" Martine continues, getting closer than she ought to, right on my heels, following my every step. "Just wait a minute, Rachel. Don't leave like this."

I approach a wall and pick up Cayce's favourite toy—a big stegosaurus.

"Leave me alone," I repeat, and it's all I can do to keep the pressure contained.

"Rachel. Seriously." Martine grabs my arm. "Just wait a min—"

At the contact of my skin, the lid blows over.

Every single shred of emotion stored in my body over the last hours, days—years—come ripping out of my bones—

I can't control it—

LEAVE

ME

THE

FUCK

ALONE

DON'T

FUCKING

TOUCH

ME

Throat raw, hands sore—

Fuck, I must have screamed that out loud—

What did I do with my hands? What's happening? How destructive is the fallout?

A flash across my mind—the wall. I slapped the wall, over and over, screaming at her not to touch me, and now she's staring back at me like a deer in headlights, and everyone's staring at me—

Oh God, oh God, no, no, no…

I bite the inside of my cheek, hard enough to taste iron, but it's still not enough to ground me here, to give me back control, and so I crumble into pieces, sobs taking over the entirety of me.

"You're fucking insane," Martine utters, but the indignation barely makes a dent in the storm of emotions that's driving me.

I can't move, I can hardly breathe, and—

"*You,*" a deep, booming voice echoes from above, "do *not* get to talk to my wife like that."

Karan.

Chapter 36

Karan

When I ran down the stairs at the sound of my wife's screams—and at the loud thump of knocking against the walls—I had no idea what to expect.

The very last thing I expected was to overhear my own mother speak to Rachel in this way.

Oh, hell *no.*

Mom's reaction is instant. She turns to me swiftly, eyes wild and bewildered. Next to her, Rachel is still crumpled to the ground and shaking, sobs taking over her entire body like waves.

It breaks my heart all over again.

"It's unacceptable," I continue.

I don't yell. I don't raise my voice to her.

I'm not my father.

But I'm firm, and I stand taller than I ever have. It's all it takes for her to shrink down.

Jocelyne is at my side almost instantly. "Karan, calm down."

I almost laugh, but I have a single edge here, and it's my calm demeanor. So I intend to keep it.

"I'm very calm, Aunt Jo."

Mom, seemingly recovered from the shock of hearing me defy her, stands tall as well, starting to wildly gesticulate towards my sobbing wife.

My Rachel.

"She's scaring me," she whimpers. "Karan, make her calm down; I was only trying to get her to talk things through. She wants to leave with the boys!"

"Then there must have been a reason."

I walk past my mother and crouch down to Rachel, who's now rocking back and forth. My heart cracks in my chest as I cradle her in my arms and stand back up.

I don't know what happened while I was out, but if there's one mistake I'm not going to commit ever again, it's to mistrust my wife. If she reacted in this way and was about to take the boys away, it can't only be to hurt me.

She wouldn't.

Something happened here.

Mom backs away into my father's arms. My father, despite him being shorter than me, somehow looks *down* at me, one arm crossed, the other wrapping around my mother's back.

Any other day, that look would have made me cower in fear.

But not today.

I'm safe. I have to make Rachel safe. I have to make my sons safe.

"Maybe I should leave," Mom says with a trembling jaw. "Give you some space. You can't just leave on New Year's Eve like this. I'll go out for a few hours, then come back when her hissy fit is over."

The blatant disrespect pricks like a thousand thorns in my back, rage spiking in my blood.

Rage and shame.

Rage at the people I've obeyed with little question my whole life. Shame that I'm only opening my eyes to the truth now.

"No. You stay here, Mom. You stay right the fuck here, and we're leaving."

"Karan," Dad says, shock cutting through the disappointment in his eyes.

I ignore him and walk past everyone, heading upstairs to find my sons, clutching Rachel tightly to my chest all the while.

She's gripping the fabric of my shirt, fisting it for it dear life. I don't care that she walked out barely an hour ago. I don't care if she seemingly gave up on us.

I haven't given up on *her*.

She's it for me. She always has been.

"I've got you," I whisper to her when I reach the top of the stairs, my words causing her to bury her head deeper into my chest as the sobs continue to rack through her.

I open door after door without discrimination until I find both Cayce and Corey, sitting in almost the same position, but in different rooms. Both have their knees to their noses with their arms wrapped around their legs, eyes red and puffy from obvious tears.

What have they done to us?

I set Rachel down on a bed, not caring whose it is, and stroke her hair. I try to look into her eyes, but though the sobs have slowed down, her gaze is vacant.

"I'm coming right back for you. I'm bringing the boys in the car. Don't move, okay? It's going to be okay."

She doesn't react to my words, but I trust that she will be all right while I pick up Cayce from this room and head to the room across the hall to get Corey.

With both boys in my arms, I come face to face with Auntie Anjali as I'm headed towards the stairs. Her eyes are big with worry.

"Do you need help?" she asks with a shaky voice.

Love for my auntie floods my veins. She could easily side with her brother and try to keep me from leaving, but she's choosing not to.

Anjali isn't the only one helping. As we head down the stairs, Corey in Auntie's arms, the cabin is in chaos below us. Jocelyne argues with my mother while Suresh and Ajay do the same with my father. Aisha rushes in to join her mother in helping me.

In no time at all, the boys, who are completely lost as to what's happening, are dressed and ready to head out.

Once at the car, I place a hand on Anjali's shoulder. "Can you get them strapped in while I go grab all our stuff?"

She simply nods with a bittersweet smile.

"I'll help you pack," Aisha adds as she follows me back inside.

As soon as I open the door, Mom rushes me, Jocelyne at her tail. "Come on, now, Karan. We can talk. Please don't leave like this!"

"Martine, let it go," Jocelyne sighs behind her.

"Please stay," Mom repeats anyway.

"I can't stay," I tell her with a shake of my head. "This isn't what Rachel needs right now."

"What about me?" All the pain in my mother's voice is a spear right through my heart. "You're my son. I need you, too."

I laugh without humour. "For the first time in my whole fucking life, I can actually see. Mom, you might need me, but Rachel's my wife. Her needs trump yours."

The words burn like acid coming out of my throat.

I hate saying them. I hate that it's come to this.

My father takes a step forward, and I recognize a similar flame in his eyes to the one currently burning through me. "You cannot speak to your mother like that."

Certainty floats through my veins when I step forward to face my father. For the first time in life, I am facing him without fear.

"I'm going to tell you the exact same thing you told me earlier today, Dad. Nothing is more important to me than my sons. To that, I'll add my wife." My gaze flits between both of my parents. "Dad, I love you, and I love Mom, but I'm not going to sit here and be a doormat while my wife gets treated like this."

"It's all completely ridiculous!" Mom screams. "She's the one who attacked me first! What am I supposed to do, then, Karan, huh? Should I be the doormat, then?"

A seedling of doubt flowers in my brain, but I don't allow it to take root.

Trust Rachel. Trust your wife.

I don't respond. Instead, I move forward, Aisha at my heels, and we move through the cabin to pick up everything my boys left behind.

Like before, my parents don't follow us upstairs when I go pack our suitcases with my cousin's help. They can't. The rest of my family has, if not entirely taken my side, at least decided that I should be allowed to leave without conflict. Them holding my parents back is enough for Aisha and me to finish packing.

Ajay arrives upstairs to help Aisha bring the suitcases down while I go get Rachel. She's now completely silent. Catatonic. Her body barely responds when I take her into my arms.

The beating of her heart against mine is enough to keep me moving forward.

Before I head through the door for the final time, I turn my head to meet Jocelyne's gaze.

"I'm really sorry, Aunt Jo."

"Don't be," she whispers, her voice nearly breaking. "Go take care of your family."

"Karan!" both of my parents cry out as I leave the cabin. I don't stop.

Anjali sits in between both of my boys' car seats, holding each of their hands. When I open the passenger door and gently place Rachel inside, both Cayce and Corey light up with questions.

"Where are we going?"

"What's going on?"

"Did we do something bad?"

"Daddy, what's wrong with Mommy?"

"It's okay, boys," Anjali coos softly, looking back at me. "Karan. I'm really proud of you."

I swallow back the lump in my throat and nod at my auntie. No more words need to be exchanged between us.

I turn to face my boys.

"You did nothing wrong. Neither one of you. We…" I fake a smile. "We're going on a little adventure, just the four of us!"

"What about Grandma and Grandpa?" Corey asks.

"They'll still be here," Anjali answers for me. "But don't worry, we'll take good care of them. You boys take good care of your mommy, okay?"

With that, Anjali slips out of the car, leaving a final kiss on each of my sons' foreheads.

The door to the house barges open behind us.

"Karan, please!" Mom cries out from the door in one final plea.

The panic in her voice shakes me to my core.

I'm a terrible son.

I'm walking back on everything I know.

How will I ever earn their love again?

No.

I've been a model son. I shouldn't have to earn anything. And I'm walking forward into the only future that I know I want more than anything…

A future with my wife and sons.

Chapter 37

Rachel

'm trapped within myself. My mind is a globe of glass, from which I can only see a blurry kaleidoscopic view of the outside world.

Where everything is muddled. Foggy. Sounds like I'm underwater.

My body, on the other hand, is on autopilot, letting Karan guide it where it needs to go. But it has no will of its own. No ability to open its mouth and speak. The words are in my brain, screaming, pleading to come out.

But they can't. They only bounce back from the glass walls and echo within me.

I want to say that I'm sorry. To Karan, and to Cayce and Corey. But especially to my boys. My actions directly ripped them away from their grandparents, and they're still so little.

How can they understand? How is this fair to them?

I did what I did to protect them. Yet, in doing so, I know that I've hurt them.

And I've hurt my husband.

My husband.

I spy him from the corner of my eye, notice his tense jaw, and how tightly he grips the steering wheel as he drives on. Who knows how much turmoil must be brewing inside his own mind?

And I'm the cause of it. If it wasn't for me—for my loss of control—he wouldn't have had to show up for me the way that he did. He wouldn't have had to confront his mother and stand up for me against her.

But he did. Oh, he did.

I'm no better than my parents, lashing out in anger like this.

The juxtaposition makes me nauseous. Never have I felt more supported and cherished by Karan. For once, he chose me. And he didn't even hesitate. He wasn't there to see why I'd begun to argue with his mother in the first place, yet he chose to believe that I must have melted down for a good reason.

He trusts *me*.

Chose me.

Karan places the car in park when we pull up in a roadside motel. I hear the boys excitedly ask if we're finally there. The sounds make it all the way to me, muffled but still present, as Karan takes the boys out of the car and walks inside the lobby, likely to get a room.

And I stay here.

Unable to move.

My husband chose me.

All the hope that I'd let wither and die mere hours ago attempts to sprout back to life. Yet, it does so in a field of ashes. Because the cost of his love for me has been substantial.

Will he resent me for it?

Maybe not now, in this very moment, but what about later, when the adrenaline fades from his bloodstream? Will he lay awake tonight, looking at me sleep, and start to doubt his decision? Will he harbour newfound anger at the way I behaved?

I keep telling myself it wasn't my fault. I tried so, so hard to keep it together, but Martine wouldn't let me breathe. And when she touched me, it all became too much.

There weren't very many times in my life that I melted down in this way. The first time was when Cayce and Corey were newborns, and I'd been completely overwhelmed. It happened a few more times when they were toddlers, and one or two times after grueling days at work, but that's it.

That's why it took me by surprise.

My thoughts get interrupted when Karan opens my car door, unclips my seat belt, and coaxes me to stand. The boys are at his heels, both of their gazes focused on me. I can tell they're worried sick. I hate to weigh on them so much. Hate the ugly rage that is an undiscernable part of me, passed down by blood from those I've cast out.

But the words won't come out yet.

Karan ushers the three of us to a small motel room with an outside door. Inside is nothing spectacular; two double beds with kitschy comforters, green carpeting, a TV, a small round wooden table, and a bathroom in the far corner. A couple cheap paintings of boats adorn the walls.

Upon seeing the room, Cayce squeals and runs to the bed closest to us, followed by Corey. They both hop on the bed and start rolling on it and laughing their little hearts out. Their worry about me seems to be gone for now.

Good.

Karan takes my hand and ushers me to the other bed. "Here, lie down, baby."

But I don't. I stay seated, my gaze focused forward on my boys.

"Okay." Karan strokes my back, so carefully that it feels like he thinks he's going to break me. "I'm going to order us some food."

"Can we get pizza?" Corey asks, his eyes lighting up.

"Yes, yes, let's get pizza!" Cayce adds, just as excited.

I sit in silence and watch my boys play together until said pizza arrives. At first, Karan focuses on the boys, setting them up with a slice of pizza each along with some napkins to use as makeshift plates on the small corner table.

But when he's done, he turns his attention to me.

"You should eat something," he says, sitting next to me with a napkin and a slice of pizza in one hand. "At least a little bit. Won't you do that for me, Rachel?"

I don't move or speak.

Karan strokes my cheek with his thumb, and my chest swells, a lump forming in my throat. "Please. Rachel. Come back to me."

I blink a few times, and finally turn to look him in the eye. With the glass globe finally vanished from my head, reality crashes into me with full force, and the tears start falling again, this time softly instead of sobs.

I don't say anything yet, but I accept the slice of pizza from Karan and take a nibble.

He smiles, though his eyes become watery. "Good. That's good, Rachel. I'm here. I'm not going anywhere."

Guilt rears its ugly head at the thought that mere hours ago, I was the one going somewhere. Intent on leaving.

I had my reasons. Now, everything is different.

I swallow the small nibble of pizza, then set it down on my thighs and look up at Karan through my tears.

"Karan, I'm so, so sorry."

"No." He shakes his head, his voice gravelly. "You have nothing to apologize for, you hear me? Absolutely nothing. So I don't want to hear it."

"You don't even know what happened."

"I don't care. You can tell me later. For now, I just want you to stop even *thinking* about apologizing, okay?" He wipes away a tear with his thumb. "My beautiful Rachel. You're the one who was right, all along. And I'm the one who's sorry it took me so long to see all the control they had over me."

"Mommy," Cayce calls from the table, his mouth full of pizza. "Are you okay, now?"

"Don't talk with your mouth full," Karan chides.

"I'm okay," I half-lie, forcing a tearful smile to share with my sons. "Mommy's going to be okay."

That's closer to the truth.

I take another bite of pizza, swallow, then set it down again and lean against Karan, letting his warmth comfort me. "Thank you."

"For what?"

"For being there for me."

"That's what we do."

"I know, but I shouldn't have doubted you. I shouldn't have stormed out earlier. I should have stayed and heard you out…"

"Rachel." He strokes my hair, placing a loose strand behind my ear. "It's in the past, okay? No matter what happens now, we're in this together."

He looks over at our sons, who are devouring their pizza, still oblivious to the conflict we've thrown them in.

"It's the four of us against the world," he adds.

"Yes. Okay."

The guilt doesn't go away—not completely, but the idea of the four of us as one strong unit gives me enough hope to at least wage war against it and keep it at bay.

Once everyone has had their fill of pizza, Karan and I both help the boys through their evening routine; bathtime, brushing their teeth, getting into their PJs, and finally, letting them crawl into bed with us. It's a tight fit, with this bed being a double and not a queen, and with Karan's size being what it is, but we make it work.

Outside, it's snowing again. Before I pull the curtains closed and head back to the bed to join my family, I stare at the falling flakes and remember that tonight is New Year's Eve. In a few hours, this year will be over, and with it, I hope Karan and I can leave behind all of the pain we've caused each other.

Maybe it's too much to ask. Likely, we'll still carry much of it with us as we move forward and continue to fix what's broken.

We put on a movie and cuddle as a family until both Cayce and Corey drift to sleep. When it's only the two of us left, Karan kisses me, reverently, oh so tenderly, before we each lay down on our pillows with the boys between us. I start to doze off with my arm on top of Corey, my hand clasped in his while his arm cradles Cayce.

"I love you," I hear Karan whisper before I drift away.

"I love you," I manage to whisper back in response right as sleep finally takes me.

And amidst the raw sensation of fear and turmoil about the future, there appears a star that outshines everything else:
Gratitude.
I have my husband back.

Chapter 38

Karan

I'm the first to wake, and I'm immediately struck by the beauty of my serene wife sleeping peacefully. A laugh attempts to escape my throat when I notice the boys, however.

Corey is completely flipped over, his head at the foot of the bed, with no blankets to cover him. Cayce, for his part, has crawled over Rachel's chest and is lying with his stomach over her, his head and feet splaying on either side of her ribs.

How Rachel is sleeping this deeply, I have no idea. Our son is five years old and actually weighs something; he's not a cat. But I shrug it off and slip out of bed as carefully as I can.

After last night, I'm confident enough about Rachel's mental state to leave her here with Cayce and Corey while I go grab breakfast. I'm careful as I get dressed and open the door.

By the time I drive back with a paper bag of warm goodies and two cups of coffee in hand, all three of them are awake. Cayce and Corey are playing tag and laughing, while Rachel sits in our bed, still dazed from sleep. Her chestnut hair ripples like a waterfall across her face when she turns to look at me enter the room and gives me a soft smile.

I smile back.

That smile from my wife is enough to keep the demons at bay, if only for now. I'm painfully aware that what awaits me today will be one of the most harrowing experiences of my life, even more so than yesterday.

For now, I get to enjoy breakfast with my family.

The twins devour their still-warm chocolate croissants while Rachel carefully nibbles on her own. When the boys are done eating and have left the table to go resume their game of tag, Rachel takes a sip of coffee and meets my gaze.

"So, what's next?"

Her tone is careful. Hesitant.

"We go home," I say.

Corey overhears me and stops dead in his tracks.

"Wait, what?" he whines just as his brother bumps into him. "You said we were going on an adventure, not home!"

"Corey, it's complicated," Rachel sighs.

"Wait, no, he's right," I chime in.

I haven't been there enough for my sons. The last thing I'm going to do is disappoint them again.

I smile at Rachel and turn my gaze to Corey. "We can take an extra day for an adventure."

"Where?" Cayce and Corey say in unison.

"Twillingate?" Rachel volunteers. "It's a good trek from where we are, but I've heard there are icebergs around this time of year."

The twins cry out in glee, and I chuckle.

"Twillingate it is." I look back at Rachel and frown. "But first, I've got somewhere to go."

The boys go back to their game while Rachel and I stare at each other in understanding.

She nods, her bottom lip quivering.

Last night, before we headed to bed, Rachel gave me the rundown on what happened with my mom at the cabin. Turns out, I was right to trust Rachel, as I should have all along. My mom, hard-headed as she is, can't accept constructive criticism. That won't fly. Not when it comes to our parenting decisions.

The last thing I want is to go back out to that place today. I crave going out with Rachel and my boys on a full, carefree adventure. But I can't do that until I've gone back.

Because Mom is right about one thing; I can't just leave like this. I have to at least *try* to make things right. And I can only hope that she'll listen to reason.

I love her and Dad too much to consider the alternative.

"Well, boys," Rachel says with what I can tell is a forced smile, "we are going to do a cozy movie morning while we wait for Dad, and then we'll go on an adventure!"

How I admire her strength. The way she can show up as a mother for our boys, even when she's torn inside.

That's what I focus on during my drive back to the cabin. Rachel's unwavering strength. The safe haven of her love. Despite having these thoughts as a balm for my mounting anxiety, my body becomes more tense, my mouth more dry as I near Jocelyne's home.

My breathing shallows, and my palms get sweaty against the steering wheel that I hold in a death grip.

When I park in the driveway, terror seizes me like a vice.

I barely have time to unbuckle my seatbelt before Mom comes running out the door, still in her pink and black polka dot pajamas, the short regrowth of her salt and pepper hair a poofy cloud around her head without her headscarf to keep them at bay.

"Karan!" she exclaims as she runs down the snow-laden steps with her slippers.

"Mom, what are you doing?" A different flavour of terror winds its way around my heart; terror for her safety.

She's going to slip and fall, break a hip, wind back at the hospital, an—

The memory of her against the drab backdrop of the hospital room, face pale, hair all gone, squeezes my chest in a painful grip.

I run to her and catch her just in time when she inevitably slips on the last step.

"Martine!" my father cries out from the door.

The next few minutes are a blur. The whole family is outside as they fawn over Mom, until we're finally ushered inside. It all happens too quickly for me to get a word in or process anything as it's happening.

Next thing I know, I'm at the kitchen table, sitting across from my parents. Dad holds Mom close, and I recognize the pained expression painted across his face as the same one I've worn for Rachel since yesterday.

Anjali sits next to me while the rest of the family simply hovers around the room. The air is heavy, the tension so thick you could cut it with a knife.

I'm the one who finally breaks the silence.

"You could have hurt yourself, Mom. Why would you rush out like that?"

Mom's lower lip trembles. Dad tightens his arm around her shoulders. "I couldn't wait another moment to see my baby boy."

I pinch the bridge of my nose. "Mom…"

"I knew you'd be back," she continues, too much hope coating her voice.

She has completely misconstrued what this is about.

"I knew you wouldn't turn your back on your own parents. I only wish you'd brought the boys with you."

"I didn't bring the boys," I start, "because I'm not staying."

"Then why are you here?" my father booms.

I resist the natural urge to flinch.

I'm safe. I'm safe. I'm safe.

"To break your mother's heart even more than you already have?"

"Surinder," Anjali warns her brother in a clipped tone.

"What? I'm only laying the truth for him to see."

"It's fine, Auntie," I reassure Anjali, carefully resting my hand against hers.

I turn my attention back to my parents and swallow past the knot in my throat. "I came here to fix this."

"Oh," Mom sighs, pressing a hand to her chest. "Good. That's good."

"Mom, Dad," I begin, bracing myself and daring to *hope, hope, hope.* "You've always taught me the importance of respecting and honouring your parents. I've always upheld those values. And I intend to do everything in my power to continue to do so."

The hopeful smiles adorned on both my parents' faces break my heart.

"But Rachel and I are parents, too." Their smiles falter, brows furrowing. "And we're raising our boys the best we can. Mom, you have to respect that we're parents in this equation, too."

"I know you're a parent," Mom says, her voice strained. "But you'll always be my baby boy, no matter what."

"That's the thing, Mom." I breathe through my nose. "It's like you do respect us as parents, until we don't do things your way. And what happened yesterday—it cannot happen again."

"So what, exactly, would have had me do, Karan? Let Rachel walk all over me after I've done both of you a favour by babysitting your children?"

"She wasn't walking all over you. She was setting a boundary."

Mom rolls her eyes at the word. "Boundaries. You're really going to take boundary advice from a woman who has turned her back on her own parents?"

"Abusive parents," I correct her.

"They never lay a finger on her," Dad chimes in.

"Oh, my God," I sigh, rubbing my beard with my hand. "I am not having this discussion with you guys. This has nothing to do with Rachel's family."

I stand, unable to stay still like this is a normal conversation. "Mom, I'm going to be crystal clear with you. You've got an issue respecting Rachel's boundaries and respecting her as a mother? Well, then, fix it. Find a therapist. Go on a silent retreat. I don't give a fuck what you do—fix your shit, or you're going to lose us for good."

My words hang in the air, everyone collectively holding their breaths. Mom stares at me. Her eyes are wide open, her jaw hanging on the floor. Dad, on the other hand, is locked tight. A stone fortress.

He's seething, but he's letting Mom break the silence.

And she does.

"All I've ever done," Mom cries out, tears beginning to stream from her face as she stands, "was to help you. But apparently, I love you too much, want you to succeed too much. Is my love for you too much, Karan?"

"No." My own voice trembles as I fight back tears.

I cannot cry in front of them. Especially Dad, who looks down at me with a stony, disappointed glare.

"I told you yesterday; I love you. I love you both."

That's the truth, because who wouldn't?

How can you not love those who loved and nurtured you from nothing?

Those who pushed you to become the best version of yourself?

Those who were once everything for you?

Once, a few years ago, Rachel's parents came up in a conversation. I asked her if she missed them. If she still loved them. I remember her tearing up and taking a long minute before she answered, "Yes."

You can love someone with everything that you are. And you can know, deep within yourself, that you have to let them go.

"If that's true, Karan, then apologize, and let's end this right now," my dad finally speaks out. "It's not too late."

Everything in my life has been orchestrated by my parents. They've been the main driving force behind every decision I've made.

Everything, except Rachel.

She's the only thing I've ever gotten to choose for myself. And Rachel chose me. We both made that very clear to each other over the last few weeks.

I'm going to choose her over and over again until the day I die.

"Be very careful what you're going to say next," I tell them both, placing my hands on the table.

"I'm not going to be made the villain here," Mom continues. "I—"

"I'm not here to apologize, and I'm not going to sweep this under the rug," I interrupt her. "You can either accept my terms, or not. It's your choice. And choices have consequences."

I look at them both, alternating between my mother and father.

"So, that's it?" Mom squeals. "All of a sudden, you're in charge, and we either bow down to your rules, or you throw us away like trash?"

"That's not how it is—"

"You're a disappointment, Karan."

My father's words echo through my ears, entering my body, and wreak all sorts of havoc inside. They bounce back and forth, destroying what I've built, the fragile confidence and self-worth that I've attempted to nurture from the scraps they've been tossing me.

There's nothing else to say, then.

This time, when I leave, I don't feel much of anything. An alien numbness slowly takes over my body like vines. Logically, I should be heartbroken, angry, scared—anything—but it's that grey quiet that engulfs me.

The only thing that keeps me from drowning in this sea of apathetic misery is the knowledge that Rachel, Cayce, and Corey are out there waiting for me.

They're the ones I'm fighting for.

Chapter 39

Rachel

As soon as Karan walks through the door, I instinctively know something's wrong.

He doesn't say anything. Even his posture wouldn't betray what's really going on under the surface; he's standing proud and tall, shoulders held back.

It's all in his eyes. Those beautiful brown eyes, so full of warmth, have always had a unique light that I've recognized as Karan's true essence.

But when he comes inside, it's like that light has gone out.

I want to ask him what happened; I want to jump into his arms and pull him into the safety of what we'll continue to build together. But the boys immediately jump from the bed, their attention on the movie gone and given to their father instead.

"Are we gonna go now?" Cayce asks, unable to contain his excitement.

"Yeah, Daddy, I want to go!" his brother adds.

Karan hugs our sons, kisses the top of their heads, and grins. "Yes. I'm all done. Let's go on an adventure."

I don't get a chance to talk to Karan alone on the route to Twillingate. The boys stay awake the entire time, and we talk and laugh as a family, commenting on the stunning, snowy mountain landscapes and the glimpses of the ocean glittering beyond. All I can do is place a hand on his thigh to show him that I'm still here, fully with him, even if we can't talk about it yet.

Twillingate is absolutely beautiful. I imagine that this charming coastal town with colourful homes, jagged cliffs, and winding roads is beautiful enough in the summer, but right now, in the heart of winter, it's ethereal.

A blanket of white coats everything, reflecting the sun like diamonds, and through the snow, we can still see glimpses of colour on the houses and businesses strewn across the coast.

The boys positively freak out when we walk along the coast and spot a large iceberg floating in the sea. On the outside, Karan shares in their glee, even picking up both twins on his wide shoulders to give them a better view. We all squeal in joy when we see a seal bobbing up and down near the iceberg.

But it's all superficial. Karan is putting on a show, as much as he tries to hide it from me. If the boys were a little older, I'm sure they'd be able to tell, too. As it stands, they're too absorbed in our fun little adventure to notice the absent look in their father's eyes.

Things start to shift on the route back toward the ferry. That superficial happiness and excitement he shared back in Twillingate slowly fades away and scatters to the wind like dust, leaving us with a quiet, withdrawn man.

Only when the boys are finally asleep in our ferry cabin can I finally talk to my husband alone.

Because we had to change the date of our tickets, we could only get a two-bed cabin, the others having all sold out already. Cayce and Corey both share the top bunk, and I'm now sliding up against Karan on the bottom bunk, trying to make the most of the tiny space.

I rest my head on his chest and close my eyes, listening to the steady rhythm of his heartbeat. That's what I focus on when I whisper the question I've been aching to ask.

"Karan, how did it go?"

He's silent at first. His body tenses, only slightly.

"Not well," he whispers back.

I wait for him to elaborate, but he doesn't. And I don't ask further questions. The fact that he's here, with us, pretty much paints the whole picture. He went back to set things straight and establish boundaries. It didn't go well.

I don't need my doctorate's degree to figure out they refused to respect his boundaries.

Our boundaries.

I wish I could bask in the pure joy that I should feel at the fact that he chose me. I wish it were that simple. But how can I do that when my husband is clearly in pain?

The next morning, as soon as the ferry lands and we've rolled out of the harbour, away from the exiting traffic, Karan parks the car on the side of the road.

"What are we doing?" I ask him, concern starting to choke me up.

"I'm setting things right," he says without an ounce of emotion before getting out of the car.

The boys start asking questions.

"It's all right," I reassure them as I unclip my own seatbelt. "I'm going to go talk to him."

I follow Karan out of the car; he's pacing on the gravel, his phone to his ear.

"Yeah, hello?" he says when I assume the person on the other end of the line picks up. "Yeah, it's me. I'm not coming back after the holidays. Consider this my final notice."

My blood goes cold, while a tiny glimmer of hope dares to show itself in my chest. Is he doing what I think he's doing?

He waits and listens, then turns to face me, our eyes meeting. This moment should be a celebration, but I'm only met with a deep abyss in his eyes.

"You can consider all that unpaid overtime I've done as the equivalent of a two week's notice."

Pause.

"No."

Pause.

"No, it's not up for discussion. Goodbye."

He hangs up.

"Did you just…" My mouth hangs open.

"Yeah." Karan sighs. "I quit that job you hate so much."

Those words should fill me with elation. Instead, my heart only sinks further at Karan's tone.

He places a hand on my shoulder. "Let's go home."

***

I don't know what I expected when we're all back home. Maybe I'd expected Karan to open up at least a little more, now that we're back in our own things, in the comfort of the familiar.

But that's not what happens.

The day after we come back, Will and Sophie bring their whole family over for dinner when they drop off Océane. Sophie insists they'll supply the food, since we'll be weary from our travels.

But when she walks into our condo with a lasagna in her arms, I'm sick to my stomach.

I don't let it show, and instead greet my friend and my siblings with a wide smile and open arms.

Karan stays quiet when he helps me find the folding chairs to accommodate all ten of us. At dinner, he makes an effort to chat and even laugh at some of Will's jokes, but I see right through him.

While I'm able to make an effort and eat some of Sophie's lasagna—which is actually delicious, despite how the idea of it turns my stomach—my husband barely touches his plate.

After dinner, Karan and Will bring the five kids to play in the living room to give Sophie and me some space to do the dishes. We're barely alone for a second before Océane walks into the kitchen and lets herself fall onto a chair.

"Okay, Rachel, what's going on with Karan?" she whispers while I grab a drying rag and Sophie turns on the hot water.

Sophie arches an eyebrow and looks over at me. "So I'm not the only one who noticed."

"You'd have to not know Karan at all not to notice something's off about him," Océane adds.

I sigh. The truth is, I don't want there to be something wrong. That pesky guilt still gnaws at my insides. If it wasn't for the way I melted down, Karan wouldn't have had to stand up for me. He wouldn't have had to make the gut-wrenching decision to confront his parents.

Then again, we wouldn't be together, either.

So, as Sophie and I do the dishes and Océane listens on, I catch them up on everything that happened. Sophie's face twists into a permanent scowl. And Océane, who is no stranger to toxic behaviour from parents, still appears shocked at how it all went down.

"Maybe I shouldn't be here," she whispers, placing a hand on her mouth, her green eyes wide.

"What do you mean?" I pause with my hands on a wet plate.

"Rachel." My sister rubs her forehead, as if she's exasperated with me. "He's going to need you to be there for him as much as possible. I'm only going to be in the way."

But you need me, I almost say until I force myself to interrupt the thoughts coalesce in my mind.

Océane is right about one thing.

Karan needs me. More than ever.

Of course he's not doing okay. Who would under these circumstances?

When I thought he would never understand what I needed from him, he finally came through. He chose me.

The least I owe him is the same courtesy.

"Yeah…" Sophie starts scrubbing her casserole dish with way too much intensity. "You two need to be alone."

"I can't just kick Océane out," I whisper, my voice breaking at the lump forming in my throat.

Océane has no one to choose her. How is this fair?

She simply grins at me. "I'm sure Will and Sophie won't mind me crashing their place for a while longer. Right?"

She looks over at Sophie.

"Oh, not just you," Sophie grunts before she finally drops the casserole dish back into the sink, abandoning the task, and places her hands on her hips. "You're sending the twins over, too."

Shock reverberates through my bones. "Wait, what?"

"Woman, I've been hearing you talk about all the issues you and Karan have been having for way too long. Now you're saying things are on the up and up between you two, but it's not going to be that way for very long if you're not there for him when he needs you most.

"His relationship with his parents was borderline incestuous. I can't imagine how devastated he must be. Or all the self-worth bullshit that must be going through his mind."

Neither can I. And it kills me inside.

"You two need all the space you can get to only be there for each other and heal," Sophie continues. "So bring the boys over. We'll handle them."

"Fuck yeah," Océane adds. "I get to play Auntie to all my nieces and nephews at once."

"Sophie, you have three kids." One of them is still a baby. "That's insanity."

"Our kids get along great! They'll love it," she argues. "Also, you can pay it back later. Maybe. We'll see."

"Sophie, I can't acce—"

"Rachel. Hear me out." From her tone, she's running out of patience with me. "I would much, much rather that you two be okay, even if it means Will and I will lose only a tiny bit of our sanity for a few days. Plus, Océane has been so great with the kids."

"It would seriously make me happy," Océane adds again.

Sophie continues bulldozing over my worries.

"We're going to be *fine*, Rachel. Just—I beg you, take the help."

My entire body is lit up with the adrenaline rush from this decision. It's a lot to take on. I don't know if Sophie understands what she's getting herself and my brother into.

My boys are my responsibility. Océane is my responsibility.

But at the same time…

Part of me knows Sophie is right. Karan is *not* okay. If there ever was a time to prove to him that I can be there for him just as he was for me, it's now.

I gather all of my courage before I speak.

"Okay."

Chapter 40

Karan

I'm underwater.

At least, that's what it feels like.

I can move, talk, see, taste, touch, and smell what's around me. But it's all got a strange coating to it, like it's been dipped in tar. Or maybe, it's me who's been dipped.

When leaving Newfoundland, I stood in front of an abyss, about to tumble below. I've fallen, and now I have nothing.

Well, that's not true. I don't have *nothing*. In fact, a pervasive shame hangs around at the idea that I probably have more than many people will ever get to have in a lifetime:

Two healthy sons that I adore more than life itself, a wife who, despite all my shortcomings, has decided to choose me, a lovingly annoying extended family.

So why, then, can my stormy thoughts only focus on what I've lost?

Because I made it my identity.

The job I worked so hard to land to please my parents?

Gone.

Those same parents?

Gone.

At least, for the foreseeable future.

I don't know if either of them will ever change their minds and come around. And I have to be okay with that if I want to keep choosing my own family.

That was a week ago now, and I don't regret my choice. But fuck, it hurts.

They were the ones to drive nearly everything I've done. With no agency, what am I even worth? Without a job to provide, how can I be the father my boys deserve?

I'm ripped from my thoughts by the soft padding of Rachel's feet against the hardwood floor of the bedroom. I look up from where I'm lying. The sight of her, hair loose, wearing monochromatic sweats in a bright teal that brings out the green of her eyes, gives my heart a temporary salve.

She's holding a cup of coffee in one hand and a plate full of *Aloo Paratha* in the other. Both emit a fragrant steam that makes its way to my nostrils.

"Hungry?" she asks, setting the mug and plate on the bedside table and taking a seat next to me.

I don't want to disappoint her. I know for a fact that she struggles with this recipe, and yet, she tried—for me. But the truth is, I'm not hungry.

I haven't been hungry for a week.

Still, I sit up and take the plate. "Thank you."

Rachel smiles and watches me take a reluctant bite, like she has for over twenty meals now. After a few quiet minutes of watching me eat without much appetite, she places a warm hand on my thigh.

"Karan… I'm beginning to really worry about you."

I get it. This time alone with Rachel was supposed to help, but I've stayed in the same sorry state instead. Try as I might, I can't will myself to roll out of bed unless Rachel coaxes me into it. She's helped me through showers, pressured almost every bite of food I've forced down my throat, and managed to convince me to take at least a couple of walks with her.

I should feel motivated to do more. To get better and bring our boys back home. To reach a mental space where I'm ready to apply for another job.

But every time I attempt to will myself into taking action, that willpower fizzles into nothingness.

"You don't have to worry about me," I reply to Rachel, though I can't prove it to her.

The smile she gives me is bittersweet.

"I don't *have* to do anything, Karan. I do it because I love you. It's just…" Her gaze flits away. "This is beginning to scare me."

My heart sinks at the thought of hurting Rachel. How long will I keep doing this to her?

"Maybe you should see someone," she continues, squeezing my thigh in reassurance. "A doctor. Or a therapist."

The fact that she's the one suggesting therapy tells me how worried she truly is.

"Maybe," I sigh, putting the plate away on the bedside table, despite having eaten less than a third of the portion Rachel set aside for me.

I've only just gotten her back. I can't lose her again. And here I am, moping around, feeling like shit, becoming a burden on her when there's already so much weighing on her shoulders.

I'm dragging her down with me when I should be lifting her up.

I need to get her out of this place.

I love her too much.

"How about this," I start, framing her face with my index and thumb. "I promise I'll think about it… if you take some time for yourself and get out of the house."

"What? No!" She grasps the hand that's on her face, squeezing it as shock flashes through her eyes. "I'm not leaving you alone."

"I think it would do you some good to get some air and some space."

"I don't *want* space from you, Karan."

I brace myself for the first lie I've ever told my wife. "What if I need space from you?"

Hurt registers all over her face and in the slump of her shoulders.

She opens her mouth, closes it, and opens it again. "Did I do something wrong?"

"No." I force a smile and kiss her forehead, lingering there for a moment with my eyes shut. "You did nothing wrong, love. I just need to be alone for a little bit. Is that okay?"

Rachel swallows and holds on to her elbows.

"Yeah, okay." She stands, picks up the untouched mug and the plate piled high with food. "But you'll call me if you need me, right?"

I nod to reassure her.

She heads into the kitchen with the coffee and food, and I listen to her move around our home while she gets ready. I treasure every sound she makes, holding on to it like a tiny treasure that I don't know I'll ever be worthy of again.

When she's finally ready to leave, she returns to the bedroom, adorned in her thick winter coat and boots.

She pulls me close, her lips brushing against mine in a soft goodbye kiss. I don't deserve her gentleness, but I let it anchor me anyway. Her arms linger around my shoulders for a moment, and I feel the weight of her worry pressing into me like a second skin.

When she finally lets go, I watch her leave, the door clicking softly shut behind her.

The silence that follows is deafening.

I wander through the condo without purpose, each step heavier than the last. The floor beneath my feet creaks faintly, the only sound in this hollow space that should, despite everything, still feel like home. My fingers trail along the walls as I pass, brushing against picture frames showcasing our little family at various stages of our lives. Happy moments frozen in time.

I wish I could dive back into them.

The kitchen is spotless, of course. Rachel's been keeping up with it, though I've all but checked out. I open a cabinet, not even sure why. The rows of neatly stacked plates and cups greet me with nothing to say. I close it again and lean against the counter, staring out the window.

It's a dreary day today. Clouds hide the sun, but it's not snowing, either. A crow perches on the power line and tilts its head at me as if it knows something I don't. I look away.

I should be doing something.

Anything.

But the weight in my chest holds me in place. It's like being trapped in quicksand. The more I think about moving, the deeper I sink. My breath feels too loud in the stillness, and I press my hands to my face, trying to ground myself. It doesn't work.

A quiet thought creeps in, uninvited. Unwelcome.

I don't want to look at it. Entertain the reality that it exists. But it's there, at the back of my mind, vying for my attention.

Go away.

No.

Get out of my hea—

No.

And for the briefest of moments, that quiet, dark thought surfaces in my brain.

It would be so easy. Everything I've lost, I wouldn't need to heal from, if I simply *stopped*. This endless weight, that sensation of being underwater—it'd all evaporate into nothingness, along with the rest of me.

You aren't worthy.

You're a disappointment.

Rachel deserves better.

For a single, minuscule moment, I actually consider it. I consider what it'd be like if I were to fall asleep and not wake up. If I simply faded away.

Those thoughts are violently replaced by the most horrifying sight I can imagine.

Cayce. Corey. Rachel.

Alone.

Dealing with the loss. The healing. The hard things that I'm now thinking of fleeing.

No.

Absolutely fucking not.

What the hell is wrong with me?

And then I'm hit by clarity like a bolt of lightning.

I need them. Just as much as they need me. Just as much as I need Rachel. I was the one who said it; it's the four of us against the world.

So, why did I let them leave me?

I need all four of us. I need sunny winter days, the laughter of my boys as they attack Rachel and me with snowballs. I need cuddles during movie night and arguments about dinner, piggyback rides and fights at bedtime.

I need Rachel's lips against mine, our bodies in sync, our hearts beating as one.

I need everything I've neglected in my life over the past year.

I run faster than I ever thought possible, back to the room, back where I know my phone lies somewhere in the messy sheets. My heart hammers against my ribs as I throw the sheets around looking for the one thing that will get me what I need, *now.*

A deep breath of relief escapes me when I finally grasp the phone. Muscle memory finds Rachel's name and dials it faster than I thought I ever could.

She picks up after a single ring.

"Rachel?"

"It's me." Her voice instantly puts me at ease. "Are you okay?"

"Yes," I breathe out, meaning it for the first time in a long time. "Rachel, I want you home. And I want you to bring back our boys."

Chapter 41

Rachel

One hour earlier

"Hey. Your son's talking to you."

Sophie's voice is what finally snaps me out of my thoughts. I look down and, as she said, Cayce is there with a toy that probably belongs to Gwen, Sophie's eldest.

"Mom, look! I want one like this, too!"

"We'll add it to your Christmas list," I say.

"But Christmas was just now!"

"Your birthday list, then."

"That's in way too long!"

I sigh, exasperated. The last thing on my mind right now is arguing about gifts.

"Cayce, you and your brother already have lots of toys at home. I'm not having this argument with you."

The twins turn six in June. If you ask me, that's the perfect equilibrium between Christmas and a birthday, but he hasn't figured that out yet.

Cayce is about to argue, but then Sophie interrupts him.

"You can come play with Gwen's toys anytime, Cayce.

You're practically cousins now!" She ruffles my son's hair, which earns her a giggle.

Seemingly happy, he goes back to play with Corey, Gwen, and Sophie's middle kiddo, Heather.

Julian, on the other hand, sits firmly on Sophie's lap, ever the velcro toddler. At eighteen months, he can walk and climb perfectly fine on his own, and even play with the older kids when they're being careful, but the energy of the others seems to intimidate him.

I grab my mug of tea from the small table and lean back against the cushy sectional. Right now, the kids are busy building a fort in the remainder of the living room. Océane is in the middle of it all, helping the kids in tasks where height is necessary, despite her own short stature. Give Gwen a few years, and she'll dwarf her.

For a moment, I'm able to stop obsessing over how Karan must be doing, home alone, shifting that focus on my sister instead. Her face is alight with laughter, her cheeks warm and pink. I can only guess what type of pain is going through her body at the moment, but despite it all, she's having a grand time with these kids.

"I've got to admit," I start, gazing back at Sophie, "Océane really seems to have thrived here. I shouldn't have been nervous at all."

Sophie winks. "Told you."

Today, her golden hair is tucked back in a mom bun, and I'm envious of how the cozy yet cute matching set of lilac sweats complements her long body.

How Sophie always looks put together even when rocking a 'mom' style is beyond me.

"But honestly, I think she's the least of your worries right now," Sophie adds.

"I know." An impossible weight sits so heavily on my chest it's a miracle that I can breathe. "But I've been there for him, Soph. I've tried so, so hard all week."

I take a sip of the herbal tea to calm myself down.

"I literally had no other focus but him. He's been completely catatonic."

"I'm really not surprised," Sophie points out, arching an elegant eyebrow. "That man and his parents were attached at the hip. Pretty sure they forgot to cut the umbilical cord thirty-one years ago. And now, he's cut that cord. That must hurt like hell."

"Yeah. I've been telling him for over a year." I purse my lips and let air out. "I only wish I could help him feel better."

"It'll come with time, I'm sure. That man had literally no control over his life, and now that he's taken back that control, it must feel alien to him."

I frown. "What do you mean?"

Sophie cocks her head. "From what you've been telling me, it was either his parents driving his decisions, or you."

"Me?"

"Yeah, girl, you."

I scour my brain, overanalyzing every tiny interaction I've had with Karan over the last fourteen years, but I don't have time to come to a conclusion before Sophie continues on her rant.

"He was either getting pulled in one direction by his parents, or in another direction by you. Is there ever anything Karan did, of his own free will, that came from him?"

"You called for me?" Will interrupts, coming in the living room with a tray of snacks he's been preparing in the kitchen.

At the sight of him—or rather, the snacks—the kids cry out in glee and swarm him.

"It's not all about you, sir," Sophie says, rolling her eyes in jest and giggling, before turning back to me. "So. Tell me. Is there anything Karan ever did that actually came from him? That wasn't a suggestion or pressure from either you or his parents?"

I open my mouth, ready to list out all the things Karan has going for him, but I find myself struggling to come up with a single one.

Fuck.

Is it really that bad? Before his parents came to the city, Karan was constantly happy. He was driven. He loved his old job.

A job I told him to take.

The weight on my chest doubles in size as a memory surges through my head.

The Ubisoft project.

Not only did they win Best Prototype, but Ubisoft also offered them a job straight out of school. Karan wanted to join his teammates and start his own indie game studio.

I encouraged him to take the job instead.

He trusted me. He took the job. It was hard work, but he thrived in that environment, like I knew he would.

Still, he didn't give up on his dreams. Whenever he had a moment to himself and the two of us weren't doing something together, I could find my husband hunched over his computer, his eyes full of stars, pouring passion into his next prototype. He wasn't multidisciplinary, so the game's looks and audio were rudimentary, but he had something.

And he loved it.

When the subject of going off on his own and starting an indie game company came up, I should have been excited. What he didn't know was that mere minutes before he told me about his idea, I'd taken a pregnancy test.

It was positive.

I didn't force Karan to get me pregnant, though. We'd simply stopped using protection a few months back, both agreeing that whatever happened would happen. It's just something we didn't think about when Karan made those plans.

But the rest?

Oh, God.

I cover my mouth with my palm. Sophie places a comforting hand on my shoulder. "Is that a no, then?"

"Sophie, what do I do?"

"You start by calming down."

Only when she says this do I notice how quick my breathing has gotten. I listen to her and take a few deep breaths.

Further in the living room, the kids and my siblings are too focused—and too loud—to pay us any attention.

Good.

Julian wriggles on his mother's lap to go join the others, probably enticed by the snacks. Sophie lets him go, but not without pressing a quick kiss on his head.

"So, yeah, I think the next few weeks are going to be tough on him," she continues. "Why do you think I told you to bring your kids here?"

"I thought it would be better by now." My voice is weak. "And Océa—"

"And let me tell you," she interrupts, wagging her index finger, "that man is not the only one with unhealthy attachments to his family, ma'am."

"What?" I look over at Océane, making sure her focus is still not on us. "Karan said he was fine with her living with us."

"Yeah, but you didn't ask him first."

"Yeah, but he agreed with it after all."

"Rachel, that's not the point." Sophie sighs and shakes her head. "You were like this with Will, too, you know. You put all of this weight on your own shoulders and somehow believe that you're responsible for everyone's well-being."

"That's because I am."

"Are you, though?"

"My parent a—"

"Are no longer in your life." Sophie clasps my hands in hers, quieting her voice, her big blue eyes bore into me. "Look at them."

I take a look at Will and Océane again, seeing that Océane is now play-wrestling with Will.

Fuck, he's going to hurt her.

No, he's not. He knows what he's doing. He's not an idiot.

Sophie chuckles. "I was about to say, look at them, and see how they're adults. But now they're acting like kids, so it's not really helping my point."

"I know they're adults."

Will is, in fact, older than me. But Océane is twenty-one years old. She's an adult, but barely. With our age difference, she was practically my baby.

"But…" I look back at Sophie, my lower lip trembling. "You said it yourself. Our parents are gone. She's got no one else."

Sophie huffs. "Oh yeah? Fuck me and Will, then."

"That's not what I mean—"

"No, that's what I'm talking about, Rach." She squeezes my hands tighter. "I know you don't mean it as an insult, and I don't take it as one. Your trauma has you convinced that you're the only one you can trust to take care of the people you love. Well, I'm here to tell you, it's bullshit.

"You are *not* alone, Rachel. You haven't been alone in a long time. And if you don't believe me…" She lifts her nose in the direction of my siblings again. "Maybe you should talk to them. See what they have to say. And actually listen instead of making assumptions about who's capable of what."

Before I have a chance to reply—or even think through anything—Sophie whistles loudly. The entirety of the room stops what they're doing and looks in our direction.

"Will. Océane. It's sibling talk time. Rachel needs some air, so why don't you go with her?"

"I do no—"

"Shut up and go talk to your family," she whispers in my ear before pushing me off the couch and forcing me to stand.

Oh, well, shit. Looks like this is happening.

***

The three of us, all bundled up in our warmest winter gear, don't say a word at first as we begin our walk down the street. Only the ambient sound of the city, along with the crunching of our boots against the crackling snow and ice covering the sidewalk, keeps us company.

I purposefully walk at a slow pace to give Océane a chance. It seems like she's having a good day, from the way she's been goofing around with Will and the kids, but still. I

308

don't want to exaggerate and take too big a risk.

It's not like we're rushing to go anywhere, either.

I'm very aware of what I have to say. The words keep bouncing around in my head like ping pong balls, and it's all I can do to keep them inside and overthink them.

Once I speak them into reality, I cannot take them back.

What if Océane thinks I don't love her as much as I once did?

What if Will isn't ready for the responsibility?

What if it all comes crashing down around me, and I lose everything?

I think of Karan, currently sitting at home alone, doing who knows what, and my stomach does a somersault. He's the reason I'm here. That's what I have to remember.

He chose me, and he's suffering for it. Now I have to choose him, too.

I grip Océane's hand and look to my left to see both of my siblings, who are already gazing back at me. Slight worry is etched on their faces.

Worry. For me. When it should be the other way around.

I never wanted them to have to take care of me.

"Océane," I start, gathering all of my courage and channeling those bouncing words in my head to finally speak them into the world. "I think, if Will is okay with it, that you should move in with him and Rachel. For good."

Both of them stay quiet. We keep walking; a police siren echoes in the background. I wait for one of them to say something—anything, really—but they only stare back at me with concern and a slight upturn of their lips.

They're waiting for me to elaborate, maybe.

For me to give a good reason.

To prove I'm not failing them.

"I…" A pressure builds up behind my eyelids and gathers in my throat.

I grip Océane's hand tighter, wishing we weren't wearing mittens so that I could feel the warmth of her hand against mine for comfort.

Whose comfort, hers or mine, I'm not too sure.

"I don't think I'm in a place where I can truly be there for you. Not like you need it." I clench my jaw to hold back the tears. "Karan needs me more than I realized. So do my kids. Océane, you don't know how much I wish I could have more to give, how much I wish I could be everything you need, but I don't have it in me. I…"

I look away so she doesn't see a lone tear fall.

"Right now, I'm not enough."

Océane squeezes my hand. I look back up at my siblings, who are now sharing a knowing look.

"You think she's done?" Will asks, raising a teasing eyebrow.

"I think so," Océane answers, the same mischievous smile on her face.

Guilt and pain turn to confusion. I stop dead in my tracks, forcing them to stop along with me.

"What?"

"Come on," Océane beckons me, pulling on my hand as she tries to coax me forward. "Let's keep walking."

"Do you guys think this is funny? Or that I'm joking? What is this?"

A hint of anger wants to rear its ugly head, but I want to give them the benefit of the doubt.

So I listen and keep walking.

"For the record, Rachel," Will starts, "you have always

been much, much more than enough."

"You literally saved me," Océane adds. "There's literally no way I could have made it out of that house on my own."

"That was the least I could do," I argue.

"Was it, though?" Will questions. "The least you could have done was what I did. Which is nothing."

"Will, you had your own shit to sort throu—"

"Yeah, I did, and thanks to you, I sorted through it." He shakes his head with a chuckle. "I've got the girl of my dreams, and a family I never dreamed I could have. You helped me get over the shame of not being there for Océane when shit hit the fan, and now we can be together without me drowning in self-loathing.

"You give, and give, and give, and you forget that once our cup is full thanks to you, we're able to give, too."

"Rachel, you are everything I've always needed and more," Océane adds. "And I'm so proud of you for finally standing up for yourself and taking what you need."

"You mean, you're not upset?" I ask through a thick throat. I shift my focus to Will. "And you…"

"We've been chatting about this with Sophie way before you brought this up," Will explains. "We all agree that you've done enough. It's time for you to lighten your load and let me do my part."

"And I'm not a child," Océane adds. "I can take care of myself for the most part. Just not alone. And we all agree that despite that, I'm going to take too much space when the four of you need each other more than you ever have before."

"But…" My gaze flits between both of my siblings in a wild goose chase for where to go.

I'm flooded with too many thoughts and feelings at once,

like a helium balloon drifting in the wind.

"The kids… they…"

"What about them?" Will asks me, genuinely confused.

"I mean, they're a handful, an—"

"So are yours, and, well, we've got a free babysitter now," he continues, giving Océane a playful poke in the ribs.

"Hey, she's no—"

"Rachel, he's only playing around," Océane reassures me. "Is it so hard to believe that I'm happy with them? And that they're happy with me?"

I'm about to say the most obvious issue—that Océane isn't Sophie's responsibility—but I'm stopped short at the realization that she wasn't Karan's responsibility either.

Or, in a sense, maybe she was. Maybe that's what family is all about. And if Sophie was against the idea, Will and Océane wouldn't be here now, swearing to me that they're all in agreement.

Sophie's kids were never Will's responsibility, yet he stepped up without even having to be asked. Funnily enough, Will, who can unfortunately never biologically become a father, has been a better father than our own ever was.

I think about our parents, who never fought to win us back. Or about Karan's parents, who prefer to hold on to their pride rather than be in our lives. And then I remember the way Karan easily adapted to Océane being in our home without me having to ask him to do it. The way Sophie took our kids in without hesitation.

Blood can only take you so far. The bonds we build—those we choose—are those that will hold us dear during our darkest nights.

I jump at the sound of my ringtone screaming from my pocket, then pull my hand from Océane's, slip my mitten off, and take my phone out as quickly as I can. When I see Karan's name reflected back at me, I gasp and answer.

"Rachel?"

There's something in Karan's voice that wasn't there when I left. But, in all of my messy emotions, I can't detect what it is for the life of me.

"It's me. Are you okay?"

"Yes," he breathes out.

I close my eyes and take a breath of relief.

"Rachel, I want you home. And I want you to bring back our boys."

Chapter 42

Karan

I'm pacing back and forth in our hallway, rubbing my beard almost obsessively, when the sounds of footsteps up the outside stairs finally make it to my ears.

They're *here*.

The door bursts open, and in a few long strides, I meet my family with wide open arms. I close my eyes as we embrace like this, and the boys somehow detect that I need this moment and decide to keep still instead of squiggling their way out of my arms.

In a deep inhale, I bask in the sweet strawberry scent of Rachel's hair and in the familiar smell of both my boys, mingled with the fresh scent of snow and cool air.

"I love you," I whisper to them.

"I love you too, Daddy," Cayce says first.

"Me too," Corey follows.

"I love you," Rachel says, "and I'm here."

I pull away from the family hug and grab Rachel's face with both hands, pressing a deep kiss on her lips.

"I shouldn't have sent you away, Rach. I'm so sorry."

"It's okay." Her hand strokes mine over her face.

"No, it's not." I kneel and pick up Cayce and Corey—one boy with each arm—to kiss the tops of their heads. "I'm going to do my best to be better from now on."

"Karan," Rachel gasps, looking at Cayce and Corey, then back at me while lowering her voice. "It's okay if you're… not okay."

She ruffles the boys' hair with a forced smile. "Boys, take off your winter stuff and go play, won't you?"

"Okay, Mom!" both twins cry out in tandem.

They both shrug out of their jackets, boots, and hats in record speed before sprinting towards their bedroom.

Rachel and I are left alone. I stand, and as soon as I've got a solid footing, I reach my arms around Rachel and bring her in close.

I'm completely blind to what the future holds. That sinking terror still has its claws in me at the thought of how I'm going to provide for my boys in the way they deserve now that I've burned the bridge at True Keys.

And I don't know if I have the capacity to do it.

I can't claim responsibility for any of my best achievements. Not when I wasn't truly in the driver's seat.

Now that the drivers themselves are disappointed in me and no longer on speaking terms with us, what do I do?

I hold on to the best thing that's ever happened to me. That's all I can do.

"Karan." Rachel pulls away from our embrace to look up at me, her green eyes glittering with unshed tears. "I've been so, so hard on you over the last year, and although I'm glad we're okay now, I'm realizing I might have hurt you more than I thought."

"You could never hurt me." I sweep a long strand of silky chestnut hair behind her ear. "You were hard on me, but it was deserved. You were right about it all."

"Not about everything." She sinks her face into my chest and sighs. "Karan, I swear to you, I wil—"

"Rachel." I tip her head back so she'll look at me again. "There's one thing I need right now, more than anything. Will you give it to me?"

"What is it?"

"All I want is a nice day with my family." Rachel returns to work from her holiday time soon, and the boys will be headed right back to school. "I don't care what we do, as long as it's the four of us."

Days from now, I'll find myself completely alone in this house during daylight hours.

I don't want to waste a single second more.

***

Rachel gives me exactly what I ask for.

I lose myself in the day and allow myself to truly feel joy. A light snow falls outside, and it's not too cold, so we make the most of it and head to Beaver Lake on Mount Royal with our ice skates and the boys' hockey sticks.

When we've all had so much fun that our cheeks hurt from smiling and laughing, we head downtown for hot chocolate at our favourite café, then head home and order Tandoori chicken and samosas from our usual place.

Then, we take out the Uno Junior cards and manage not to kill each other before the boys are almost on the edge of collapse from exhaustion.

When I kiss them goodnight, I linger for a moment on each of their foreheads. I absorb all of the love I can get, letting it seep through my skin and into my bones.

Everything is going to be okay.

By the time they're both asleep, I'm ready to collapse on the couch. Rachel is already there, both legs folded up underneath her, when I make it to the living room. A pleasant scent hits my nostrils, and I notice two steaming mugs on the coffee table.

"Made us tea," Rachel says with a smile.

I sit next to her and grab a mug. "Thank you, love."

I bring the mug to my lips and let the sweet and earthy notes of the herbal tea dance on my taste buds. When I swallow, its warmth travels down to my belly, and it almost feels like it spreads throughout all of me.

I set the mug back on the table and open my arm to beckon Rachel closer. She nuzzles into my side, just as I'd hoped she would.

"So, was today everything you were hoping for?" she asks me.

"It was wonderful, Rachel." I allow my fingers to weave through her hair.

For a second, that sinking feeling of worthlessness hooks itself into me. I can't quite push it away, but I focus on the silky strands of Rachel's hair, on her steady breathing against my chest, on the knowledge that my boys are safe and sound asleep in their room, hopefully dreaming of better things than I will tonight.

"But?" Rachel finally asks, the slight tension that overtook my muscles a moment ago telling her what I didn't dare say.

She knows me better than anyone.

"But…"

If I speak this into existence, will it make it more true? Or will it instead air out my wound and let it breathe so it can finally start to heal?

"I don't know what I'm going to do, Rachel."

I expect her to reassure me, like she usually would. But instead, she peers up at me through those dark eyelashes of hers, and she waits.

She listens.

"I doubt I can get another job in software. Not after the stunt I pulled. My boss is going to spread the word around to let everyone in the industry know I'm unreliable."

Now that I've opened the valve, the words come pouring out of me like pus.

"And even if I could, I doubt I can make it work. We've both seen what happens when I try to make it work." I scoff. "There are probably some people who can balance things right, but not me. So I obviously can't cut it in that industry.

"That leaves video games. But I've got no guarantee Ubisoft would take me back. There would need to be a new project, or someone who recently left, and right now, with the state of the world, and all these mass layoffs I've heard about from my old colleagues, it's not exactly raining jobs out there."

My breath hitches.

"And that's exactly why I wanted more for Cayce and Corey. Neither of us can guarantee what the world will look like when they're grown up, so I wanted to at least guarantee that we could give them as big a safety net as possible. Now I don't know how I'm going to do that. And…"

I realize my breathing is shallow.

"Karan." Rachel strokes my shoulder and back. "You are capable of so much more than you give yourself credit for. And I love that about you. I love how smart you are, how hard you work, especially for us. But for fuck's sake, Karan…"

She chuckles, and all I want is to capture that breathy laugh into my mouth and lose myself in her, but we have to see this conversation through.

"Am I nervous about the future, too? Of course. I'm terrified. But no matter how much money we have, there's nothing we can guarantee. And that's the hardest part of being a parent.

"We are going to make it through, Karan. You'll do wonderful things, and you'll be there for your boys, and even if you don't get them the trust fund you're trying to build for them, you have to trust that our hard work as parents will pay off and that they're going to be okay."

"I want them to be more than okay." I choke back a sob. "Rachel, I want so badly for them to have everything they could ever dream of."

"So do I. So you know what?" She strokes the side of my face. "Let's show them what it's like to build their own happiness by being the best examples we can be."

My wife stands, gives my shoulders a brief squeeze, and heads toward the hallway.

"Wait, what?" I ask as I watch her leave. "Where are you… I mean, what are you doing?"

"I'll be right back," she promises. "Stay here."

I'm left to my own devices as time stretches to a standstill while she's gone. I'm facing the precipice again, on the edge of breaking down, but everything is on hold. It's like I'm only fully living when Rachel is next to me.

What could she have meant by 'build your own happiness'?

I let the breath I'd been holding finally go when she traipses back into the living room, her bare feet carefully padding the hardwood floor as quietly as she can so as not to wake the boys. There's something nestled under her armpit, but I can't tell what it is. Her lips are upturned in a quiet smile.

And her eyes. They shine like diamonds.

Whatever she's holding, it's got her excited.

Rachel sits next to me and takes out what I now recognize as my old laptop. I used to take that bulky thing with me everywhere, in case I'd get a few minutes of free time to work on my game project.

A rush of nostalgia floods my veins, and my stomach sinks. I miss the man I used to be. The man Rachel fell in love with, who had dreams of starting his own game studio. I miss this project, which was part farm sim, part space exploration and survival. I gave up its development completely when I left Ubisoft and took the job at True Keys.

And with it, I think I gave up part of myself, too.

"Why do you have this?" I immediately ask, my voice a tad bitter.

It's not that I'm upset at Rachel for bringing this thing out. Rather, I'm bitter at the reminder of everything I've lost.

Rachel places the bulky laptop on my lap. "You know, one of my favourite parts of our old evenings was to walk in on you working on this thing. Plugged into its second screen in our bedroom."

The desk and second screen she's talking about have lain untouched for nearly a year.

"Lots of wives would be upset at how much time you spent working on this, but I always loved to see how your eyes came to life. And it was never at my expense, or at the kids' expense, either. I always loved you so much for that."

I stare at the laptop without grabbing it, feeling its cool surface permeate through the fabric of my jeans.

"I know," I say simply.

It's the truth.

I knew this was a part of me Rachel adored.

And I let it die anyway.

"Karan." Rachel places a hand on my thigh, near the laptop. "It's not too late for you to pursue this."

"There's no time," I argue. "I'll have to get another job, and job hunting alone is going to be a hell of a ride."

I look at her and soften my expression.

"And the rest of the time I have, I want to spend it with you."

Rachel cocks her head sideways and sighs at my comment.

"And I appreciate that so much, Karan. But that's not what I meant." She touches the laptop again. "I meant pursue this professionally. Start your own studio. Apply for grants. The whole thing."

My heart skips a beat, then starts hammering against my chest. It takes longer for my brain to process what Rachel is suggesting, and when it does, the words are out of my mouth faster than I can anticipate:

"No. Rachel, no."

"Why not?"

"I… I can't."

I pick up the laptop and set it aside, then grab both of Rachel's hands. The moment Rachel told me she was pregnant all those years ago was the moment I knew it was already too late for this, and things haven't changed.

"I'll be on minimum wage for at least a year, probably more."

There's a government grant for business owners in the creative media sector that provides us with mentorship and a minimum wage, but that doesn't cover additional wages for other team members I'll need. And getting additional grants can take years.

"There's no guarantee I could ever make enough to get the kids through college. No… I'll just get another job in the game industry. Not in software…" I squeeze her hands. "I promise."

"Karan." Rachel's brow furrows. "No. You've given up every opportunity you had to achieve your dream, because of me."

"It wasn't because of yo—"

"It was." She bites her lip. "I was the one who told you to take the Ubisoft job."

"It was a sensible decision." One my parents would have made, even if the games industry isn't one they respect. "It was a good decision."

"It wasn't your decision, though. I took that choice away from you." Rachel leans closer to me. "But what if you had the chance to pursue what *you* want, for once?"

I look away. Allow myself, just for a moment, to dream.

"That… would be wonderful."

My heart leaps at the thought of having my own studio. Pursuing my own vision.

The thought withers and dies as quickly as it came to life.

"But it's too big a risk."

"It's really not," Rachel argues. "I've been thinking about

it all day. We could sell the condo and move to the South Shore, off the isla—"

"Rache—"

She places a finger on my lip. "Shush. Hear me out, please."

I sigh, not daring to truly hope yet, and nod.

"This place is worth a ton more than what we paid for it, and it's in a prime area," she continues. "There's no need for us to live right here. On the South Shore, we'll still be close to our family…"

Her voice trails off as she seemingly remembers that we won't be talking to *my* family anytime soon.

"I'll be close to Will and Océan—"

"Océane? Isn't she living with us?"

"Will's going to take her." My eyes go wide, but Rachel continues. "I know you were okay with it, but I should never have made that decision without you."

"Rachel…"

"So, the South Shore, or somewhere similar. I can find a job in another pharmacy. In case you've forgotten, Karan, I make a shit ton of money, too. You're not the sole provider. It's not all on your shoulders."

Her thumb traces circles against my hand.

"With a much smaller mortgage and our savings, we'll have more than enough of a cushion for you to pursue this project. You can even do freelance work if it makes you feel better, to help make ends meet; Logan can help you out with that and show you where to find gigs, or connect you with the right people."

The vision starts to form in my head. This goes against every instinct in my body. Before we had Cayce and

Corey, I'll admit, I did have the drive to make this a reality. But everything changed once I knew I was going to be a father. My responsibility to them as a provider came before everything else.

My chance for my dream had passed. I would have to wait at least two or three decades, and even then, would I still have the energy and drive left?

But what Rachel is proposing… it could work.

In theory.

But it could also fail spectacularly.

And the cost of that failure…

"Rachel, we could lose everything." I press my forehead against hers, trying to hold myself together.

Part of me is trying so hard to keep the small breath of hope that she gave me alive.

The rest of me wants to smother it before it grows too large. Too uncontrollable.

"If I fail, if it never works out…"

Rachel weaves a hand behind my neck, tangling her fingers in the loose hairs of my nape. "We'll deal with it together."

I draw in a ragged breath.

"It's time to put what you want first," she continues, holding me close. "You chose to fight for me, Karan. Now I'm choosing to do the same for you. It's just like you said in Newfoundland. It's us against the world. So let me fight for you, Karan. Let me do this for you, when you've already done so much for me."

Do I dare to let myself hope? With her holding me like this, I feel safer than I ever have.

The weight of all my fears…

The crushing pressure of the responsibility, the expectations that I could never truly live up to…

The gnawing doubt that I could ever make this work…

They're still there.

But for the first time in years, I allow something else to shine through:

A flicker of possibility.

A spark of the man I used to be—the one who can dream without limits.

I exhale, my breath shaking, and press my lips to hers.

Rachel melts into me and tightens her fingers in my hair, her body leaning into mine as if she's trying to fuse us together. And just like that, the dam breaks.

We kiss with everything we've been holding back since those days alone at the A-frame cabin. My ribs ache from the pressure of it, my throat tight with the weight of everything unsaid. Her lips are warm, and oh so soft, but my hands are shaking, my pulse thundering in my ears like a storm.

There's salt on her skin, salt on mine, the taste of tears that I've finally let loose mixing with the bitter tang of tea still clinging to her mouth. My chest is too full, too tight, like I've been holding my breath for years and only now remember how to exhale.

Her fingers dig into my shoulders, nails biting through fabric. Her heartbeat slams against my own ribs, fast and uneven, like a bird trapped in a cage. My own breath comes in ragged bursts against her mouth, my lungs burning, my skin too hot, too alive. Every touch is a spark.

Her palm against my jaw.

Her thighs tightening around my waist.

The way her breath hitches when I press her closer.

And when she sobs against my mouth, I do too, because there is no other way out.

"Okay," I gasp when I pull my mouth away from hers for just a moment.

"Okay?"

I'm terrified, and I hold on to her for dear life. I stand, lifting her with me. Her legs wrap around my waist as her arms lock around my neck.

"Rachel," I groan against her neck. "Thank you."

I slowly make my way to the bedroom, kissing along her jaw, the crook of her neck, that spot behind her neck that she likes.

"Thank you."

"I love you so much, Karan." Her breath comes in little gasps against my kisses along her skin.

When we reach our bedroom, I place her down on the bed carefully. We undress each other slowly, reverently, and each little sound of fabric rustling, my belt unlatching, sends a hot shock through my spine.

I've never needed her more than I do at this moment.

Rachel's skin is so warm and soft under my hands, even softer than I remember from a week or so ago—or maybe I've only forgotten what it feels like to touch her, to savour her, without the weight of the world pressing down between us. The silk of her thighs against mine as I settle between them sends a shudder through me, not just desire but something deeper, something aching and sweet.

I pause and rest my forehead against hers. "Rachel."

The sole act of saying her name is enough. It says all I need her to know.

"Karan." She lifts her hips, pressing into me, and the heat of her is too much, too perfect.

And then I'm sinking deep into her, slowly, letting her adjust to me. But she's already there, meeting me, her body arching up to take me deeper. The sound she makes—soft, broken—unravels something in my chest.

I bury my face in her neck and revel in the sensation of her legs tightening around me, her heels digging into my back, the warmth and friction of her so exquisite. The groan that escapes me elicits a moan from her.

She's so responsive. Has always been. But in this moment, it means so much more.

It means everything.

I lose myself in the rhythm of her, in how achingly good she feels. With every thrust, a part of me heals. With every gasp from Rachel's lips, I become a little more whole.

Her breath comes in sharp little gasps against my ear, her fingers digging into my shoulders like she's trying to crawl inside my skin. The way her body tightens around me, the way her hips rise to meet mine, is my salvation.

"I've got you," I murmur against her collarbone, my lips brushing her silk-like skin as I weave a hand in between us, touching her exactly where she needs it. "I've got you, Rachel. Come for me, baby."

Her back arches off the bed as the first wave hits her, her nails raking down my back as her body clenches around me. The sound she makes—fuck, that sound, my name torn from her throat—shatters something inside me. I sense her pulse against me, feel her body trembling as the orgasm rolls through her, and white-hot pleasure sears right through me.

I come with a groan that sounds like her name, my

forehead pressed to hers as my body locks up. I can hardly breathe, even as we're both coming down from this high.

Yet I've never felt more alive.

Rachel just gave me a gift I didn't know to ask for. Now, with her in my arms, the scent of the two of us lingering in the air, I'm whole. There's still a gaping hole where my parents used to be, but for now, this has got to be enough.

It will be more than enough.

Chapter 43

Rachel

Two months later

"Here, let me get that for you."

I stop struggling in vain against the heavy box I'm trying to lift and step aside, letting Karan handle it for me. It's a box of books, and it's one of the last remaining boxes in the condo before we truly empty the place out.

I watch, entranced at the sight of his forearms bulging as he grips the heavy box and lifts it without breaking a sweat. My bear of a husband. I love him so much that it sometimes still scares me.

In the background, the sounds of Cayce, Corey, Gwen, and Heather running across the empty condo echo through the rooms. They've never had this much fun in this place, despite all their toys being at the new house already. It's crazy how much a child can make out of nothing—in this case, a whole lot of space.

The condo sold at a price I hadn't dared dream of. What was more difficult was finding a house just as quickly. There were tons of homes for sale along the South Shore, but they'd get snatched up so fast we barely had time to think.

But in the end, we found it. The place we hope will be our forever home. I hadn't ever dreamed of owning a house—a house, with a yard, imagine that—and when I walked inside, everything immediately felt right.

It's a small bungalow with a brick facade, a finished basement, three bedrooms, and a simple backyard complete with a patio, located in the heart of beautiful Chambly. It's nearly half the price of what we sold the condo for. Living off the island will be a change of pace, but not necessarily an unwelcome one.

I've already got a job lined up when we're done with the move. And we're a five-minute drive away from the coworking space Karan will use to start his own indie game studio.

"The only boxes left are book boxes," I tell Karan, letting a harsh breath go through my nose. "I can't let you do all the work."

"You can, and you will." Karan winks at me before heading towards the door.

"He's not doing all the work," Will chimes as he walks into the living room and proceeds to pick up another box. "Besides, you and Sophie said you were fixing dinner, right?"

"I still can't believe you don't want to just do beer and pizza, like normal people," Sophie exclaims when she joins us in the room, little Julian in her arms like usual.

"With a kitchen like that?"

I picture the wide counter spaces, huge island counter, and top-of-the-line stovetop and oven waiting for me in our new house. The old couple who owned the place included them in the price of the house because they're headed to a retirement home.

"No way we're ordering food. I'm christening that kitchen first thing when we get there."

"I think you're grossly overestimating the energy you'll have when we get to that point," Sophie laughs.

I'm about to retort something when my phone rings. I grab it from my pocket and freeze when I see the name flash across the screen.

Martine.

"You good?" Sophie asks, inching closer to me.

I can't breathe.

The past two months have been nothing short of harrowing. Although I managed to convince Karan to make the big move and chase his dreams, he's been understandably melancholic for large stretches of time. We're undertaking the most exciting project of our lives, and his parents, the people he looks up to the most, aren't in our lives to witness it.

A thousand questions battle for attention in my head.

Why is she calling?

Why is she calling *me?*

Should I expect more insults? Or begging?

I have to pick up.

I make a small gesture to Sophie to tell her to wait, then pick up and bring the phone to my ear as I quickly make my way to the bathroom.

"Hello?"

"Rachel?"

The voice on the other end of the line is frail, unsure. Meanwhile, my heart's beating so fast I can feel it in my throat.

"Yes. It's me."

Silence echoes for a beat. "Could we… talk?"

I want to run away. Throw up. Close my eyes and not have this conversation.

The last time we spoke, Martine witnessed me at my worst. And she didn't like what she saw.

Is she ever going to respect me again?

Then I think of Karan, and all my discomfort, my anxiety over speaking to her, seems like nothing compared to what he must be going through.

"Um, sure."

"In person?"

"When?"

"Is now a good time?"

I grit my teeth. If I delay this conversation, it's going to weigh on me the entire time.

I won't be able to think. And Karan will see right through me.

"Somewhere neutral," Martine adds. "I thought of *La Fabrique de Bagel* near your place."

Now that's surprising. I'd expected Martine to invite me to her house. The consideration needed to think of a neutral space like the cozy café she suggested is something I didn't think her capable of.

What has been going through her head over the last two months?

I'll have to make up an excuse for why I'm walking out of our own move for a good hour. Karan cannot know about this—not right away. There must be a reason Martine is reaching out to me first, and until she tells me, I don't want to get Karan's hopes up.

"I can be there in half an hour," I reply, my throat dry.

"Okay. I'll be there." Another beat of silence. "Thank you."

She hangs up.

My fingers are shaking as I place the phone back in the pocket of my jeans. When I open the bathroom door, Sophie's standing there, her brow furrowed.

"Who was that?" she whispers.

"Martine," I mouth, hardly letting a sound escape my lips.

Sophie's eyes go wide. "Holy shit."

"Shit," Julian repeats after her with a giggle as he grabs Sophie's ponytail.

"Oops." Sophie makes a face, but lets it go. "What did she want?"

"To meet. With me."

"What did you say?"

"I agreed."

"Holy…" Sophie looks at Julian and abstains from cursing a second time.

"Yeah."

My whole body feels like it's on fire, and I'm struggling to keep my breathing steady.

"I'm gonna tell Karan my old work called me for some paperwork they forgot to have me fill out, and you're going to corroborate what I say because you overheard the entire call, right?"

Sophie arches an eyebrow. "Did I?"

"You did."

"Right."

I find my winter gear and get dressed in a daze. When Karan comes back up for more boxes, I repeat my excuse, which tastes bitter on my tongue. I hate lying to my husband, even if I know it's only for a short time. And when he kisses me goodbye, my heart sinks to my feet.

The weather is mild enough for me to walk, so I do, hardly sensing the slight chill in the air against my cheeks the entire way. Even when I arrive and walk inside, the smell of freshly baked bagels and coffee that permeates the air doesn't faze me.

Because she's already here.

Martine sits alone in an armchair that seems to swallow her up. She's holding a steaming mug of coffee, and she's no longer wearing a headscarf, letting her short silver curls out in the open. A second mug sits on the table in front of her, facing an empty armchair that she saved for me.

At first, she doesn't hear me walk towards her; her gaze is fixed forward, her brows deeply furrowed. It looks like she's lost in thought. I hesitate when I'm ten feet away. If she were to turn her head slightly, she would see me standing awkwardly.

I can do this.

I take a deep breath and step forward, taking a seat in the empty armchair. My arrival rips her out of her daze. She blinks several times, then looks me up and down before finally meeting my gaze.

"Rachel."

"Is this…" I point to the second mug on the table. "For me?"

She gives me a small, hesitant smile. "Yes. Just how you like it. I hope that's okay."

I nod and pick up the mug. We're both quiet for a moment, unsure of how to break the ice. It should be her. After all, she asked me to come. And I don't want to say the wrong thing and seem 'insane' to her again.

"Thank you for agreeing to meet," Martine finally says.

There's nothing aggressive or off-putting in her tone. It doesn't feel like she's trying to build up to an argument.

"I know we didn't leave things on the best of terms."

"What do you want?" I blurt out.

I immediately cover my mouth, shocked by my own rudeness. I've let the pressure get to me.

Martine recoils, her eyes going wide for an instant.

"I'm sorry," I immediately say. "That came out rude."

"No, I understand," she stammers. "I was completely out of line in the way I treated you at the cabin, Rachel. I'm here to apologize."

The world drops below my feet.

Of all the things I could have expected…

This wasn't it.

Martine laughs, if a little nervously. "Well, don't look so surprised.

"Do you blame me though?"

She pinches her lips. "Not really."

I shift uncomfortably in my chair and take a sip of coffee. It's good. I try to focus on the bold flavours dancing on my tongue, but it can't overshadow everything else.

There are so many things I want to say. I want to be mean. I want to cower and say that it's okay. I want to scream for Karan's sake.

But I say nothing. *She* reached out to *me*. She can be the first to speak.

"I've been going to therapy." She grips her mug a bit tighter than before. "At first, I didn't want to go. But it was Surinder's idea that we both go."

I can't hide my surprise at that. Martine smiles.

"Yes, he surprised me, too. But I gave in, and, you know,

it wasn't as bad as I thought." She shrugs. "Well… Not all of it, anyway."

"That's good," I say, just to stay engaged.

Because what else can I say?

"Going through that process made me realize how badly I treated you." She looks at me with a quivering chin. "It wasn't about you, Rachel. I've always loved you like a daughter."

And I always loved you like a mother, I want to say.

"I always wanted a big family." Her gaze moves up, and for a moment, I see something wistful in her eyes, like she's lost in a vision of the past. "Jocelyne and I lost our parents very young. She never wanted kids. I wanted so many of them so that I could grow the happy family I missed. But Karan's birth was too hard on my body."

Her eyes become watery, yet she holds her tears back. "Look, none of this excuses my behaviour, Rachel. I'm not trying to give you excuses so that you forgive me. I only want you to know all there is to know, so that maybe you can one day come to understand why I am the way I am. I realize I cling to Karan, sometimes too much."

She laughs without humour.

"Surinder and I put so much on his shoulders, and it's not fair. It's not his fault he's carrying the dreams of every child I wish I'd had."

"He took it really, really hard," I tell Martine, looking straight into her eyes. "It's not just me you hurt."

Karan is doing so much better, but it doesn't erase the pain they inflicted on him. And that's without even mentioning the years and years of pressure that turned him into a shell of himself.

"I know that. God, do I know." Martine looks down, then back up at me. "But I'm apologizing to you first, Rachel. I'm so sorry I reacted the way I did at the cabin. I'm sorry I didn't listen when you asked for space. My therapist, she… She told me you most likely had a panic attack. I didn't know what those were before, and I…"

She pauses for a breath.

"I'm here, with you, because it's your authority as a mother that I tried to bring down. So I'm apologizing to you first out of respect."

When I'm quiet for a beat, Martine continues.

"You don't have to forgive me right away. I only hope that you can, in time."

I'm still wary of Martine, and even of Surinder. But if I've learned anything, it's that most of us are genuinely trying our best to do good by those we love.

Sometimes, that love can be destructive. But other times? It can be the most healing experience you'll ever go through.

"I can forgive you under one condition," I say, my voice quiet.

Martine lights up. "What is it?"

"Apologize to Karan. Make things right with him. And…" I give her a small smile. "Be proud of what he's about to do."

***

Karan

We've already been in this house for two days, and I feel like we've hardly gotten through any of our boxes.

Rachel says she hates to pack but loves to unpack. She enjoys the opportunity to choose where everything goes and start clean. Well, I hate boxes, period. I can't wait until we're fully settled and everything has its place.

I only wish Mom and Dad could see it, too.

Cayce and Corey are already in bed, so I'm making the most of this time to unpack all my office-related stuff. We don't have a separate room for an office, but I've set up a small desk in the basement living room. At least, I'm trying to. We tore the desk apart to make it easier to move, but now I can't find the screw that's supposed to hold the last leg to the main table.

The stairs creak, and warmth floods my chest at the thought of seeing Rachel. It thaws even my deepest frustrations about this stupid desk.

But when I gaze up at her, she stops in the middle of the stairs. Instead of the loose pajamas she'd usually be wearing once the kids are in bed, she's in jeans and a knit lavender sweater, her hair tied back in a neat bun. And a strange expression paints her face.

"What is it?" I ask her. I immediately straighten my back and go on full alert.

"Don't freak out, but your parents are here."

The words hit me like a ton of bricks as I immediately start to freak out. Conflicting emotions seep into my bloodstream all at once; fear, joy, embarrassment, uncertainty.

Hurt.

Rachel completes her path down the stairs and heads to me while I'm still trying to make sense of what's going on. She grabs hold of my arm and pulls upward; I follow her lead.

"What are they doing here?" I finally manage to say.

"I talked to your mom the other day." I stop dead in my tracks, blood rushing to my ears. "She wanted to talk to me first. I didn't tell you because I didn't want you to make yourself sick over the anticipation of seeing them again."

"You handled that alone?"

Rachel's gaze falls, guilt flashing across her face.

"I did."

But I'm not mad. I grab her chin to lift her head and press my lips to hers for a soft kiss.

"I love you so much," I tell her.

I love the way she took on that situation for me. I love the way she's here for me now, as we both head upstairs, together.

I love her more than anything.

I grip—maybe too tightly—onto her hand when we finally make it up the stairs to see both my parents seated at our kitchen table. They stand in unison, and I remain there, motionless, the three of us—no, the four of us—at a standoff.

I don't breathe. They don't move. The quiet could drown us.

My father is the first to break the silence. His face crumples, and his arms open wide.

"Beta…"

I'm next, and in the blink of an eye, we're suddenly all on our knees, the four of us, sobbing in each other's arms. They both whisper their sorries through tears, but I don't even need the words, because I can *feel* it, draping over me like a warm blanket.

Plenty of time for words will come later. But now, in this moment, all I feel is love.

Epilogue

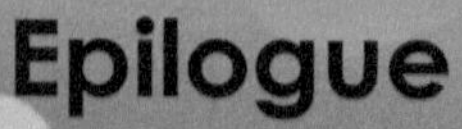

Eleven years later

There were many times over the last decade when I thought I finally understood what went through my mother's head. Why she held on so tightly to me, to the point where it all boiled over that one day at the cabin.

But only now, as I hold both my boys in my arms and have to hold back the sobs that want to rip through me, do I truly understand.

All around us, the Montréal–Trudeau International Airport is rife with noise and commotion, as it always is. How many hundreds—if not thousands—of lives are changing forever around us today?

Mine feels like it's about to end, though I should know better.

"Okay, Dad, we really have to go," Cayce says as he tries to pull away.

Corey, on the other hand, lingers a moment longer.

"I know," I say, my voice breaking.

I sense Rachel's hand on my back as a silent support. She's as torn about our boys moving away as I am, and, unlike me, her tears fall freely, staining her cheeks red. But that small touch gives me the final boost of courage I need to let my sons go.

I back away and take a final look at them. They've grown so fast, I can hardly comprehend it. They're tall, but not quite as tall as me, although, at seventeen, there's a good chance they're not done growing just yet. I think the right word to describe them right now is 'lanky'.

But it seems like just yesterday, they were small enough for me to lift them both in my arms at the same time.

And despite them being identical twins, right now, they look nothing alike. Cayce has let his straight black hair grow to his chin, and the beginnings of a beard are peppered across his jaw, while Corey is clean-shaven and never lets his locks get over two inches long.

Cayce doesn't mind the glasses they both need, while Corey prefers his contacts. Both still play soccer, but only Corey still plays seriously, and the difference in their build is staggering.

Under all accounts, my sons are set up for success. No, they don't have the huge trust fund I originally wanted to build for them. But with Corey's full-ride sports scholarship at the University of British Columbia—home of arguably the country's best college soccer program—he will barely need to dip into his college savings.

And although Cayce is taking a sabbatical year to tour Europe, he has worked so hard at his part-time jobs throughout high school that he can easily swing it.

Still, I'm terrified the savings we gave them won't be enough. My video game studio has launched a few successful games by now, but it's by no means making me rich. I haven't yet been able to give myself the same salary I would be earning by now if I'd stayed in the software industry.

But with Rachel's support, and regular therapy appointments, the anxiety has been manageable.

Corey looks me up and down, and, seeming to detect my worry, hugs me again.

"We're going to be okay, Dad," he whispers in my ear. "You prepared us for it. We're both ready."

"I know," I repeat when he pulls away, alternating my gaze between the two of them. "I'm so proud of you both."

"We both are," Rachel says through her tears. "Oh, I love you both so much."

I'm proud of how they're both pursuing their own dreams, unapologetically. They don't struggle with the same separation anxiety that plagued them when they were little, but still, the choice to go their separate ways was a painful one.

One they took anyway.

By the time they've gone through their gates, both headed to a layover in Toronto before they're then headed in completely different directions, a few tears manage to break their way past my defenses. And when Rachel and I drive away from the airport, we're both bawling like babies, so much so that I have to exit the highway to park on the side of the road.

But Rachel makes me feel safe, even in the moment when I feel the most vulnerable. The most broken.

When we've both settled down, enough that I can drive again, Rachel places a hand on my thigh.

"Corey's right," she tells me in a contemplative tone. "You couldn't have prepared them for the world any better."

"We both did," I reply. "It's still us against the world, right?"

Rachel grins at me, ever the beauty, with the two strands of white hair now framing her face.

"Always."

***

Rachel

An hour later, I'm knocking on Sophie's door, still depleted from the day's emotions. Karan's hand is wrapped around mine.

My heart is utterly broken, but a warm inkling of love and hope sparks within to nurture what grows from the ashes.

I don't think I was ready for my boys to leave.

But *they* were ready. And that's what matters.

Sophie opens the door with a bittersweet smile.

"Oh, come here," she sings, pulling me inside her home by the arm before she wraps me in a tight hug.

"You're next," I whisper to her, cry-laughing.

"Ugh. Don't remind me. In my head, Gwen's still a baby."

She pulls away, and I look towards her kitchen, where the rest of tonight's company sits on stools around the island counter. Will, Océane, Avery, Logan, and even Tania and Nolan are all here.

No kids tonight. Or rather, no teenagers. Gwen, Heather, and Julian headed to Avery and Logan's place to hang out with Avery's son Nathan and give us adults some space. The last thing Karan and I needed tonight was a reminder that our friends still have their kids with them.

The gang greets us, and Tania offers us a plate of

scrumptious-looking pastries as Logan plays bartender and mixes us a drink.

"I could never say no to those," I tell Tania as I grab one of her sinful croissant cube delicacies.

"You're not the only one," Nolan says with a laugh. "We're thinking of opening a sixth location. From what our market studies have told us, Val-d'Or would be a good place."

"Ooh, you should," Karan agrees while grabbing his own croissant cube.

Over the last decade, Tania's café bakeries took off in the province, and they now have a total of five locations. I can't say I'm surprised. Every time I see Tania and Nolan and they bring their delicacies, I probably gain about five pounds.

I lose myself in casual conversation with my dearest friends and family. The entire time, Karan doesn't leave my side. Tomorrow, there's a good chance we'll wake up with sore hearts, but we still have each other. And we have the knowledge that we did our very best to send our boys off into the world equipped with what they need to thrive.

Eventually, we settle down to eat. Sophie prepared a delicious caramelized onion Flammekueche—or rather, she prepared two, with the help of Océane, who, by all means, seems to be having one of her really good days.

Logan and Karan sit next to each other and talk shop, like they always do. Shortly after Karan started his own studio, Logan joined him, so they probably spend the most time together out of all of us.

I take the opportunity to chat up with Avery, who's sitting in front of me.

"So, how does it feel to work in an actual office again?"

Avery chuckles, then swallows her bite of food. "You know, it's actually refreshing. My colleagues are some of the best people I know, so it makes it easier that I'm not nervous to be around them."

She winks and lowers her voice. "Plus, all psychotherapists are a little bit weird and messed up. That's why we do what we do."

A few years ago, Avery got the devastating news that her father had died. By then, it had been nearly a decade since they'd last spoken. She had hoped they would one day reconnect, but he had his own demons to deal with, and Avery prioritized her own mental health—and that of her son.

Finding out he had died without her being able to reconnect with him sent her to a dark place for a long time. We were all there for her, none more than Logan. But when she eventually climbed out of that hole, she'd decided she had to change her career.

"It's weird, but despite my anxiety, it doesn't make me feel anxious to talk to my clients," she continues.

"Not even a little bit?" I ask.

"Well, okay, a bit. And I was definitely more anxious with the first few real appointments I took." She takes a sip of her drink, a sweet, pink thing that matches her demeanor. "But helping other people through their fucked up family shit gives me an actual purpose. It helps me cope to know that I can help people in a way that I wish someone could have helped me, you know?"

Logan takes a beat from his conversation with Karan and gazes over at the love of his life, making sure she's okay, before shifting his focus back to Karan.

"Shouldn't we wait after dessert?" I hear Will say from across the table.

My brows furrow as I gaze over to him and Sophie, who, from their tense body language, seem to be arguing.

"I just… I can't hold it in anymore," Sophie responds.

"Hold in what?"

The table goes silent. I don't think Sophie meant us to overhear. All of us were engrossed in our own conversations. Now, every eye is turned towards her and Will, the weight of expectation palpable.

"Well, I guess you can go for it, now," Will says, one corner of his lips turning up as he gives Sophie a sideways glance.

Sophie takes a deep breath, presses her palms to the table, and sweeps her gaze over each of us. "We're, uh… we're retiring."

A collective gasp rips out of the room.

"Retiring?" Avery asks, eyes wide. "So, selling the business?"

That's what she has to mean. Eight years ago, Will quit his consulting job to join Sophie at her party planning business full-time. To say that it's been thriving over the last decade is an understatement.

"Yup," Sophie says, looking down towards her lap.

"But that's great news!" Tania exclaims. "Isn't it? You've been wanting to spend more time with the kids, no?"

"We're leaving Montréal."

This time, no gasps echo through the room. Only shocked silence.

Sophie meets my gaze. "We've been talking about doing this for a long time. And the whole family agrees. Even Gwen. We're going to take some time to travel as a family."

I don't know what shocks me more—the fact that I won't see my sister in law for who knows how long, or the fact that Gwen, who has a single year of high school left, agrees to leave her friends behind right before graduation.

"That's… amazing, guys," Karan says to break the long, awkward silence.

"It really is," I add, though all I can think is, *My boys are gone, and now so are my brother and my best friend.*

"But… wait just a minute."

My gaze flits between Sophie and Océane.

"Where will you go?" I ask my sister, my throat threatening to clog up.

Océane beams. "Sammie asked me to move in with her."

"Oh."

I'm flushed with conflicting emotions. Sammie is a wonderful woman, and yes, they've been together for nearly five years. I've known her for much longer; she's about to celebrate her ten-year anniversary working at Karan's studio.

But I can't help but wonder if she can take care of my sister in the way she needs.

"Don't doubt our sister like that," Will chides me. "I, for one, am proud of her."

I look at Océane, her cheeks flushed, her smile big. And I realize Will is right. She's come a long way in dealing with her trauma. Yes, her fibromyalgia will always be a part of her, but her mental health is miles from where it once was. Under all accounts, she's thriving.

There's no reason she can't thrive with the person who seems to be the love of her life.

"You guys are going to love it," Avery says, her voice breaking as she fights back the flood of tears threatening to spill forth. "Traveling like that was the best experience Logan and I ever went through."

"I'm going to miss the fuck out of all of you," Sophie continues, now also on the verge of tears.

"Me too," Tania adds.

That's something we can all agree on.

We make the most of the rest of the evening and bask in the joy of being together, now knowing that it's going to be the last time in a long, long while.

It hurts, but the memories we make are going to be little treasures I hold onto as tightly as I can.

That night, Karan and I take a stroll around our neighborhood after we park in our driveway before heading inside, neither of us ready to face the empty house yet.

Hand in hand, we head out to the Chambly canal, the stars a glittering blanket over our heads.

"I'm so proud of Océane," I say as I look out to the dark horizon, watching the reflection of the moon ripple across the surface of the water. "She's been dealt a shit hand, and look what she's made of it."

Karan wraps his arm around my waist. "She's had the right people in her life to give her the support she needed."

"Hmmm." I lean against him and close my eyes, reveling in this simple gesture, this simple moment. "And I'm proud of you, too, you know that?"

"Why?"

"Today was hard. And you made it through."

"It was hard for you, too."

"We both know it isn't the same."

More than a decade ago, Karan's anxiety over the boys' future almost took everything from us. Today, he has overcome it with a resilience that I love him more deeply for.

"Maybe. But I'm proud of you, too." He turns and bends towards me for a kiss.

"I love you," he whispers to me.

"I love you, too," I whisper back, meaning every word more than ever before.

This never gets old.

Never.

Twenty-five years together, and I haven't stopped craving the feel of his lips against mine, the warmth of his body, losing myself in his arms.

This life hasn't been perfect. But the best moments have deeply outshone the rest. And that's all you can hope for, is it not?

The End

Want to read Sophie and Will's story? Fall Into You is a single mom, forced proximity romance where she hates him (and he pines after her) set in Montréal during the fall.
Get Fall Into You

Looking for a second chance, friends-with-benefits story set in a cozy sugar shack? Read Tania and Logan's story of overcoming grief and finding love again in Springing Back Together.
Get Springing Back Together

Interested in checking out Avery and Logan's story? Summer Kind of Love is a summery friends-to-lovers romance with a cinnamon roll MMC, anxiety rep, and small-town coastal vibes.
Get Summer Kind of Love

Sign up for my newsletter to access the first two chapters of Summer Kind of Lover & first dibs on ARC signups, launch promos, and more!
subscribepage.io/charlene-newsletter

If you enjoyed reading this book, please consider leaving an honest review! Reviews are the lifeblood of indie authors, and I'd be incredibly grateful if you took your valuable time to share your opinion.

And keep reading for a preview of my next book, a lakeside, forced proximity romance featuring Karan and Logan as side characters!

Acknowledgements

Seasons of the East Coast has come to a close, and I've got so much to be thankful for.

My first thanks go out to my lovely developmental editor, Swati, who has been with me throughout this entire series. You've allowed my words to shine and for the stories I've had buried inside me to become the best they could be. Reader, I'll tell you right now, you would NOT have wanted to read the initial version of this book. I don't think you would have wanted Rachel and Karan to even stay together! I also need to thank Swati for the insight into Indian culture to help bring Karan to life. Any mistakes are purely my own.

To my line editor and proofreader, Lloyd. At first, seeing your comments pop up in my inbox on my manuscript, I was terrified. You asked questions and made comments no other line editor ever has before. But your thoroughness and detailed insight helped me choose the right words to dive even deeper into what Rachel and Karan's story should be. Thank you so much for your work.

To my amazing ARC readers who've shown up for every book so far (and to the new ones, too)... your words of encouragement, engagement on social media, and love for my books is what keeps me going. Seeing how these stories resonate with even a single person gives meaning to my writing. From the bottom of my heart, thank you.

Sierra Ward, thank you so much for all of your illustrations for the covers of this series. I get so many compliments on them, and I can't get enough of the night sky and mountains for this latest piece. And, of course, thank you to Rotoscope Design for the beautiful cover design and interior formatting.

To my best friend, Elissa, for being a constant cheerleader of my books and even taking a trip to help me out with decorating my table at my very first author signing event (on her birthday weekend, too!), thank you, thank you, thank you. I was probably 85% less nervous about this signing event thanks to your advice.

I always finish out these acknowledgement sections by thanking my partner, Jay. And it's especially fitting here. Although Rachel and Karan are completely different people from you and me, there's a lot of us in their relationship. A lot of, "If we'd made different choices along the way, what would have happened to us?"

Rachel and Karan allow their trauma to make choices for them, before they finally gain the strength to take back control of their lives. But you've always made me feel safe enough to overcome my demons and choose you, over and over again. I love you, always.

Finally, to you, Reader… whether you're an ARC reader, a new reader, an old reader, or simply reading because you know me in real life and want to support me… Thank you, again and again, for making my childhood dreams come true.

A preview of Game Jam, a lakeside, forced-proximity romance…

Chapter One

I'm bottlenecked.

If you've ever gotten so lost in a song that you came out of it in a daze, unable to pinpoint how much time has passed, you'll understand the intense fugue state that gamers fall into. A good video game will envelop you in its soothing arms the same way a good piece of music would.

But in a game, if you let yourself fade out of the illusion—if you let yourself remember that none of this is real, and thus lose your focus—you die.

Of course, that's okay. At least, at first. You come back to life. That's the beauty of games. You get to try over and over again. You get better at it a little bit each time. But when you're bottlenecked like me, you'll also die, again and again, little by little, every time you remember what your real life looks like.

Life is supposed to be like a video game. You're supposed to build over time. Get better at things. Find your purpose and get closer and closer to it. But not for me. I've reached the limit of how much progress I can make. I've hit the bottleneck.

Yeah, this is as good as it gets.

'This' being quite literally staring at the bottleneck of the empty twelve-pack from last night.

"Are you sure you're okay?"

My father leans back against his worn leather armchair, the same one he's had even before Mom died. In other words, an eternity ago. The twelve empty bottles are lined next to said chair in a crooked formation.

It's 1 pm, and yet, there's a half-empty beer bottle stuck in his grip. Surprisingly, it's only his first today.

I blink a couple of times to fade back into reality.

Another tiny death.

"Yeah. I'm fine."

The last thing I want is to make Dad nervous right before I leave him alone for the entire weekend. I'm already worried for him enough as it is; I don't see why it's necessary to make him sick with worry, too.

Muffles rubs against my leg. I bend my knees and give his short tuxedo coat a good rub. From the worn suitcase leaning against the apartment door, my cat can tell I'm going somewhere.

Not that it happens all that often, but still. He's soaking in all the love he can get while he still can.

"You remember where his food is?" I ask Dad.

"Yup."

"And that he gets his portions three times a day."

"Yes, Dom."

"It's really important." I straighten my spine and cross my arms, facing Dad full on.

To his credit, he's paying attention. His eyes are on me, and they're not glazed over yet.

"And you have to remove the leftover food after one hour," I add. "Two max."

"I got it." He raises his bottle to me. "Seriously, Dom. Muffles and I will be just fine. Weren't you supposed to leave five minutes ago?"

I stomp over to the fridge one final time. Dad is right, but I'd rather that Karan and Logan be just a tad upset with me for making them wait a few extra minutes in the car than leave without being fully certain Dad is equipped to survive on his own.

I almost never leave this apartment overnight. Let alone for over forty-eight hours.

The fridge looks no different than it did when I checked it five minutes ago; it's still fully stocked to the brim with fruits and veggies I've chopped up for him, plus individual plastic containers with ready-to-eat meals that Dad can heat up in the microwave. There's almost no space for the beer bottles lining the bottom row, but he managed to make them fit.

Satisfied—or, at least, as satisfied as I'll ever be—I close the fridge door and turn to face Dad again. He's peering at me with a bittersweet smile.

"I wish you wouldn't worry so much, Dominique," he says.

I resist the urge to scoff. Instead, I walk over to him and bend over for a hug. His longish, greasy hair tickles my neck, and when I feel his arms tighten around me, I shut my eyes and hold my breath.

I should have taken some time to pressure him into showering before I go. Too late now.

"Try to enjoy yourself, at least," he whispers in my ear. "Keep your mind off your old man for a weekend."

I wish it were that simple. The truth is, I've been looking forward to this game jam for months now. Two days of pure creation with my friends.

Yet, the anticipation is a two-sided coin. One cannot exist without the other.

On one side, the yearning for a few days of escape. Of freedom.

On the other, a clawing fear that I won't be there if catastrophe befalls him.

It could be so many things. Dad could go overboard again and choke on his own vomit. He could slip and fall, bump his head, with no one here to find him. He could take it upon himself to ignore the cooked meals I've prepared for him and try his hand at cooking, only for him to forget in a drunken haze and set this apartment ablaze.

I pull away from him, more than a little reluctant.

Deep breath in.

"Okay. I'm going. But don't hesitate to call or text if there's anything."

"I love you, sweetie," he replies, his deep brown eyes, so dark they're nearly black, just like mine, crinkling with his smile. "Now go."

He shoos me away with a gesture of his liver-spotted hand.

I bite my bottom lip, take a final look at Muffles staring at me from his seat on the kitchen chair, and nod.

"Love you too."

When I open the apartment door, my small suitcase in tow, the sun's rays hit my skin and fill me with a momentary delight. Their warmth across my face and bare arms gives me a taste of the weekend to come. Sure, game jams aren't known for being outdoorsy. Stick a handful of game developers in a building, give them a theme, and let them come up with a complete, functional video game from scratch in forty-eight hours; that's usually how it goes.

This jam is different, and it's why Karan, Logan, and Sammie's hounding finally got me to accept to come along.

From the rickety metal balcony, I spot Karan's Toyota parked across the street. Karan waves at me from the driver's window, a goofy smile lighting up his round face. He's sporting his usual look; long black hair pulled back in a bun, and a matching beard neatly shaped and combed around his jaw.

I head to the back of the car and open the trunk to drop my suitcase inside. I'm about to head to the passenger's seat, but I interrupt my own stride when I see Logan has already claimed that spot.

Seeing Logan seated next to Karan is almost comical. Logan isn't just a head shorter than Karan. He's also got the complete opposite build. While Karan is built like a bear, broad-shouldered and solid, with a frame that carries both strength and softness, Logan is lean and angular, his frame almost wiry.

Their contrast doesn't stop there—Logan's pale skin is already starting to turn bronze in the light of June, while Karan's warm complexion has begun to deepen into a rich brown tone.

"Hey, boys." I slide into the back seat, not allowing the nervous energy to creep into my voice.

Logan turns in his seat to face me.

"I'm pinching myself over the fact that you're actually here, Dom." He smiles, then presses his glasses back up the bridge of his nose and turns back around.

"Right?" Karan echoes, putting the car back in drive. "It's about time we got her out."

I force a small giggle. The truth is, Karan, Logan, and Sammie are my closest friends. Yet, they know nothing of my home situation. All they know is that I live with my dad.

I've always come up with excuses for why I don't like leaving my place for too long. It's not too difficult to blame it on anxiety. They're just clueless as to the true origin of said anxiety.

"It's been a long time since the four of us have worked together on the same project," I say, looking out the window to see the city of Montréal whiz by. "I missed it."

"Uh. About that," Karan starts.

"What?" I ask, my attention now pulled away from the outside sights.

"Sammie called when we were on our way to your place," Logan says, and my stomach sinks as I can already see where this is headed. "She's not gonna make it this weekend."

"Is she okay?"

Thoughts of her recent surgery pop into my head. If she weren't okay, like, truly not okay, we wouldn't still be headed outside the city to this game jam, though, would we?

"She tore through her stitches," Logan explains. I wince. "So traveling is a no-go."

"Shit." My heart goes out to Sammie, who was so nervous about this surgery in the first place.

But an additional nagging thought comes to join it immediately.

"Wait, so it's just the three of us?"

I'm not just going to this game jam to make a cool game in forty-eight hours. I'm going to win.

And winning's going to be impossible without an artist.

My mouth goes dry. Breathing becomes just a tad more difficult. As nervous as I am to leave Dad on his own, I *need* this. I'll suffocate without it.

And I need that prize.

Just the idea of not winning feels like a chokehold at my throat, squeezing all the air out of my lungs. A dark cloud looms over me.

"Oh, not at all," Karan says, interrupting my rumination. He merges onto the highway to exit the island. "Logan called up a guy we know."

"He's really good," Logan reassures me. "His name's Nick. We hired him a while back to help Sam with rigging and skinning. He specializes in that, but he's also a great modeler and texture artist."

A jack of all trades who also masters one of the most difficult aspects of video game animation? Looks like we lucked out after all.

"And he had nothing else to do on a nice summer weekend except to jump on this last minute?" I ask, incredulous.

Whoever this guy is, his social calendar must be sparse.

"I don't know. He didn't hesitate at all." Karan chuckles. "He's taking his own car, so you'll get to meet him once we arrive in Sainte-Agathe."

"Think we'll get along?" I can't help but ask.

"I do," Logan says, looking back over at me. "On top of being an artist, he's a huge audiofile, so I'm sure both of you will geek out over music theory and all that shit."

"You mean the shit that makes your eyes glaze over when I go on a rant?"

"Hey, listen, I love music as much as any other guy," Logan defends himself with a smile. "But I'm self-taught. All that theory goes way over my head."

"Says the programmer."

"Software engineer."

"Same shit."

"Is not!" Karan calls out, and we all laugh a little.

Both of them are software engineers, but it was Karan who founded the game studio that has quickly become my favourite to freelance for.

I peer through my window and watch the cityscape slowly transform into the blue and green mountainous expanse of the Laurentides. The verdant, breathtaking peaks. Homes nestled between the trees at dizzying heights. Lakes scattered across the landscape aplenty, like a thousand blue mirrors reflecting back the surrounding beauty.

I quickly snag the moment, cradle it lovingly in my chest, take a deep breath to truly feel it all, and put the moment away in my pocket, just in time before an intrusive thought crashes through to interrupt my rare moment of joy.

Working with Karan, Logan, and Sammie was *nothing* like the first few paid audio design gigs I did. By then, I'd done a few other unpaid gigs to build up my portfolio, and even swallowed the fact that one team didn't credit my work at all.

The first paid gig I ever landed was cool overall, but there was this guy. A guy who, unfortunately, shared my name. And who seemingly couldn't stand me.

Dominic Kaczmarek nitpicked every single one of my songs and sound effects at every sprint review. Even at points when no one else had anything to say about my compositions, he'd bring at least one bit of criticism, if not more.

To add insult to injury, he sat as far away from me as possible for lunch and at group outings. It did wonders for my self-esteem. Add to that the fact that this guy was my type—good-looking in a scruffy kind of way, taller than me (which is a rarity with my 5'11) with sandy curls, long black lashes, and honey-colored eyes that reflected the light in the most tantalizing way—and the way he seemed to hate my guts felt like utter rejection.

I shouldn't have taken it so hard. After all, it's not like I'm in a position to date anyone.

But Karan's studio was different. I felt utterly at home there. Even though I'm not a full-time employee, they've since then hired me to do the audio for every project they do, and the four of us have become fast friends.

I can only hope that Nick's arrival doesn't disturb the sense of family I've come to love about this group. Not when I need this so much.

Having left before the rush of traffic that overtakes the greater Montréal area every Friday, it only takes us an hour and a half to reach Sainte-Agathe-des-Monts. Karan navigates through the small town and finds the smaller roads that lead to the lakehouses, and when he pulls into our destination, I catch the first glimpse of sprawling windows reflecting the afternoon sun off the lake.

And then it hits me:

For the first time in years, I'm somewhere my father can't reach me. There's still a deep bubble of anxiety at that thought, but there's also a jubilant excitement.

It's just going to be me, my music, and forty-eight hours to pretend I'm the kind of person who gets to want things for herself.

About the Author

Charlène Boutin writes swoon-worthy stories that will make you laugh, cry, and most of all, will warm your heart. Originally from Val-d'Or, Québec (Canada), she spent six years in Red Lake, Ontario, and six more years in Montréal, Québec, giving her fodder for both small-town AND city-driven love stories. She now lives in Granby, Québec, with her partner, son, and tuxedo cat, Clapton. When she's not reading or writing, you'll find her boulder climbing or spending quality time with her family.

www.ingramcontent.com/pod-product-compliance
Lightning Source LLC
Chambersburg PA
CBHW020903060726
47591CB00004B/1058